Praise for the Ghost Hunter Mysteries

"A bewitching book blessed with many blithe spirits."
—Nancy Martin, author of
the Blackbird Sisters Mysteries

"Ms. Laurie has penned a fabulous read and packed it with ghost-hunting action at its best. With a chilling mystery, a danger-filled investigation, a bit of romance, and a wonderful dose of humor, there's little chance that readers will be able to set this book down."
—Darque Reviews

"M.J.'s first-person worldview is both unique and enticing. With truly likable characters, plenty of chills, and even a hint of romance, real-life psychic Laurie guarantees that readers are in for a spooktacularly thrilling ride." —*Romantic Times* (4½ stars)

"A great, fast-paced, addicting read."
—Enchanting Reviews

"A great story." —MyShelf.com

Praise for the Psychic Eye Mysteries

"Victoria Laurie has crafted a fantastic tale in this latest Psychic Eye Mystery. There are few things in life that upset Abby Cooper, but ghosts and her parents feature high on her list . . . giving the reader a few real frights and a lot of laughs." —Fresh Fiction

"Fabulous. . . . Fans will highly praise this fine ghostly murder mystery." —The Best Reviews

"A great new series . . . plenty of action."
—*Midwest Book Review*

"An invigorating entry into the cozy mystery realm . . . I cannot wait for the next book."
—Roundtable Reviews

"A fresh, exciting addition to the amateur sleuth genre." —J. A. Konrath, author of *Dirty Martini*

"Worth reading over and over again." —Bookviews

The Ghost Hunter Mystery Series

What's a Ghoul to Do?
Demons Are a Ghoul's Best Friend

The Psychic Eye Mystery Series

Abby Cooper, Psychic Eye
Better Read than Dead
A Vision of Murder
Killer Insight
Crime Seen
Death Perception

GHOULS
JUST HAUNT
TO HAVE FUN

A GHOST HUNTER MYSTERY

Victoria Laurie

AN OBSIDIAN MYSTERY

OBSIDIAN
Published by New American Library, a division of
Penguin Group (USA) Inc., 375 Hudson Street,
New York, New York 10014, USA
Penguin Group (Canada), 90 Eglinton Avenue East, Suite 700, Toronto,
Ontario M4P 2Y3, Canada (a division of Pearson Penguin Canada Inc.)
Penguin Books Ltd., 80 Strand, London WC2R 0RL, England
Penguin Ireland, 25 St. Stephen's Green, Dublin 2,
Ireland (a division of Penguin Books Ltd.)
Penguin Group (Australia), 250 Camberwell Road, Camberwell, Victoria 3124,
Australia (a division of Pearson Australia Group Pty. Ltd.)
Penguin Books India Pvt. Ltd., 11 Community Centre, Panchsheel Park,
New Delhi - 110 017, India
Penguin Group (NZ), 67 Apollo Drive, Rosedale, North Shore 0632,
New Zealand (a division of Pearson New Zealand Ltd.)
Penguin Books (South Africa) (Pty.) Ltd., 24 Sturdee Avenue,
Rosebank, Johannesburg 2196, South Africa

Penguin Books Ltd., Registered Offices:
80 Strand, London WC2R 0RL, England

First published by Obsidian, an imprint of New American Library,
a division of Penguin Group (USA) Inc.

First Printing, March 2009
10   9   8   7   6   5   4   3   2   1

For Leanne Tierney,
a great friend and my personal hero

Acknowledgments

A couple of years ago I got a call from my agent, Jim McCarthy, telling me that a producer had been in touch with the agency to see if I might be up for participating in a cable TV special on haunted possessions. The way they envisioned the show was *Most Haunted* meets *Antiques Roadshow*.

"It sounds goofy," I said after hearing the pitch.

"Think of it like free advertising for the books!" he encouraged.

"Yeah, but these things never make the psychic look good," I argued. "You know they can do anything they want in that editing room."

"But think of how many books you could sell!" he countered.

I had a feeling Jim had a one-track mind on this one. Finally, however, after a whole lotta back-and-forth I conceded, with one condition: Jim had to fly to California with me and hold my hand during the shoot.

And everything was moving forward until Jim found out that the location of the shoot and our accommodations would be aboard the *Queen Mary*, aka the most haunted ghost ship in America. After that little tidbit came out, the excuses began:

"Uh, about going to California with you . . ." he said.

"Mmm-hmm?"

"Yeah, well, you see, the thing of it is . . . I might not have room in my work schedule after all."

"You don't say?"

"And I think I have some other personal conflicts that weekend."

"I see. . . ."

"And"—cough-cough—"I may be coming down with a cold." Sniffle, hack, wheeze, sniffle. "And you know how they say to avoid flying when you have a cold. . . ."

So it came to pass that Jim weaseled out, which, truth be told, was a good thing, because I didn't have a great feeling about attending either and we eventually informed the producers that we were no longer interested in participating.

A few months later I saw a small clip of the actual show, and all I can say is *thank God* I backed out! There were some crazy happenings going on during that clip that I knew I'd have been totally freaked-out over. (Just 'cause I can communicate with the dead doesn't mean I don't find it creepy at times.)

Still, the concept of a haunted possession intrigued me enough to use it in a story with my favorite ghost hunting team of M.J., Gilley, and Steven. And now you know that I'm much braver, sitting in my nice, quiet, decidedly unhaunted home writing about things that go bump in the night rather than hunting them down myself. ☺

To that end I would like to thank all those who helped me along the way:

My fabulous editor, Kristen Weber, who is so easy to work with and full of enthusiasm and encouragement. Thanks for taking such great care of me, Kristen. It means a lot!

Thanks as well to everyone at Obsidian for their efforts on my behalf, and that list includes Leslie Henkel and Rebecca Vinter, along with many, many others who work so diligently behind the scenes. Please accept my boundless appreciation for all you do for me.

My agent, Jim McCarthy, who always has my back (unless it involves spending the night on a ghost ship), and who is simply the best damn agent in the biz! Also, thanks to the entire staff at Dystel and Goderich, Literary Management, for their advice and support over the years.

And I'd like to thank my family for their continued support and encouragement, along with all my friends who cheer every time I show up on their doorstep with a new release. I usually name you all individually, but that list is getting a bit long, so know that if you think I might be including you, I definitely am!

One small individual mention here, and that is to Leanne Tierney, to whom this book is dedicated: Leanne, you're simply wonderful, and every time I talk to you it's like getting an adrenaline shot of sunshine. Thank you for being a great friend and providing such inspiration. You amaze me with your attitude, boundless enthusiasm, and continued strength and determination. Hugs and love, gal pal!

Chapter 1

Here's some free advice: *Never* go into business with your best friend. And if you happen to ignore that initial advice—then, by God, make *sure* you have some sort of an escape clause.

How am I qualified to give such advice?

I'll tell you: I'm the idiot who went into business with her BFF and barely lived to tell about it.

Gilley Gillespie has been my best friend for twenty years—and he'd been driving me crazy for nineteen and a half of them when I ignored all reason and good sense and formed a small ghostbusting business with him as my partner. The plan had seemed sound at the time. I'm a psychic medium with a good reputation and lots of experience, Gilley is a computer and gadget whiz, and New England is chock-*full* of haunted houses. We thought it was the perfect blend of talent meeting opportunity.

But, sadly, what we found after hanging out our ghostbusting shingle was a whole lot of skepticism and folks who weren't bothered by bumps in the night as much as we thought they'd be.

Still, our prices weren't cheap, so the jobs we did

manage to book we were at least well compensated for, and that left us with a lot of free time waiting for the phone to ring. I liked to fill these periods surfing the Web or scoping out the latest gossip rag, while Gilley liked to think up new ways to increase business. (Enter the need for an escape clause. . . .)

So when I came into the office suite I shared with Gil on a cool Friday morning in late September, I noticed right away that my best friend might have had way too much time on his hands recently, and that meant I was likely in trouble.

You see, Gilley looked guilty. Of what exactly, I wasn't yet sure, but something was up, and I had a feeling it was probable that my breakfast would consist of a cup of coffee, a bagel, and a side of aspirin. "What'd you do now?" I groaned as I put my jacket on the coatrack.

"Something that will bring us *tons* of new business!" he announced with a flourish.

I shot him a skeptical look over my shoulder as I headed into my office, tucked just behind the front lobby of our suite. "Why do I have the feeling that I'm not going to like it?"

"Because you never like any of my ultracreative ideas."

For the record, Gilley's idea of "ultracreative" ways to increase our professional ghostbusting business have included a man dressed up as Casper waving to pedestrian traffic outside our office, and a late-night cable TV commercial featuring Gil and a half dozen of his fellow queens (I should mention that Gil is *decidedly* light in his loafers) doing a mock-up of Michael Jackson's "Thriller" video while someone in a cop uniform rushed around "busting" the walking dead.

"I never like any of your crazy ideas, Gil, because they all cost money and don't return on the investment. We're still paying for your thirty-second stint on late-night TV," I pointed out.

Gilley got up from his desk and hurried into my office. With a flick of his hand he dismissed my pessimism. "That's the beauty of this idea, M.J. It won't cost us a penny. In fact, it will actually pay us *handsomely*!"

I sat down with another sigh and picked up the mail Gil had laid on my desk, sorting through the envelopes. "How much does handsomely go for these days?" I asked casually.

"Five hundred dollars a day!" Gil said, and clapped his hands happily.

I arched an eyebrow at him. "That's less than we get paid for a bust."

Gilley took a seat in one of the chairs opposite me. "Yes, but it's free advertising! We'd actually get *paid* to tell the world about our business! And the exposure will be national. I tell you, this could be big!"

I set the mail down and eyed him critically. "I always know I'm in for a rude awakening when you play this stuff up."

"Not this time," he insisted, his knees bouncing with excitement.

"Fine," I groaned. "What's this latest brainstorm?"

"I just got off the phone with a Hollywood producer—"

"Hollywood?" I interrupted. "Isn't that commute a little far?" We live just outside Boston.

"Well, of course we'd be flown in," he said impatiently. "Anyway, as I was saying, this Hollywood producer is putting together this really cool new show for Bravo. You know how we love to watch our Bravo!"

"Uh-huh," I said, sitting back in my chair and crossing my arms. So far I wasn't too impressed, even though Gilley and I were avid fans of the cable channel.

"It's an assembly of talent, the best mediums the world has to offer," Gil continued. "This producer has scoured the U.S. to find the greatest psychics in the biz, in fact."

"Who's attending?" I was pretty up on who the best intuitive mediums in the country were. I was good friends with Rebecca Rosen from Colorado, and Theresa Rogers from California, not to mention that I'd actually met both John Edward and James Van Praagh in person, and if any one of them were in, then I might consider the idea.

"Bernard Higgins," Gil said.

I searched my memory banks. "Never heard of him."

"How about Heath Whitefeather or Angelica Demarche?"

I rolled the names around in my head and came up empty. "Have *you* heard of these people?"

"Sure!" he said, in that high, whiny way that told me he was a big, fat fibber.

I rubbed my temples and glanced at the clock on my desk. Nine a.m. and I already had a headache. It was a new record. "The answer is no," I said flatly.

"But you haven't even heard the whole pitch!" Gilley wailed.

"I don't need to," I warned, leveling a look at him. "It's goofy, whatever it is."

"It is not!"

"Fine." I sighed. "Then tell me what this great assembly of *talent* is all about."

"It's about helping people," Gilley said earnestly. "And isn't that really what we're all about?"

"Who are we helping?" asked a deep baritone from the lobby.

Gil and I both looked up to see six feet of tall, dark, and yummy. "Hey, Steven," I said. Dr. Steven Sable was my significant other and our financial backer. In other words, he was ridiculously wealthy and had enough dough to blow on some rather eccentric "entertainment." That's right—Gilley and I were the "entertainment."

"I'm trying to talk to M.J. about the TV show."

"With the things that are possessed?" he asked. Obviously he was more in the loop than I was, which could mean only that Gil had told him in order to help warm me up to the idea.

"Possessed?" I asked, shifting my attention back to Gil. "You know I don't believe in exorcisms."

"No, no, no!" Gilley said quickly. "It's not like that at all. Listen, this producer has an idea about a show where he gathers some mediums and has them tune in on objects that the owners feel are possessed with either good or bad spirits. Think of it as a haunted *Antiques Roadshow*."

"Again," I said to Gil, "the answer is no."

"M.J.!" Gilley wailed. "You can't say no!"

I stood up from my chair and laid my hands flat on my desk. "I thought I just did."

"But I am all packed," said Steven.

"What do you mean, you're packed?" I asked.

"Gilley gave me the itinerary yesterday. He said we would need to be at the airport by noon today."

"Whoa," I said, shaking my head in disbelief. "Gilley, you already told this producer guy *yes*?"

"It's all arranged," Gilley said quickly. "And I've cashed the first check. They sent us a three-hundred-dollar bonus for signing the contract."

"Wait a minute!" I yelled. "I haven't signed any contract!" And then a flicker of memory burbled up in my mind. Two weeks ago I'd been on the phone and Gilley had swept in, placing some documents in front of me with little "sign here" tabs. Gil and I were in the middle of refinancing our condos for a lower rate—we lived in the same building, one floor apart—so I'd just assumed the papers had to do with the mortgage application.

To confirm that my memory was accurate I saw Gilley picking at his sweater, avoiding my eyes, and I knew I'd been had. "You're fired," I said, doing my best Donald Trump hand-like-a-cobra impression.

"You can't fire me," he said calmly. "We're partners."

"I won't do it!" I snapped. "Get us out of this, Gilley, or so help me, I'll . . ." I was so angry I couldn't think of what I'd do, but I knew it was something big.

"M.J.," Steven said, coming into the room to take a chair next to Gilley, "I think you should do it."

"Easy for you to say," I groused. "You're not the one doing some goofy show on television that's going to make you look like a loony tune!"

"I don't think it will be so bad," Steven said, his

voice calm and soothing. "And I can tell you from my own personal experience that when I watch you work I am memorized."

I should also mention that Steven was born in Argentina and raised in Germany. He's new to both the States and English. "*Mesmerized,*" Gilley whispered out of the corner of his mouth.

"Yes, that too," Steven said. "The point here is that the show is a good opportunity for your business, and to prove to people that you are a gifted medium able to communicate with the dead."

"Think of it," Gilley added. "I mean, how many people have some object in their home that they think might have bad energy associated with it? M.J., this could be a whole new business for us! It's not just about busting someone's home anymore; now we're talking busting that old hairbrush or picture frame or whatever."

I sank back down in my seat. I was outmanned, outmaneuvered, and outsmarted. "What happens if I don't show up?"

"They'll sue you," Gil said. "Breach of contract and all."

I closed my eyes and pinched the bridge of my nose. "How long is this going to take?"

"Including tonight, it'll take three days. We land this evening, and they start shooting tomorrow at eight a.m. sharp."

"So we're back here by Monday?" I asked.

"Yep."

"And there's no new business on the calendar?" It had been a slow couple of weeks.

"Nothing. Not even a nibble."

"And you've already made arrangements for

Doc?" Doc was my African Gray parrot. I'd had him since I was twelve.

"Mama Dell and the Captain are going to look after him." Mama Dell and her husband, known only as "the Captain," owned the coffee shop across the street and were good friends of ours.

I looked from Steven to Gilley and back again, hoping one of them would come to his senses and back me for a change. Finally I rolled my eyes and sighed. "*Fine.* But I swear to God, Gil, if this in any way makes me look like an ass, you're going to pay for it."

"Don't I always?" Gilley muttered, but quickly flashed me a big, toothy smile and clapped his hands. "It'll be fun!"

I gave him a dark look, and he wisely hurried out of my office, muttering something about heading to my condo to pack a bag for me.

"He's right, you know," Steven said after we heard the front door close.

"About this being fun? Don't count on it."

"No, about it being good for the business."

"Or it will be really bad for business," I countered, still irritated at having been hoodwinked.

"What is your worry over this?" he asked, genuinely curious.

"I'm worried that this program is exploitive, that the intent isn't to educate as much as it is to disprove, and that the producer will use every opportunity to showcase any miss I get and call me out on national television as a fraud."

"But you're not a fraud," Steven said gently. "You are the real McCain."

One corner of my mouth lifted. "McCoy," I corrected. "And I know that, but you should see what goes on in the editing room, Steven. I mean, they can take so much out of context that they could make Einstein look stupid."

"Maybe you are taking this too seriously," Steven reasoned. "It seems to me the show is about entertainment, not about making some sort of ideological point."

My eyes widened in surprise. "May I say that your English is really improving?"

"Thank you," he said modestly. "I've been practicing." He got up then and came around my desk, lifting me up out of my chair and pulling me into his wonderfully developed chest. "I have a feeling you will look very good on camera," he said, and kissed me lightly on the lips. "You have a face for the television."

I smiled a little wider. "So if this thing turns ugly, you promise to get me out of there?"

"Mmmm," Steven said, and kissed me again. "Yes, I will rescue you," he added, caressing my back.

We did some heavy petting and smooching until we heard an "Ahem" from someone in the lobby. Neither of us had heard anyone come in. I stepped quickly away from Steven and spotted Mama Dell, looking very uncomfortable in the doorway. "Hey, there." I coughed, straightening my clothes and patting my hair, which I knew was likely tousled.

"I'm so sorry," Mama Dell said, color rising to her cheeks. "I didn't know you were . . . uh . . . busy."

"Mama," Steven cooed, waving her into my office, where he pulled out a chair for her. "It is always a pleasure to see you."

Mama smiled, blushed some more, and took a seat, looking at me expectantly.

"Is there something you need, Mama?" I asked.

"Gilley said to be here by nine thirty to pick up Doc," she explained.

Just then the door opened and Gilley reappeared, struggling through the entrance with a large covered birdcage. From inside the cage we could all hear a scratchy, high nasal voice singing the lyrics to "In the Navy."

"Ah, the Village People," I said. "Gilley loves to play their greatest hits for Doc."

Mama Dell looked over her shoulder. "Does he sing all the time?"

As if on cue, Gilley pulled up the cover on Doc's birdcage and Doc stopped singing abruptly. He regarded all of us for a minute and then said, "Doc's cuckoo for Cocoa Puffs!"

Gilley smiled tightly and dropped the cover. "I've got some of that cereal packed for you, Mama. He likes Cocoa Puffs with fruit."

Mama Dell got up and stepped toward Gilley. "You're sure he'll be all right with me?"

"Of course," Gilley said, reassuring her. "He's met you before, and he seems to love you, so I'm sure he'll be fine. Plus, he's pretty good about entertaining himself. Just set his cage up in front of a window and let him out for a little while at dusk, and he'll be just ducky for the few days we'll be gone."

"Well, all right then," said Mama, adding, "I've got a lovely spot in my house next to the window where he can look out while the Captain and I tend to the coffee shop. Speaking of which," she said, glancing at her watch, "I'll need to hurry back. My husband can handle the morning crowd by himself for only so long before he gets cranky."

Gilley helped Mama Dell out to her car with Doc's cage and loaded it in for her. He was back a few moments later and said with a knowing grin, "By the way, M.J., your lipstick's smeared."

We headed to the airport after tidying up the office and packing our luggage for the trip. Steven left his Aston Martin—aka the Batmobile—in our parking lot, and we all piled into the company van.

We found a spot in short-term parking and made our way to the e-ticket kiosk for JetBlue. Once we had our boarding passes we got through security and found our gate without much hassle. "Not many travelers this late in the morning," I said as we took our seats.

"Most people travel early on Fridays," Gilley noted. "Here," he said, sitting next to me and handing me a file. "In there is all the correspondence between Gopher and me."

"Who?"

"The producer of the show," Gilley explained.

I groaned loudly. "A guy calls you up and pitches you a show about haunted possessions, tells you his name is Gopher, and you take him *seriously*?"

"No," Gilley said, pulling out a book from his backpack. "I took his money seriously. He wants to fly all three of us out to the West Coast, put us up at the Duke Hotel for three days, pay all our travel expenses, food, lodging, et cetera, *and* pay you five hundred a day for your troubles? Where do I sign?"

Something dawned on me then. "Wait a minute. What are you and Steven going to do while I'm shooting the show?"

Gilley opened his book, pulled it up to his nose,

and pretended to read. He muttered something into the pages that I didn't quite catch.

"What was that?" I asked, pulling the book down.

"The hotel is smack in the middle of downtown, and you do know how I loves me some San Francisco."

My mouth fell open. "You mean to tell me that you signed me up for this stunt for the free *vacation* it could offer you?"

"No," Gil said meekly. "I mean, I'll be there for moral support, M.J. It's not like I'm going to abandon you or anything."

I gave Gilley an even look. He and I both knew that San Francisco was like Disneyland for the gay man. "Oh, you'll be there for moral support, all right," I said. "In fact, I want you in my line of sight at *all* times, Gilley. Since you tricked me into this, I am holding you personally responsible for making sure that my lighting is right and the camera angle plays to my good side."

Gilley pouted. "You really need me there at all times?"

"Oh, yeah," I said, opening the manila folder. "At allllllll times, my friend."

While we waited for the plane I read through the e-mails and downloaded Web pages that Gilley had printed out. Apparently this guy Gopher wasn't as goofy as his name. The show was the brainchild of the coproducer, Roger Evenstein, whom the e-mails suggested would not be at the actual shoot. While doing a documentary on the infamous Russian prison camp where Aleksandr Solzhenitsyn spent his internment and from his experiences wrote *The*

Gulag Archipelago, Roger came across one man who had survived six years alongside Solzhenitsyn in the freezing temperatures of the Siberian wasteland. The man was especially interesting to the producer because he claimed that a family heirloom—a small silver cross—smuggled in to him by a relative had saved him. He claimed that the cross had kept him warm during the bitter temperatures of the Siberian nights, and that whenever he took the cross off, he became cold—chilled to the very bone—but as long as he wore it, the cold did not penetrate his skin, and he was saved from freezing to death through six agonizing subzero winters.

Roger was ready to consider it a simple case of mind over matter: His body worked harder to maintain its temperature because the man's belief in the talisman was so strong. But to show the producer that he was not imagining it, the old man offered him the cross to try out. Roger wrote:

From the moment I placed the cross around my neck I felt a sense of physical warmth that permeated to the very marrow of my bones. This happened as a gradual warming of my extremities and ended with me sweating as I sat across from the old man while he shivered in the thin coat he'd worn to meet with me.

A few years later Roger had teamed up with Gopher on a project about another documentary involving a scientist at the University of Arizona who was doing electronic brain scans of mediums and psychics during reading sessions for strangers. While working on that project, Roger had shared his story of the cross with Gopher, and the idea for the show was born.

The two men wondered what other everyday objects could contain such power, and whether that power was limited to only good or positive energy. In their research they came across all manner of items that were claimed to possess special, amazing, or even evil energy.

And it was the folks who claimed to own an evil talisman that concerned the producers the most; these people, Gopher described in his notes to Gilley, were completely imprisoned by the object in question. They believed strongly that it haunted them and that there was no way to get rid of it without bringing on a catastrophe for either themselves or some other poor soul who happened upon the possessed thing they had thrown away.

The show had arranged for an assortment of guests to showcase their "haunted" items to the team of "experts" or mediums invited to the show. Gopher emphasized that his hope was to help those people anchored to this so-called "evil" object to let go of its hold over them or dispose of it in a safe manner, while tracing the root of power for those objects that had "good" energy.

As I read the production notes, I had to admit I was intrigued. But I was also highly skeptical. I know more about things that go bump in the night than just about anyone, but the idea that a ghost or spirit could inhabit something as small as a hairbrush was a bit far-fetched for me. Most ghosts need territory to walk around in: a room, or a house, or a field, or a barn. Every once in a while you'll see them cling to an instrument—usually one of destruction, like a sword or a pistol—but even then they'll still stomp around in the area where the instrument is kept. They don't contain themselves to the item; they contain themselves to the area *around* the item.

But the story of the old Russian man and his cross wouldn't leave me, and as our plane began to load and people lined up to board I decided this might not be so bad after all. At least it would provide me with a little more education and experience, because, trust me, in the ghostbusting business, just when you think you've seen it all—you become acutely aware that you ain't seen nothin' yet.

We landed at four thirty Pacific time. While we waited for the cab that would take us to the Duke Hotel I stretched my legs and arms. It had been a long flight.

Steven and Gilley had slept through most of it, while I'd continued to read through the folder, becoming more and more curious about this little adventure. We were next in line for a cab when Gilley gave me a sideways glance and said, "You still mad at me?"

I smiled. "Nah. But I am a bit surprised that you agreed to come along and sleep in the lodgings provided."

Gilley's look turned puzzled. "Why?"

I opened my eyes wide at him. "*The* most haunted hotel in America?"

"What's the most haunted hotel in America?" he said, his face going a teensy bit pale.

"The Duke Hotel," I said. Oh, this was too good to be true! Gilley obviously hadn't read the literature on our accommodations.

There was a look of panic in Gil's eyes as the rest of the color drained from his face. "You're lying," he said breathlessly.

"Am not," I sang, and swung the pamphlet over to him. Despite being in the ghostbusting business, Gilley is actually terrified of ghosties. Oh, he's great about observing things from the remote safety of the van when I need him, but ask him to actually *enter* someplace haunted and that *POW!* you hear is the sonic boom created by Gilley breaking the sound barrier on his way out the door.

Gilley tore the pamphlet from my hands and scanned the contents as we hustled into the cab that had just pulled up to the curb. "Oh, no," Gil moaned as we got settled into the backseat. "All I heard was that we were staying in some luxurious accommodations! No one told me this place is *haunted!*"

Steven and I laughed, as he'd been listening in and was thoroughly enjoying Gilley's reaction. "What'd you expect?" I said. "That they'd shoot something about haunted possessions at the local Starbucks?"

Gilley didn't reply. He was too busy hyperventilating. Steven pulled out a small plastic bag from his messenger bag and handed it to Gil. "Breathe into this; it will help."

Our cabdriver looked in his rearview mirror. "Is he okay back there?"

"He's fine," I said. "Just being a drama queen. How long will it take to get to the Duke Hotel?"

"About twenty minutes," he said, still looking skeptically at Gilley, then at me, as though I should do something.

Under the cabdriver's disapproving glare I was

motivated to rub Gil's back. "It'll be okay," I said to him. "I'll protect you."

Gilley wheezed into the bag and glared at me. I . . . left . . . my sweatshirt . . . at . . . home!" he said, gasping.

On one of the busts that we'd done in the early summer Gilley had been attacked by a vicious brute of a ghost. To protect him, I'd rigged a sweatshirt with dozens of refrigerator magnets (ghosties *hate* magnets). Looking at him now, all red and hyperventilating, I gave in. "Driver? Can you please take us first to a sporting goods store and a hardware store before you drop us at the hotel?"

An hour later, and with a huge cab fare tab, we finally arrived in front of the Duke Hotel. I had been hurrying to glue on enough magnets to the inside of the sweatshirt we'd purchased for Gilley to hold him through the front lobby. I would finish it once we were checked in to our room.

As we were pulling up to the grand structure, Gilley squeaked in that way that said he was both excited and nervous.

"What?" I said, concentrating on gluing down a magnet.

"We're here," he said. "And there's trouble."

I glanced up just as Steven said, "There are a lot of police and an ambulance up there."

I squinted through the windshield. The curved driveway leading to the front door was lined with police and rescue vehicles, and the area was blocked off. An even longer line of cars had slowed in front of the commotion. Some were being directed by a traffic cop to move on, while others were waved into the hotel's underground garage.

I could also see several uniformed bellhops in red jackets with gold piping who looked distinctly out of place among all the police and medical crew.

"Wonder what happened," our driver said.

"Something bad," I whispered, feeling a shiver.

"What would you like me to do?" the driver asked, turning his head to look at us over his shoulder. "It's gonna take a while to move up this line. Or I can let you out here and you can make your way to the lobby if you'd like."

"We'll get out here," Steven said, reaching for his wallet.

Meanwhile, I was transfixed by the scene up ahead. Handing Gilley the sweatshirt along with the extra magnets and glue, I reached for the door handle.

"M.J.?" he said, obviously noticing my withdrawn appearance.

"I'll be back, Gil." And I got out of the cab.

"Wait a second and I'll come with you!" he said, gathering up his things and struggling with the sweatshirt and magnets.

"No!" I snapped, then reined myself in. "You can't," I said gently. "Or at least, you can't bring that sweatshirt along."

"Why not?"

"What's happening?" Steven said, coming to stand next to me on the sidewalk after paying the driver.

"There's a girl up there who needs my help."

"A girl?" Steven and Gilley said together, while they looked from me to where I was pointing, up near the mass of police.

"Yeah. She says someone entered her room and

hit her over the head. She's been trying to tell the police, but she can't get any of them to listen to her."

"How did you hear a girl from inside the cab?" Steven asked.

Out of the corner of my eye I saw Gilley mouth the word *ghost* to Steven.

"Ahhh," Steven said, nodding. "I will stay with Gilley. You go help the girl."

"I'll be back in a minute," I confirmed, handing Steven my backpack and looking at my watch. We'd landed an hour and a half ago and already I was doing my first bust. Little did I know that over the next few days, it certainly wouldn't be my last.

Chapter 2

I wound my way through the mix of onlookers and men in uniform to get as close to the girl as I could. It was tough going, as many of the gawkers didn't want to give up their places at the front of the crime scene, and no one in uniform would let me cross the yellow tape and orange sawhorses marking the area off-limits to the public. Finally someone in the exact spot I needed to get to shivered as if they were cold and moved aside, letting me slide into place at the very top of the crime-scene tape and close to a blanketed figure lying prone on the driveway.

Right next to the body I could see the slightest of haze in the atmosphere, and I knew that the woman who told me about being struck over the head in her hotel room was right now trying to figure out who the body on the driveway belonged to. *Yoo-hoo!* I called in my mind to get her attention.

I had this sense of the woman considering me curiously for a few seconds before making her way over. Immediately the five feet around me became cold as ice, and people crowding around shivered, rubbed their arms, and unconsciously moved away from where I was standing, which was a relief, because I was beginning to feel really scrunched.

What's your name, sweetheart? I asked. Her answer was clear; it sounded like the words *so* and *fee. Hi, Sophie,* I said pleasantly. *Can you tell me what happened to you in the hotel room?*

Immediately a series of disjointed pictures played out in my mind. I was looking at a brass plate hung on a door with the numbers three, two, and one on it. Then I had a very quick glimpse of a room decorated with celery green and yellow–striped wallpaper, cream carpet, and dark wood furnishings. On a table in the center of the room was a mess of papers. I had the sense of searching for one particular item within all that clutter, but something shiny shook loose and fell to the floor, where it caught the light and sparkled. As I reached down to pick it up I became aware of footsteps right behind me, and before I had a chance to react I felt a searing blow to the back of my head, followed by the fuzzy, confused haze of where I stood now.

I reached out to grab the column the police tape was secured to, feeling very wobbly on my feet.

"Ma'am?" someone said to me. "Ma'am, are you all right?"

I blinked a few times and rubbed the back of my head, then realized that an EMT was standing quite close to me with a concerned look on his face. "I'm fine," I said, eyeing the body on the ground. "What happened to her?" I asked him, thinking about feeling that hard knock to the back of my own head and how Sophie had ended up here.

The EMT looked me over again, probably to assess whether I really was okay; then he said, "Looks like she might have jumped from the roof."

"She *jumped*?" I asked.

The EMT nodded. "Right now they think it's probably a suicide. Cops are trying to figure out the trajectory of jumping off a six-story building, but the angle's right."

I gulped. "You sound like you've seen this before."

"I've been an EMT for twenty years. You see a lot in this line of work."

I looked back to the body, then up at the building. My eyes hovered around the third story. I also became aware that the EMT was still talking to me. ". . . cops are looking into whether she was a hotel guest or just someone who managed to find a tall roof to jump off of. No one saw her do it, so it's tough to tell."

"She was a guest," I said. "Her name was Sophie, and she was staying in room three-twenty-one."

"You knew her?" the EMT asked in surprise.

"Only casually," I admitted, very much aware that Sophie had gone back to the covered figure lying on the pavement, utterly confused about her surroundings and why she felt such a strong connection to the body beneath the blanket.

That was when I also became aware that the EMT was calling over one of the cops. "Yo! Ayden! This woman knows your vic!"

One of the faces in the crowd of officials turned and eyed us. He was about Steven's height, with thin black hair and square features, and I gulped as I realized his sharp blue eyes were focused intently on me.

He walked toward me with purpose, and I braced myself for the encounter, knowing I was very likely going to get a whole lot of resistance to the fact that I'd just picked up that tidbit of info about the woman under the blanket from her dearly departed soul.

"Afternoon," he said when he got to me. "I'm Detective Ayden MacDonald. You knew our victim?"

"Er . . . not really," I said honestly. "I've actually just flown in from Boston, but the woman contacted me when our cab pulled up to the hotel and told me her name and the room she was staying in."

"Excuse me?" he said, those blue eyes blinking hard to follow along. "What do you mean, she 'contacted' you?"

"I'm a psychic medium," I explained. "I'm here to do a show for television on haunted possessions."

MacDonald's face looked like he was waiting for me to get to the punch line. When I didn't comment further he turned somewhat serious and said, "I see. And this woman's ghost told you *what*, exactly?"

"She said her first name was Sophie and she was a hotel guest staying in room three-twenty-one. She showed me that she was in her room trying to sort through some paperwork when someone came up behind her and hit her on the back of the head. The next thing she knew, she was out here on the driveway surrounded by police."

MacDonald turned and regarded one of the uniformed policemen behind him. "Stanslowski!" he called. When a beefy-looking cop with a receding hairline looked up, MacDonald said, "Go inside and ask the desk clerk if there's a woman, first name Sophie, staying in room three-twenty-one."

The cop nodded and hustled away. We waited

in a tension-filled silence as the scene continued to buzz with people and energy. From inside I could hear the sound of jackhammers and construction, and for the first time I noticed a small poster on the outside of the hotel that begged patrons to excuse the noise and the dust.

After just a few minutes Stanslowski came back out and hustled up to MacDonald. "Desk clerk confirms a Sophie Givens is staying in room three-twenty-one, Detective. Do you want me and Reynolds to track her down?"

MacDonald glanced at the body on the pavement, then back to me. "Yeah," he said, his eyes wide with surprise. "Have management take you up to her room and see if she's there. If not, see if you can find some photo ID and bring it back to me."

"On it," he said, and whistled to another uniformed policeman.

"Mind if I ask you a few questions?" MacDonald asked me.

"I figured you'd say that," I said wearily. "And I'd love to answer them all, but I have a condition."

"A condition?" he repeated with an arched eyebrow that told me I didn't fully comprehend the precariousness of my position.

"Yes," I said, undaunted. "If I answer all of your questions, and if you discover that my story checks out, I want to cross this tape before they take her body away."

"Nope," said MacDonald, and his tone suggested there was no room for negotiation.

I looked at him for a long moment, wanting to argue but struggling with that motivation. Finally I opened my purse and handed him my boarding pass. "My plane got in an hour and a half ago," I said, digging around in my purse again. "From that point on we went on two errands, here and here." And I handed over the receipts from the sporting goods store and the hardware store. Going back to my purse I scrounged around for my card and one of the e-mails from Gopher to Gilley that I thought was particularly interesting.

"What's this?" said MacDonald as he took the e-mail.

"That's some correspondence from my business partner to the television production team that has invited me here to San Francisco," I said. "I'm the real deal, Detective, and the issue here isn't proving that to you as much as it is needing to get Sophie to understand that her body has died and that it's all right to move on, because right now her soul is suffering. It's clear to me that she hasn't made the connection that her body has stopped working and she can never come back to the land of the living. And the longer you and I stand here and trade credentials, the longer her suffering continues."

Just then the detective's cell phone beeped. He answered it quickly, and the voice coming through the earpiece was loud enough for me to hear.

"It's Stanslowski," said the voice. "I'm up here in room three-twenty-one, and we got ourselves a crime scene, Detective. There's blood on the carpet, and the place has been ransacked. Also, we found the lady's purse—her passport photo matches the woman on the pavement, sir."

MacDonald's eyes bored into mine, and his lips became pencil thin. "Secure the scene, Art," he said. "I'll be up in a minute."

I smiled at him and motioned back to the area where Sophie's body lay. "All I want is two minutes over there. I won't touch the body; I can even stand on that patch of lawn next to the ambulance. I just need to get close enough to grab her attention and send her on her way."

"You can actually talk to this girl?" asked the detective, his eyes traversing her body.

"I can."

After a moment he sighed and said, "Fine." Then he took my arm in one hand as he lifted the crimescene tape with the other, instructing, "I'll take you over there, but before you send her wherever you need to send her, I'll need to ask her some questions about what happened to her."

I pulled my arm out of his grip and stood back. "It doesn't work like that, Detective."

"What do you mean, it doesn't work like that?" he asked, still holding up the yellow tape.

"I mean that my primary directive is not solving your case. My job is to relieve her suffering. Right now she's completely lost and confused, and if I don't get to her quickly, she's going to start to panic and freak out. Trust me on this: There is nothing worse than watching someone stuck in a ghostly state as they have a complete mental breakdown when they realize no one can hear them and no one can help them. She'll soon become unreasonable and even inconsolable, and I won't be able to help her until she calms down again—which could be *years*.

"So you see, sir, I'm not going to risk sending her into that state of terror by giving her the third degree. If she's willing to listen to me, I'm going to get her over to the other side. Pronto."

MacDonald lowered the tape and stood up tall. His eyes seemed to be taking my measure. Glancing down at my card, he said, "The way I see it, Ms. Holliday, you don't have much of a choice. My lieutenant would eat me for lunch if he knew I let you close to the body, so if you don't have anything else to offer me, then I'm afraid I'm going to have to follow protocol."

I looked over again at Sophie's body, and I could see a thin vapor hovering around the crime scene. The vapor was shifting back and forth, and I realized that she was already beginning to get anxious. I could sense her emotions building and the panic beginning to form. "Damn it," I swore, and looked back to the detective. "Fine, have it your way. I'll ask her your questions, but the moment she begins to get too upset, Detective, I'm going to get her to move on, with or without your case wrapped up."

MacDonald lifted the crime-scene tape again. "After you," he said pleasantly.

I ducked low and stepped under, with MacDonald right next to me as he took firm hold of my elbow again. I resisted the urge to roll my eyes—the guy obviously thought I was some kind of liability ready to trample all over his crime scene—and I allowed myself to be guided over to within five feet of the sheet covering Sophie.

We got a few curious looks from the uniformed cops and CSIs standing nearby, but MacDonald didn't explain anything to them and ignored their inquisitive stares. "Okay," he said softly when we came to a stop. "See if you can get her to tell you how she came to land faceup on the pavement."

I closed my eyes and reached out to Sophie. *So-*

phie, I said in my mind. *My name is M.J., and I'm here to help you. Can you hear me?*

There was a kind of mental nod in my head. I had her attention.

That's great! I encouraged, but even then I could feel her energy drifting back to the sheet, as if she were distracted by it. I knew she was uncertain as to why she felt such a strong connection to it. So far she hadn't put two and two together, and I planned on keeping it that way for just a bit longer. *Now, Sophie,* I said, *I understand something happened up in your hotel room.*

The energy wafting back to me registered confusion, or rather, it felt a bit slow on the uptake, so I elaborated. *I've sent someone to check your hotel room,* I explained. *They say that they found it to be a mess. Do you remember someone coming into your room and maybe threatening you or trying to hurt you?*

Sophie's vapory energy began to shimmer with alarm.

"What's she saying?" asked the detective.

I opened one eye and scowled at him. "*Shhh!*" I hissed. "I'm trying to work here!"

He frowned but nodded. Sophie, however, was starting to make some noise. *Where is my file?* she demanded. *I had it in my hand! He's stolen it!*

Who's stolen it? I asked. *Honey, if you tell me who came into your room, I promise I'll help you find your file.*

Something's wrong with my head, Sophie continued. *He hit me! He hit me and stole my file!*

I could feel Sophie's increasing agitation. I knew I was pushing it and decided to ask one more time before I focused on trying to get her across. *Sophie,*

I said gently in my mind, *I'm so sorry he did that. But I've got the police here, and they're ready to take your statement. Just tell me what the man looked like and we'll get them to find your file.*

And then I could feel something like shock reverberate across the ether, and I knew that Sophie was now fully aware of all the police and the CSIs around her. Her surroundings were becoming clearer, and the fog was starting to lift. The dots were going to connect in the next instant, and I knew I was about to have a hell of a time doing anything for her if I didn't say something else, and quickly.

SOPHIE! I yelled as loud as I could in my head. And it worked; I got her attention. *I need you to listen to me, and listen carefully. You've been in a terrible accident,* I said. *And it's time for you to leave us. You have to realize that there is nothing more you can do here, and you've got to let go. Do you understand?*

My file! she said. *He can't get his hands on that file! I need to turn it in to the authorities, or he'll get away with everything!*

I've found it! I lied. *I've given it over to the police and it's safe. But you need to move forward now.*

Sophie's energy went back to the covered form on the pavement. *Is that me?* she asked, the tone in my head sounding pitifully sad.

Yes, my friend, I said carefully. *It is. I'm so sorry.*

Sophie's energy seemed to shudder, and I hoped the realization wouldn't throw her into a state of panic. Finally, however, she asked, *What do I do now?*

I felt my shoulders sag with relief. She was a strong woman; that was for sure. *If you look up, you'll see a beautiful ball of light about ten feet above your head,* I instructed.

There was another slight hesitation, and then I felt a sort of mental gasp. *I see it!*

Excellent! I encouraged. *Sophie, that ball of light is your magical elevator ride, and it will take you to your next destination. All you need to do is call it down to you—just think of it descending slowly around you, and when you're completely surrounded by it, you'll be taken away from here to reunite with your deceased loved ones.* I waited two heartbeats and felt Sophie follow my instructions. *That's it!* I said to her. *Now, we only have a few seconds*, I said quickly, *so when you feel it completely envelop you, I'll need you to let go. Just let the light take you. I promise you'll be safe and sound, and you'll arrive home on the other side in no time. Okay?*

Again I felt that mental nod and also the lowering of the light around Sophie, and then there was a *whoosh* feeling all around me, and in an instant she was gone.

I let out the breath that I'd been holding and opened my eyes. MacDonald was looking down at his arms and the hair that was visible where his shirt was rolled up. "Something just happened," he said, indicating the way all the hairs on his arms were standing straight up on end.

"Yep," I confirmed. "She's gone."

"What'd she tell you?" he asked, and the look on his face suggested he thought I'd tricked him.

"She said that someone broke into her room and stole an important file she had in her possession, and that's why she was attacked and murdered."

The detective's brows furrowed. "A paper file or a computer file?" he asked.

I shrugged. "I've no idea," I said wearily. Already it'd been a long day.

"M.J.!" I heard from near the entrance, and I looked over to see Gilley and Steven standing just on the other side of the crime-scene tape. "Is everything okay?" Gil said.

I nodded. "I'll be there in a second," I reassured them before turning back to the detective.

"So, she's gone for good?" he said to me, and I smirked at the way his eyes were roving around, as if he were looking for her.

"She is," I said. "I got her across when she started to panic. The only thing she told me about what happened was that some unidentified man came in and took her file."

"Did you give you a name or tell you if she knew this guy?"

"No," I said. "Again, I really couldn't get much out of her."

"Not very cooperative, huh?"

"Well, how cooperative would you feel if someone had just murdered *you*?" I asked seriously.

That got MacDonald to smile. "I see your point," he said, then looked up to the third floor, where Sophie had likely been pushed out of her window. "Say, can you use your magic powers to come up to her room and maybe get an impression about what happened? You know, like those psychics do on TV?"

Great. Now I was a novelty item. I sighed tiredly, not exactly feeling very charitable after that kind of statement. "You know, that's not really my forte. And besides, I'm pretty tired after traveling cross-country."

The detective's face fell. "Okay, fine," he said. "Sorry I asked."

I felt the guilt seep into the middle of my chest. "Okay, okay," I said grudgingly. "Just let me tell my business associates what's going on so they can at least get me checked in, all right?"

MacDonald guided me again over to the crime-scene tape (I was seriously starting to feel like an errant child with all this leading-around-by-the-arm stuff), and, after he left me with my friends, I explained quickly what had happened and why I needed to leave them again.

"What do you think you can pick up in the room if you've already crossed this woman over?" asked Steven.

"Well, probably a lot," I admitted. "The more violent the act in that room, the better I'll be able to feel it out."

"How?" he wondered.

I thought for a moment about how best to explain it. As I was thinking, Gilley—who's had a lot of experience with paranormal research—explained. "Think of it as if the space all around us is one giant sponge, and it can absorb physical actions like a liquid or a stain. Some stains are faint—your simple everyday routine, for instance—hardly noticeable. But other things, like a car accident or a violent outburst that causes intense pain or an act of murder, are darker, more acute stains that people like M.J. can clearly pick up on. They're able to describe the event because it leaves a more intense impression on the sponge. Am I right, M.J.?"

I smiled at Gil. "You are," I said. "That was a great analogy."

"So, you are going to clean up the stain?" Steven asked, and I could tell he hadn't quite gotten it.

"No," I said. "I'm going to go into her room and hopefully tell them how the event unfolded. The atmosphere up there should have acted a bit like a movie camera—if we're lucky, it should have recorded the event that took place there, and I might be able to visualize the images for the police."

"Ah, now I am understanding," said Steven with a nod. "We will get you checked in and take your luggage to the room. I will send a text to your cell phone to let you know what room we're in."

"Awesome," I said as Detective MacDonald came up to me again carrying a duffel bag.

"Ready to go, Ms. Holliday?"

"Let's do it," I said, and we left Gilley and Steven to make their way to the check-in counter.

MacDonald led the way over to the main elevator through the various cones set up in the mezzanine to steer patrons away from construction zones. "Hotel's doing a major renovation. Seems they've got a bunch of old wiring and plumbing that's not up to code," MacDonald commented as he handed me some rubber gloves.

"What are these for?" I asked.

"In case you need to touch or hold anything in the room," he said, before reaching into his duffel and pulling out some little blue booties. "These go over your shoes," he added as the elevator door opened and we got on.

"I feel like I've just stepped onto a movie set," I mumbled as I leaned my back against the elevator wall and popped the booties over my boots.

MacDonald didn't comment as he did the same, and when we reached the third floor he led the way to room 321. It wasn't hard to find; there were about three uniformed policemen close by. One was sealing the area around the room with yellow crime-scene tape, while another was knocking on doors, and yet another was interviewing a man in the hallway.

MacDonald stopped in front of the uniformed cop setting up the tape, and the two whispered in low tones just out of my earshot. The uniformed officer looked curiously back at me a few times, and I saw his eyes ogle me a bit. I sent him what I hoped was a winning smile and waited to be allowed into the room.

Not long after that MacDonald waved me forward, and I approached with my hands clasped behind my back. Even though I now wore gloves, I didn't want to be tempted to touch or disturb anything. MacDonald stepped into the room first, and I followed him warily.

My eyes roved the room, which appeared to have been hit by a tornado. The sheets on the bed had been torn off and lay in a messy, trampled pile to one side. Several pillows were strewn about, and the mattress itself was pulled entirely off the bed and was leaning against the far wall. Long gashes had been sliced into the mattress, and the stuffing lay in large, fluffy tufts all about the floor.

Drawers from the two nightstands had been tossed aside, much like the pillows, and the table that, by the indentations in the carpet, had once resided by the window was now overturned and in the middle of the room.

Dresser drawers were pulled open, and clothing had been thrown about like confetti. The television had even been gutted, and even though it was still perched on top of the dresser, it was now facing backward with its wires pulled out like it had undergone an electronic autopsy. "Jesus," I whispered as I stared around the room.

MacDonald too was taking it all in, and I saw him out of the corner of my eye making a quick sketch on his notepad, marking with little arrows where things were. He didn't say anything, so I figured he must be waiting for me to do my thing. I braced myself and focused all my energy on picking out whatever might be lying about in the ether of the room.

My eye went immediately to the table, and almost subconsciously I walked to it, barely resisting the urge to pick it up. I left it where it lay and went over to where it had once rested, by the window. Here I had a clear impression of Sophie working on a laptop, and I looked around the room, but no computer was evident. "Did they find a laptop?" I asked MacDonald.

"Hmm?" he murmured, looking up from his sketch.

"Did your uniformed cop find a laptop in here and take it out of the room?"

MacDonald turned to the cop he'd first sent up here to investigate room 321. "Art, did you guys find a computer?"

"No, sir," he said, "we didn't."

I looked back at the empty space and turned in a circle. A broken chair lay in three pieces behind me, and I shuddered. My eye then darted over to the bed, and I approached the crumpled remains of the comforter on the floor. I bent down and carefully held my gloved hand just above the comforter, wincing, while my other hand went up to my throat, and I found it difficult to swallow. I stood up then, and my head snapped over to the sliding glass door to the balcony, which was closed, but a section of the curtain had been caught in the door when someone shut it.

"I know how it went down," I said gravely.

"Spill it," said MacDonald, flipping the page in his notebook.

"She was working on her computer," I began as the impressions sorted themselves out in my mind. "She has a connection to Europe," I added, "England specifically, but London most specifically."

MacDonald shot his eyes over to the uniformed cop in the doorway, whose jaw, I noticed, had dropped a fraction.

"Her passport lists her current address in London," he confirmed.

"There was a knock on the door," I continued, pointing over to where the cop was. "Sophie answered it and right away things got bad. I feel like she was shoved violently onto the bed, and her attacker began to strangle her. There was a struggle, but she was really outmatched. Somehow she got out from under him and she tried to flee. He grabbed that chair," I added, pointing now to the remains of the chair on the floor, "and whacked her over the head with it. He then ransacked the place and was about to leave when I think she either woke up or showed signs of coming to. That's when he took her out to the balcony and tossed her over the railing."

No one spoke for several seconds, and truthfully, I was grateful. The events that played in my mind and the carnage of the room made me want to find a shower and scrub myself from head to toe. I hated being in that room, and really wanted to leave.

Finally MacDonald said, "Can you describe the guy?"

I shook my head. "No." When he looked at me as if to ask why not, I explained, "I don't see these things quite the way you think I would. They don't happen like a moving picture in my head—it's more like the sense of something, as if I were watching something through a haze where the finite details get obscured. I know he was tall. I know he was much stronger than she was, but other than that, I can't give you a mug shot."

"Do you think she knew him?"

I frowned. I had an urge to say yes, but I realized I wanted to say that because I was afraid of what it might mean if he were some creepy stranger prowling the hotel for innocent victims—after all, I was staying here tonight. "I don't know," I said after considering it. "There is something familiar about his energy with her. Almost like she knew him, but might not have recognized him at first."

"What do you think he was after?" MacDonald asked me next, and he pointed his pen around in an arc at the chaos in the room.

"Her file," I said simply. "Only now I really think it was a computer file, and I don't think he found it on the computer. I think she might have put whatever it was on a flash drive and hidden it. Whether he found it I can't say, but I do know she was really worried he'd stolen it, so that tells me it must have been here in this room."

The detective scribbled some more in his notebook, then looked up at me and smiled kindly for the first time since I'd met him. "Thank you, Ms. Holliday. I won't take up any more of your time for now, but can I call on you in the next day or so if we need you again?"

My first impulse was to say no, but then my conscience got the best of me. "That's fine," I agreed, feeling the pocket where my cell phone was buzzing. Pulling it out, I looked at the screen and said, "My associates have just let me know I'll be in room four-twenty-one. You can leave messages there until we're finished with the shoot and head back home day after tomorrow."

"Great," said MacDonald. "We probably won't need you, but I appreciate it."

As I left Sophie's room and took off my booties and gloves, I had the distinct impression that I hadn't seen the last of MacDonald or this investigation, and this thought unsettled me for some time.

Chapter 3

I met my partners in the hallway just outside my room. "How'd it go?" Steven asked.

"It went okay." I sighed. "Hopefully they won't need me again, but for right now all I want to do is get into my room, take a shower, and have a really good power nap."

Gilley, who was standing in front of me holding out my key card, blanched. "Yeah," he mumbled, "about that."

I groaned and hung my head. "Please don't tell me that we have to do something for the show right now."

"Okay," he said.

"Okay, *what*?" I growled, picking my head up to look at him.

"I won't tell you, even though we're due downstairs in the lobby in five minutes to meet the producers and the other mediums."

I narrowed my eyes at my partner, and without saying a word I grabbed the room key out of his hand and moved off into my room, making sure to slam the door a little after I entered.

Steven's luggage was already in the corner next to mine, and I was actually glad he was going to be hanging with me. I'd need someone to vent at when this thing became a pain in the ass . . . like now.

Sighing, I went into the bathroom and splashed some cool water onto my face, then freshened up and made my way back into the hallway. Steven and Gilley were waiting for me, Gilley looking really guilty, which actually made me feel better. "Come on," I said to him. "Let's get this over with."

Just a few minutes later we were down in the lobby, which was abuzz with people talking about the girl who had fallen out of the third-story window. The overwhelming consensus from the chatter that I overheard was that she had committed suicide, something I knew to be completely false, but it wasn't my place to correct these things—that job fell to the reporters also hovering around the area.

As we approached a group of folks who looked like they belonged in television, one of the reporters interviewing a woman snapped his head in my direction, much like a lion sensing an injured antelope. "Uh-oh," I whispered.

Gilley glanced over at me. "What?"

I motioned with my head over to the reporter, who was now ignoring the woman talking in earnest to him as he rudely began to click through the photos he'd taken earlier on his digital camera. "Crap," I muttered when he seemed to find the one that he was looking for and his head snapped back over to me.

"Do you know him?" Steven asked.

"No, but we're about to be introduced." No sooner had I finished that sentence than the reporter

. excused himself from the woman he'd been interviewing and hurried over to intercept us.

"Excuse me!" he called, waving at us across the lobby. I had a moment when I thought about running, but really, where was I going to go? So I paused and waited for the reporter to trot over to us. "Hi, there," he said with a winning smile that I didn't trust for a nanosecond. "I'm Trent Fielding with the *San Francisco Chronicle*," he added, extending his hand for me to shake.

I shook it and gave a cool, "Hello."

"I was wondering if I could ask you a few questions about the tragedy that happened here today," he said, motioning with his head to the front door, where we could all see the CSI techs still gathering evidence, although I was thankful that Sophie's body had been taken away.

I listened politely but declined the opportunity to give him any details. "I'm sorry, Mr. Fielding, but no. My associates and I were just about to meet our friends, and I'm afraid I have nothing to contribute to your story."

I turned to go, but Fielding took a step forward and blocked me. "Really?" he persisted, again flashing that winning smile. "See, that's funny, because I've got a photo here that begs to differ." With that he showed me the viewfinder on his camera and hit a button. A digital image of me standing next to MacDonald appeared, with Sophie's covered body in the foreground.

I resisted the urge to shove my way past the reporter and settled for making my voice sound as firm as possible. "As I said, I have *nothing* to contribute. Have a good afternoon." And then I did push forward, brushing him with my shoulder just a little to get my point across.

From behind me I overheard the reporter ask, "What's her name?"

Gilley's enthusiastic voice replied, "That is M. J. Holliday, spelled with two Ls. She's a gifted medium. She's going to be on television, you know."

I whirled around. "*Gilley!*" I hissed. But Gil was busy looking over Trent's shoulder to make sure he spelled my name correctly.

"What is this problem you're having?" asked Steven on the other side of me, and I realized he didn't understand that I was about to be sucked into the Twilight Zone.

"A *medium?*" Fielding was saying. "You mean the 'I see dead people' kind of medium?"

Gilley nodded his head vigorously. "That's right. She sees them, she hears them, and she busts them."

"*Gilley Gillespie!*" I hissed again, but Gil was on a roll, and his new best friend, Trent, couldn't write fast enough.

"When you say 'bust,' I'm assuming you're referring to ghostbusting?" Fielding clarified.

"I am, indeedy!" said Gil, working himself up into a good story. "And let me tell you a bit about our most recent buh—Eeeeeow!"

I had Gilley by the ear and I wasn't letting go until he stopped talking. "Come. With. Me," I ordered, separating each word so there could be no doubt about how pissed off I was.

"Hey!" Gilley howled. "That hurts!"

"Then promise to walk over there without saying another word and I'll let you go," I demanded. I had little sympathy for my partner at the moment.

"Okay, okay!" he whined.

Gil hurried away from Fielding as Steven and I followed close behind over to a set of wing chairs and a small coffee table. Only when we were out of the reporter's earshot did I let go. "What the *hell* is wrong with you?" I snapped.

Gil rubbed his ear and gave me a dirty look. "Usually I have your time of the month circled on my calendar, but I must have miscalculated."

"Why do you *insist* on making a mockery of me?" I asked, ignoring his cheap shot. "Don't you realize that the last thing I want is for the press to get hold of who I am and what I do?"

Gilley crossed his arms over his chest and pouted. His look told me he didn't give a rat's ass about what I wanted. "It's good for business," he insisted.

"*How* is being shaded as a nut job by some local reporter going to be good for business *exactly*?" I said loudly. A few people nearby turned to look at us, and I lowered my voice back down to a shrewish whisper. "Seriously, Gil! Have you no scruples? Will you just pimp me out to anyone with a pen and a story to tell?"

"Maybe it will not be so negative for you?" Steven suggested helpfully.

"Don't be naive," I growled, but felt bad when I saw him raise his eyebrows before tossing his hands up in surrender and giving Gilley and me some room.

"What would you have me do, M.J.?" Gilley snapped as Steven walked away. "Would you have me continue to run around Boston with *flyers*? Or maybe I should rehire that Casper guy? Because in case you haven't been paying attention, girlfriend, our business is drying up faster than a woman in menopause, and I for one would like to continue to pay the light bill!"

"Again," I said angrily, "how does making me look like an idiot benefit us? I mean, it's not like we live out here and can just gas up the van and zip on over to bust any of the local-yokel ghosts!"

"Oh, stuff gets thrown up from these newspapers onto the AP all the time!" Gil argued. "And this kind of story, well, it's juicy enough to go *national*! Think of it, M.J.!" Gil gushed, before dropping his voice down a few octaves and saying in his most serious broadcaster voice while his hand moved in short jerks, "'Ghost hunter helps police solve local murder. Film at eleven.' You can't *pay* for advertising like that!"

"If you think there's any chance of that reporter doing a legitimate article on us, you are as naive as you are light in the loafers! There's no way he'd be objective! And it would compromise any amount of assistance I could offer the police. Think about that detective who took a chance by letting me help Sophie cross over. Think about the little bit of good I did by feeling out the energy in her hotel room and offering the police a direction on where to start looking, and how you just shot all of that straight to hell. If the press connects the dots that I'm helping the investigation in *any* way, the SFPD is likely to toss out all of my impressions. That could seriously damage the case they're trying to make to solve her murder! How could you be so incredibly stupid, Gilley, as to jeopardize all of that for the sake of a small bit of *useless* publicity?"

I was so angry I could feel my face starting to

flush. Gilley's expression told me that he finally realized why I was so uptight, and he dropped his eyes. "Well," he said, uncrossing his arms to tuck his hands into his back pockets, "when you put it like *that . . .*"

I didn't say anything more. Instead I turned away from him in disgust and headed over to the group that we had initially been walking toward. The first guy I came to was wearing a funky-looking hat and a cashmere scarf with dark sunglasses, even though it was rather dim in the lobby. "Hello," I said, extending my hand and working hard to compose myself. "I'm M. J. Holliday."

"Ah, Miss Holliday," he said. "I'm Peter Gophner, but most folks call me Gopher. I have to say, I'm mighty impressed with your résumé."

"Thanks," I said, noticing that Gilley and Steven had just come up to stand next to me. I decided to play nice and introduce them. "These are my associates, Dr. Steven Sable and Gilley Gillespie. I believe you and Gilley know each other through e-mail quite well by now."

"Gilley!" Gopher said, and I was actually surprised when he reached out to hug my partner. "It's great to finally meet you, man!"

I felt myself smile when I saw Gilley's delighted face. I knew he thought that Gopher was hot, and to get such a warm hug from a hot guy . . . well, I could pretty much figure Gil was already mentally picking out the china pattern.

"You too, Gopher!" my partner said, squeezing the producer in a tight embrace. I figured Gopher had about five seconds before Gil began some inappropriate groping.

Steven cleared his throat, and Gopher pulled himself out of Gilley's arms. "Dr. Sable," he said, extending his hand to Steven.

"A pleasure," Steven said, and my smile broadened. Steven has the most delicious accent. Coupled with his deep baritone voice, it's a wicked combination that always makes me feel a little googly inside.

Turning back to me, Gopher said, "M.J., I'd like to introduce you to our other mediums."

"Super," I said, working really hard to muster up some enthusiasm. However, when I saw a gentleman with a receding hairline and a horrible combover wearing—I kid you not—a cape, it was really, *really* hard to keep a straight face.

"This is Bernard Higgins," Gopher was saying, and Bernard looked me up and down from toe to chest—where his eyes just stopped—and gave me a little bow.

I bent my knees and cocked my head, attempting to make eye contact. "Mr. Higgins," I said, offering my hand.

Bernard took it, but instead of shaking it he turned it over and gave my palm a wet, slobbery kiss. "Enchanted," he said.

Grossed out, I thought.

"And over here we have Madam Angelica Demarche," Gopher added, moving over to a woman I'd guess was anywhere from thirty-five to sixty-five. Looking at her face, it was impossible to tell. We're talking Botox, face-lifts, and collagen up the yin-yang.

"Nice to meet you," I said, offering her my hand, which she regarded with all the enthusiasm with which she'd probably regard a rat.

"Hello," she said, looking down her nose at me and refusing to shake my hand.

I pumped it up and down anyway, as if I were shaking an invisible hand, to show her just how rude I thought she was being. Yes, I'm a smart aleck, but only in the face of blatant impropriety.

Gopher didn't seem to notice; instead he moved me over to a young, good-looking guy with shoulder-length black hair, olive skin, high cheekbones, lots of turquoise jewelry, and a small white feather dangling from one earlobe. "And this is Heath White-feather," he said.

Heath reached out his hand first and we shook, exchanging big, toothy smiles. "Hi!" he said, and I immediately liked him.

"Hi, yourself," I said.

"Now that we're all here," Gopher announced, addressing the entire group, "let's head next door for dinner."

We all tagged along behind Gopher toward the Salazar Bistro, adjacent to the Duke, and my stomach growled as I caught a whiff of something delicious wafting out from inside the restaurant. "Man, am I hungry," I said as we approached.

"All food is included, so feel free to chow down," Gilley said to my right, and I noticed he was keeping a bit of distance from me. I gave him a smile that said we were on better terms, and he melted. "I'm really sorry!" he whispered, moving in to give my shoulder a bump with his own.

"I know," I said gently. "Just next time, sweetheart, can you please think first and talk second?"

"You know that's always been a challenge for me." He grinned.

"Yes, but the challenging part isn't just for you; it's for the rest of us who suffer for it."

"Okay, okay," he said. "I get it. Now let's drop it and enjoy dinner."

"Deal," I agreed.

The hostess led our troop to a table at the back of the restaurant large enough for everyone to sit down without feeling cramped. Gilley chose a seat right next to Gopher, (*quelle surprise*), and I went for the seat next to Gil. My chair was pulled out for me, and I turned my head to see Steven doing his usual chivalry thing. "Thanks, sweetie," I said, and he gave my cheek a buss before taking the seat next to me.

Across from me I noticed that Bernard had taken his seat just to the left of Madam Hateful, and on the other side of him sat Heath.

I tried to ignore Bernard's renewed attempts to ogle my chest (I'm "blessed" in that area, and I find that around lecherous old guys my boobs have the magical ability to lower a few IQ points) and opened my menu with enthusiasm, while using it as a prop to block Bernard.

"What looks good to you?" Steven murmured after a moment of looking at the menu.

"Everything," I said with a grin. "But I think I'm going to go for the sautéed monkfish."

"Good choice," he agreed. "I was trying to decide between that and the braised short ribs."

"Ooh," I said, darting my eyes down the menu. "That sounds really good too. Why don't you get that and I'll get the monkfish and we'll share?"

"Perfect," Steven said, closing his menu.

I set mine down too, and that was when I became aware of the buzz around the table. "Yes, I agree,"

Bernard was saying to Madam Hateful. "I too picked up a suicide."

"Her lover left her," said Angelica, and the way she spoke you couldn't help but think she found herself incredibly important. "There was another woman, of course, and this caused the poor wretch to leap to her death."

Out of the corner of my eye I saw Gilley staring at me the way a hungry dog stares when it really, really wants to take a bite out of your steak. I turned my head and lowered my eyebrows in that *don't you dare say a word!* way, and he dropped his eyes to the table and sighed.

Gopher said, "Angelica and Bernard, do you think you might be able to contact this poor woman?"

"Oh, but I already have," replied Madam Hateful with a wave of her hand. "She came to me in my room, you know, clearly distraught. She told me the whole sordid story and begged me to help her. But, as you know, there is little one can do for a suicide victim."

By now I was playing with the corners of the napkin in my lap. It was taking a lot not to comment on the load of baloney coming out of Madam Hateful's mouth, but I knew I needed to resist. Sophie deserved a little respect, and my ego didn't need to be pumped up by dragging out what had really happened to her for these folks to feast on.

On the other side of the table, however, a voice of reason piped up. "You know, I don't think it was a suicide," Heath said thoughtfully.

My eyes shot over to him. "Really?" I questioned.

He nodded, and his eyes held a faraway look. "I think she was murdered."

Heath now had my full attention, but Madam Hateful and Captain Comb-over were unimpressed.

"Murder!" scoffed Bernard. "Ridiculous. No, I agree with Angelica. The girl clearly jumped to her death."

"Oh, I don't know," I said, unable to resist poking the tiger now that I had an ally. "I actually agree with Heath."

"Of course you do," said Madam Hateful, and she and Bernard exchanged knowing glances. "Perhaps when you've had a bit more practice you'll be able to distinguish between a suicide and a murder," she added, looking pointedly at Heath.

Heath turned red and took a sip of water, clearly intimidated by the odd couple. I was about to argue his point when our waiter appeared and began taking everyone's order. After he left, the conversation changed to talk of the show. "Tomorrow I'll need you four mediums to meet me down in the lobby no later than eight thirty. We've reserved one of the larger conference rooms at the Duke, and when we meet in the morning I'll lead you there."

"Can you talk a little bit about how this is going to unfold?" I asked.

"Certainly," said Gopher. "I think initially we should set you up in groups of two. We've got a great inventory of haunted possessions for you to give your impressions on, and we'll have these displayed one at a time on a table, with the owner of the item in question, who can verify or disprove your conclusions, on the other side of the table."

I glanced at Gilley, and I could tell he knew I wasn't liking that whole "disprove your conclusions" part.

"When you say you have the owner there to authenticate or disprove the medium's findings," Gil said, taking the lead for me, "do you mean that this person will be well versed in the object's entire history? And the reason I ask is that M.J. can often pick up even the subtlest energies, some lost to history or to anyone living."

Gopher nodded. "Yes, we've been very careful to research each and every haunted possession so that we can easily identify whether you mediums are reading accurate information. Trust me, if you're all as talented as I think you are, this should be a walk in the park."

But I still had my doubts, and they lingered all through our delectable meal and into the oh-so-delicious hot-fudge sundaes that followed.

Over dessert Gopher told us a little bit about his background. "I used to work as a producer for *60 Minutes*," he bragged. "Did some really great stories there, but you know how it is at those news shows."

Everyone looked at him curiously. Apparently we didn't all know how it was.

"They burn you out quick," he advised. "Then I kicked around for a while out in L.A. I had some great offers to work on some pretty cool stuff—you know, reality TV is where it's at these days—but I wanted to do something hipper, not another *Idol* retread or *Big Brother* knockoff. That's when I met Roger, and he and I had the same philosophy, know what I'm saying?"

Again all eyes around the table looked curiously at him. We didn't.

"We wanted to push the envelope, man!" Go-

pher said. "So we came up with this idea and went
to almost every studio in town with it. Eventually
Bravo said yes, but they needed it done quick. Since
Roger's stuck in the Sudan right now on another
documentary, I just had to pick up the reins and run
with it."

"I thought I saw Matt Duval in the lobby," Heath
said. "Is he part of this show?"

It took me a moment to place the name, but eventually I remembered that Matt Duval had been the
spunky teenager on a popular TV family sitcom back
when I was in high school. And if memory served
me correctly, tabloid reports had had him in and out
of rehab ever since the canceling of that show.

Gopher leaned back in his chair and smiled. "He
is," he said. "Matt and I go way back. We were college roomies at Berkeley. He's actually doing me a
favor by hosting this show. He's got some real irons
in the fire that he's put on hold just to come out here
this weekend."

Somehow I doubted that, but I kept my thoughts
to myself, and eventually our little party broke up
and we left the restaurant to head back to the hotel.

Throughout dinner I'd become more and more
impressed with Heath, and I discreetly asked him
to join us for a cocktail in the lobby area of the hotel.
He smiled shyly and trailed after us as we found a
couch to settle down on and have a nightcap.

Steven played waiter. "What would everyone
like?" he asked, reaching for his wallet, and again
I was struck by how much I liked him for always
being quick to take care of any company he found
himself in—especially Gilley and me.

After he'd gone to the bar to fetch our drinks

I turned to Heath and said, "So tell me about yourself."

"Well," he began, and I could tell that like many of us legitimate psychics, he was a bit shy. "I was born in New Mexico and raised in Santa Fe. My mom is Native American, and we lived on one of the reservations until I was nine, when she married my stepdad and we moved to one of the nicer suburbs."

"What was it like living on a reservation?" asked Gilley.

Heath thought for a minute before answering. "It was really awesome and terrible at the same time," he explained. "Like, I loved learning about my heritage and culture, but it was also very confining. The atmosphere of the reservation was pretty antiestablishment, and none of the leaders wanted us to mix with any of the white kids in the area, so we stuck to ourselves and kept our heads down, and because there weren't a lot of kids my own age on the reservation it was pretty lonely.

"I think that's why I developed my skills as a medium. I was starving for people to talk to, and the only people I could find were some of the spirits that walked the land."

"Who did you end up talking to?" I asked, fascinated by Heath's history.

"What are we talking about?" Steven interrupted as he came back with our drinks and took a seat next to me.

"Heath was just telling us about how he grew up on an American Indian reservation, and that he used to talk to spirits on the land."

"Like who?" Steven asked.

"Billy the Kid for one," he said. "And Kit Carson

for another. He was hated by my people, but in actuality I really liked his spirit, if you'll pardon the pun."

"That is so cool," I said with appreciation. "I'm a direct relative of Doc Holliday."

"No way!" he said.

"Way." I smiled. "He was my great-great-uncle."

"That is so awesome!" Heath said.

"My grandfather was the mayor of Valdosta," Gilley piped in proudly.

Heath nodded, as if he already knew that. "His name was Abner, right?"

Gilley's eyebrows shot up. "Wow!" he said. "You're good!"

Heath blushed, then turned to me. "M.J., can I pass along a message for you?"

I felt my heart quicken, and before he even said another word I knew who was likely knocking on Heath's energy. "Sure," I said, my voice cracking.

"Your mom has been all over me since we first sat down to dinner," Heath explained. "Her name began with an M, but I think her middle name was Lynn, right?"

I felt my eyes water, and I tried to get it together before answering. "Her name was Madelyn."

Heath's eyes brightened. "Duh!" he said, as if he should have put that together. "Anyway," he continued, "like I said, she's been all over me since dinner, and she wants you to know that she's really, really proud of you. She says she talks to you, but usually you tune her out." Heath looked at me with a curious expression, and I understood that he wanted to know why I did that.

It took me a moment to gather my voice and explain. Even though my mom's been dead for more than twenty years, I still deeply mourn her loss. "You know how this sixth-sense thing works," I began. "If I let my mom in to talk to me, I'd only want to hear from her. Plus, this stuff is so subtle, I think that I'd start to doubt whether it was really her or not. If she came to me, I'd assume it was my conscious mind making it up because I miss her so much."

"I get it," Heath said with an understanding smile. "I'm sort of that way about my grandfather who passed away about ten years ago and my stepdad, who died just last year. Anyway, your mom says she's been having a great time looking in on . . . ." Heath paused, and his eyebrows furrowed as if he were checking with my mom to confirm what he was seeing. "Do you have a pet bird that needs to go to the vet?"

Gilley laughed and slapped his knee. "That's Doc!" he said. "Yes, M.J. has a pet parrot named Doc."

"Oh," said Heath. "I get it. She kept showing me this parrot and pointing to a man in a lab coat—I just assumed she was referring to the vet. I didn't realize she was talking about his name!"

I was pretty speechless at this point. It's one thing to connect with someone else's loved ones—there's a distance created that takes the emotion out of it. But to have someone just as talented tune in to my own mother . . . well, it almost undid me.

"She's also saying she really likes Steven," he said, glancing at my boyfriend, who smiled broadly and gave me a squeeze. "But she's saying she thinks you should go easier on him."

I barked out a laugh, because I can be a little tough

on him, especially when I'm working. "I knew she'd take his side," I muttered with a smile.

"Your mother is a smart woman," Steven remarked.

I focused back on Heath, who looked as if he were concentrating really hard on something. He then looked at me curiously and said, "She also thinks that coming here wasn't such a hot idea."

I laughed. "Tell me about it, but I had no choice; I got suckered into participating." Gilley turned red and suddenly became very interested in his shoes.

"Yeah, I kinda got the same message from my own guides," said Heath. "But it's good exposure, right?"

"Let's hope so. What do you make of the other two?" I asked. "Bernard and Angelica?"

Heath rolled his eyes. "How the hell did they pass the screening test?" he wondered. "I mean, I don't want to talk trash about anyone, but they don't appear to be very talented."

"I agree," I said with a nod. "So, why don't you and I pair up tomorrow during the taping? I think we both operate in the same way, and we're probably going to complement each other during the shoot. It might be a good way to ensure we're not portrayed badly when this thing broadcasts."

"I like that line of thinking," said Heath with a wink. "And what was your take on that whole freaky scene this afternoon with the woman who died outside?"

"Exactly the same as yours," I admitted. "She was murdered, just like you said."

"I keep getting the letter A associated with her killer," said Heath. "I wanted to say something to the police when they were here, but I didn't want to freak them out."

I stared in awe at this young, incredibly talented man. "You know what?" I said to him. "Even I didn't tune in to an initial. And I *did* say something to the police. So, because I've already broken the ice with the lead detective, would you mind if I mentioned that clue to him?"

"You're involved in the investigation?" Heath asked, and I could tell he thought it was cool.

"More by accident than by invitation," I admitted. "But I believe they think I'm credible, and every little bit of info helps, so we might as well give them this intel about the initial A too."

"Absolutely," Heath said, before he seemed to think of something else. "M.J.?"

"Yeah?"

"After we're through filming tomorrow, would you maybe like to put our heads together on the woman's murder and see if we can't pull a few more clues out of the ether?"

Gilley looked as though he were about to burst with happiness, and I knew my partner was thinking only about the headline *Psychic Dynamic Duo Solves Local Murder Mystery. Film at Eleven.*

I gave him a cautionary look but told Heath, "That sounds like a great idea. But let's keep it on the down-low until we're sure we've got something solid to offer the investigators, okay?"

"I hear ya," said Heath. "I've always wanted to work with the police," he admitted. "I'm addicted to those psychic detective shows."

I laughed, and Gilley couldn't resist telling Heath, "M.J. has solved a few murder cases."

"You have?" Heath's eyes went wide with surprise.

"Two," I said, trying to downplay Gilley's enthusiasm. "It hardly makes me a psychic detective."

"Still, two is better than none," Heath reasoned, still clearly impressed. "What were the cases?"

I told him the history of solving the homicide of Steven's grandfather and the serial murder cases of some poor young boys in upstate New York.

"That's awesome!" Heath said.

I smiled and tried to stifle a yawn. It had been a really long day. "I think we should get you to bed," Steven whispered in my ear, adding the smallest purr.

I felt my face flush, and I cleared my throat. Making a show of looking at my watch, I said, "Might be a good idea to turn in for now if we have to get up early for the shoot."

Gilley and Heath looked a little disappointed, but both of them nodded and stood up. "Good night," said Heath, extending his hand. "I'm really excited to be working with you."

I ignored his hand and moved in to give him a brief hug. "Thank you for passing on that message from my mother," I whispered. "I really miss her."

Steven and I gave our good-nights and headed up to our room. We left Gilley eyeing the front door, and I knew he wouldn't be able to resist the lure of the San Francisco night scene. I imagined he'd head out for an evening of dancing and flirting and crawl back to the hotel for an hour of shut-eye before it was time to get up. Gilley had a reputation for being able to get by on very little sleep—especially when cute men were calling.

When Steven and I reached our room he took the

key card out of my hand and picked me up dramatically. "Allow me," he said, moving in to kiss my neck.

I felt that tired feeling leave me immediately, replaced by raging hormones. The man *knew* how to turn me on. I heard a small click, and Steven had the door open and was carrying me across the threshold.

The room was dark, but there was enough light to make out the bed, and Steven moved from nibbling my neck up to my lips. The man is an amazing kisser, and I heard myself moan as my fingers found the buttons on his shirt.

He laid me gently down on the bed, and the heat between us rose a few degrees. I felt his fingers curl into my hair, and I couldn't seem to get his shirt off fast enough. I ached something fierce to feel his skin.

Steven shrugged out of his shirt, and I ran my fingers through the small tuft of hair along his chest. He gave a soft moan when I thrust my pelvis up into his, and responded by deepening his kiss.

My shirt came off along with my bra, and just as things were getting *really* interesting there was a tremendous crash against the room door, followed by the shouting of two angry men clearly intent on killing each other.

Chapter 4

Steven was off of me in a hot second and racing to the room door. It took me a little longer, as I didn't want to flash the "ladies" by running out into the hallway half-naked, but I joined him a moment later, wriggling into my shirt.

Steven was trying to get the door open, and having a hell of a time of it. "What's the matter?" I shouted, my voice trying to rise above the commotion in the hallway.

"The door won't open!" Steven said, pulling fiercely down on the handle and trying to yank it away from the doorjamb.

"Is it locked?" I asked, flipping on the light so that he could see better.

Steven grunted as he again attempted to heave the door open, but it wouldn't budge. Meanwhile the fight outside seemed to be raging on, full force. "I'm calling the front desk," I said, hurrying to the phone on the nightstand. "Look out the peephole, Steven, and see if you can give me a description so I can have the desk alert security."

As I lifted the phone and pressed 0, however, the

noise from outside our door vanished, and with a whack I heard our door open so quickly that it hit Steven right in the face.

"Ungh!" he said as he fell backward to land flat on his back.

"Front desk," announced a woman's voice into the earpiece of the phone.

"What the hell?" I gasped, looking at Steven clutching his forehead and swearing in both Spanish and German.

"Hello?" said the desk clerk. "Can I help you?"

I opened my mouth to say something, but the situation was so freaky I didn't know where to begin. Finally I said, "There were two men fighting outside our door, and I think they hurt my boyfriend!"

"How badly is he injured?" asked the desk clerk, clearly alarmed.

"Steven," I said, bending down next to him and pulling at the hand covering his forehead. "Let me see, honey."

Steven resisted for just a second, still swearing; then he sat up awkwardly and moved his hand. I sucked in a breath as I spotted the deep vertical gash right above his left brow and told the clerk, "He's going to need stitches."

She responded by speaking rapidly to someone nearby, but she was obviously covering the mouthpiece, because it was muffled. Then she said, "I'm sending security right up, ma'am. Please stay in your room and lock the door until he arrives."

I leaned out over Steven and spied the open door. No one was evident out in the hallway, and as my mind tried to grapple with what had happened our door abruptly slammed shut so hard that it rattled the walls. "Holy crap!" I screeched, jumping to the side. It was then that I became aware of the goose bumps running up and down my arms.

"Steven," I whispered hurriedly while tossing aside the phone, "honey, I've got to move you over to the bed."

"My head," Steven said, his bloody hand going back to his brow. "Jesus," he added. "I'm bleeding."

All of a sudden my chest became tight, as if my heart were caught in a vise. "Oh, no!" I said, feeling my breath quicken. "Steven!" I insisted, tugging at his arm. "Get . . . to . . . the . . . bed!"

"What's the matter with you?" I heard him say, but focusing on him was now intensely difficult. The tightening in my chest grew worse, and I felt as though I could barely breathe. "Someone's trying to take me over." I gasped. "You've got to get away from me!"

"What do you mean, take you over?"

I gasped again and felt myself being tugged backward, as if a black hole had suddenly taken hold of my energy. "Leave . . . me . . . alone!" I managed, trying to pull back from the incredibly powerful energy tugging at every fiber of me.

"M.J.?!" Steven said in a voice filled with urgency and alarm. "What's happening to your face?"

I tried to focus on him, but my vision began to close in, and the tunnel I felt I was looking out of seemed to lengthen. "*Get . . . away!*" I shouted, willing myself to stay in control of my body. But the energy that had jumped into mine and was attempting to literally hijack me wouldn't let go.

As if from a distance I felt myself being shaken, and Steven's voice echoed into my thoughts. "M.J.!" he was yelling. "What's happening to you?"

"Nooooooo!" I said, curling my fingers around his arms, struggling with everything I had to hold on and resist the sensations assaulting me.

The next few minutes were a bit of a blur. There was a hideous voice that kept echoing loudly through my brain, and I felt my lips moving and strange sounds coming out of my mouth, and then someone was pounding on the door, and I focused as hard as I could on the sound, like a drumbeat calling me back.

Finally I felt the shivers, and such a deep sense of cold that I didn't think I'd ever feel warm again. And then my vision came back, and I could see Steven clearly again, his gash bleeding badly and such a look of concern on his face that it shocked me.

"Is she having a seizure?" I heard another voice ask.

"I don't know," Steven said, relaxing just a bit when he saw my eyes blinking at him.

"I'm okay," I finally managed to say as my teeth chattered.

"Can you hand me the bedcover?" Steven asked the man standing in the room wearing a gray shirt with a badge and black pants, who was obviously hotel security.

The security guy yanked the coverlet off our bed and helped Steven wrap me in it. "Sir, you're bleeding pretty bad," the guard remarked, getting up and hurrying to the bathroom.

He returned a moment later with a washcloth and a towel. "Maybe I should call an ambulance for you two?"

"No," I said, sitting up and clutching at the coverlet. "I'm fine." But then I realized that Steven might be more hurt than he looked, so I quickly added, "Unless, Steven, you feel you want to go to the hospital by ambulance?"

My boyfriend took a long time to answer. He'd let go of me and was holding the wet washcloth to his forehead, applying pressure to his head wound. The look on his face was both frightened and suspicious. "No," he finally said. "No ambulance. I brought my bag with me," he added, his eyes roving to the small medical bag he usually carried everywhere he went. "I've got medical glue in there that I can seal the cut up with."

"You a doctor?" the security guy asked. Steven nodded absently. There was an awkward silence before the guard asked, "Would either of you two like to tell me what happened?"

I looked at Steven and he looked at me, as if to ask each other who wanted to explain the unexplainable. I took the lead. "We heard a fight break out in the hallway. It sounded violent, and my boyfriend here went to investigate, but the door got stuck and wouldn't open. And then it gave way, and it hit him in the forehead."

"Did you see who was fighting?" asked the guard.

I shook my head, and Steven said, "No. We didn't. But it definitely sounded like two men."

"It was so loud I can't imagine we were the only ones who heard it," I added. "If you knock on a few of the other guests' doors, I'm sure they heard it too, and maybe they saw something."

"Okay," said the guard, taking out a small pad and jotting down a few notes. "I'll ask around. Ma'am," he added, looking at me with concern while I shivered in my coverlet, "are you sure you're all right?"

"Of course," I said, and realized I probably didn't look convincing, so I tossed in, "I'm hypoglycemic— low blood sugar. Sometimes it can give me the shakes."

"Can I get you a candy bar?" he suggested kindly.

I forced a smile. "That'd be great, sir. Thank you."

The guard quickly left, promising to return in a few minutes, leaving Steven and me alone in awkward silence. "You sure you don't want to go to the hospital?" I finally asked.

Steven shook his head. "I can fix this, no problem." I noticed he was still looking at me oddly. "M.J.?"

"I was hijacked by a spirit," I explained before he had a chance to ask the full question.

"What is this 'hijacked'?" he asked.

"It's only happened to me one time before," I explained, remembering a tricky bust Gilley and I had done when I was still fairly new to this medium stuff. "Some ghosts are superaggressive, and when given the opportunity they can attempt to literally take over your body."

Steven's jaw dropped in horror. "You were possessed?"

That made me chuckle. "Not exactly," I said. "At least, not like they portray it in the movies. But I suppose that technically, yeah, I was a little possessed. Usually spirits who do this sort of thing can only hold on for a short period of time, but while they take over your body, you're completely unaware of what's going on."

Steven's expression looked haunted. (Forgive the pun, but it really did look like that.) "Something happened to your face. You looked . . ." He paused as if he were searching for the right word. ". . . masculine."

"I did?"

"Yes," he said with a nod. "Your face was angry, and your eyes . . . M.J., I swear they turned *brown*."

For the record, my eyes are naturally gray. "That is *freaky!*" I said, half fascinated, half completely creeped out.

"And your voice changed too," Steven added. "It got very deep, and you started speaking Portuguese."

I felt my brows shoot up. "Really?" I was now very interested. "Could you understand what I was saying?"

Steven's lips pressed together, and he gave a curt nod. "It was some scary shit. You said you were the eater of flesh. That you were looking forward to a meal of virgins and babies. That you wanted to quench the blood thirst of your ancestors."

I gaped at him. "Whoa," I whispered after a long pause. "This guy is one sick son of a bitch."

"It was most upsetting," Steven agreed.

"Did he mention a name? Did he tell you who he was?"

"No. After telling me you wanted to eat the babies, your face changed back to look like you, and then your eyes rolled up, and you fell back on the floor."

"That must've been when I was able to fight him off," I said with a shiver. "I felt him leave my body right when the security guard began knocking on our door."

"Is this spirit still here?" Steven asked, his eyes warily roving the room.

"No," I said, feeling out the area with my antennae. "He's gone."

"Do you think he'll come back and do this hijacking again?" Steven whispered nervously.

"I sure as hell hope not," I said, rubbing my neck, and when I noticed that Steven still looked intensely worried I added, "Now that I know this character is on the prowl, I can do things to make sure he doesn't take me over again."

"Like what things?"

"Well," I said, getting up and moving over to my suitcase, searching through the zippered pocket to find a certain crystal I'd brought along. "This is sphalerite," I said, holding up a gray, knobby rock for him to see and feeling an immediate sense of heaviness all through me, as if an invisible weight were pressing down on me. "It's an ore found in zinc. As long as I keep it close by, my energy is too heavy for this creepy spirit to want to bother with me."

Steven got up too and went to peer at his wound in the mirror above the dresser. "I don't understand," he said. "The stone is heavy?"

I came to stand next to him as he inspected his gash. "Not exactly." I winced as he dabbed at the blood still leaking out of his wound. "But it does make my aura heavy. See, normally my energy is really light—I sort of raise my vibrations so that I can communicate with other spirits. And this is what is so attractive to negative spirits like this hijacker. I'm fairly easy to take over because my energy is vibrating so fast. But this little crystal slows those vibrations way down, and it's much, much harder for someone to enter my auric field when that happens."

Steven moved over to his bag and began lifting out tubes and a small bottle of antiseptic. "Are you sure it will work?" he asked, and I could tell he was still unnerved by what had happened to me.

"Yes," I said softly, pulling out a chair and motioning for him to sit down. When he did I took the antiseptic from his hands and began to gently clean around the gash for him. Once I'd wiped up the blood, the cut on his forehead didn't look nearly as serious as I'd thought.

"Let me see," he said, and swiveled toward the mirror. Poking around the edges of the wound he said, "This is not too bad."

"I should get you some ice," I offered, and at that moment there was a knock on our door and the security guard stepped back in, along with another gentleman who looked like he'd had a rough day.

"I got you a Twix," the guard said, holding out the candy bar to me. "And this is Murray Knollenberg, the general manager of the Duke."

"I understand you were injured this evening, Dr. Sable?" said Knollenberg. "I'm terribly sorry," he added when Steven turned to face him and the GM got a good look at the gash on his forehead. "Can I provide you with transportation to the hospital?"

Steven shook his head. "I'm fine," he insisted, grabbing his medical bag and moving toward the bathroom. "I'll just need a few minutes in front of the mirror with some light. If you'll excuse me," he said.

"Do you want some help?" I offered.

"No," said Steven, giving me a small grin. "You stay with these men and tell them what happened." And with that he closed himself inside the bathroom.

"This is all very distressing," said Knollenberg. "I've never had so many disturbing incidents happen at the Duke in one day."

"Well, they say bad things come in threes," I said, then realized I'd said the wrong thing when Knollenberg's face visibly paled. "But that's just an old wives' tale, I'm sure," I added, clearing my throat and ripping off the wrapper of the Twix to take a bite.

"Mr. Knollenberg and I have secured this floor," said the security guard. "There are very few guests here due to all the construction we've got going on, and whoever was fighting out in the hallway has apparently gone."

"Have you asked any of the other guests if they heard anything?" I asked.

Knollenberg turned to the guard. "That's right, Gary. You were going to do that next."

"I'm on it," he said, and headed out the door.

"Again, I'm very sorry that your evening has been so disrupted," said the GM while wringing his hands. I really felt for the guy.

"Mr. Knollenberg?" I asked, thinking of something.

"Yes?"

"I know the Duke is haunted," I said, thinking back on the notes Gopher had sent to Gilley. "But in the literature I read, all of the spirits that have been identified did not include anyone from Portugal, correct?"

Knollenberg blinked at me for several moments, his eyes roving from the Twix bar in my hand up to my face, as if waiting for me to deliver the punch line. Finally he said, "I'm afraid I don't quite understand your question, miss."

I sat down on the bed again and shrugged out of the comforter now that I wasn't shivering anymore. "There are several ghosts that haunt the Duke, correct?" I asked, again referring to the literature.

Knollenberg nodded, and his face flushed. "According to legend, yes," he conceded. "Sir Phineas is said to be one. His daughter, Sara, is said to be another, along with Mickey O'Reilly—he was a bellhop who worked here for nearly sixty years—and then, of course, the unfortunate woman who committed suicide in 1987."

"She committed suicide?" I asked, thinking that I knew one of the ghosts was a rather recent addition, but I didn't realize she'd committed suicide.

"Yes. Carol Mustgrove," said Knollenberg. "That was the first year I began working at the Duke as a desk clerk. I was actually the person who checked her in to the hotel."

"What happened to her?" I asked.

"Her fiancé left her for another woman," Knollenberg said. "She arrived at the Duke on the morning of what was to have been her wedding day, Friday, April sixteenth, 1987, for a three-day stay. She then went on a shopping spree and rang up ten thousand dollars on her fiancé's personal credit card, which she had apparently stolen. That night she came back to her room, placed a Do Not Disturb sign on the doorknob, and settled herself in the bathtub with a pillow over her chest before shooting herself in the heart with a small handgun."

"She really wanted to make a statement, didn't she?" I couldn't help thinking how sad it was that this poor woman had made such a bad choice.

"She did," agreed Knollenberg. "One of our chambermaids found her two days later."

"No one heard the shot?" I asked.

"No." Knollenberg frowned. "At least, no one reported hearing it. And it's likely that if anyone did, they either didn't want to get involved or thought it was the television."

"What room did this happen in?" I asked as a thought occurred to me.

Knollenberg opened his mouth, then caught himself. His eyes grew large as something triggered in his memory, and I knew immediately what room it was. "Room three-twenty-one," he whispered, confirming my suspicion.

"Freaky!" I exclaimed, because it really was.

There was an odd little silence before Knollenberg spoke. "You know, I've never really believed in ghosts. That is, until a few months ago, when I was working very late and I kept hearing a man just outside my office call out the name Sara over and over. Each time I went to investigate there was no one around, until about the sixth or seventh time. I was really angry and I stormed out into the hallway, only to come face-to-face with this man dressed in formal attire who asked me if I'd seen his daughter, Sara. When I said that I hadn't, he vanished in front of my very eyes."

"Let me guess," I said, somewhat amused.

"He looked just like the portraits of Sir Phineas, correct?"

"The spitting image," Knollenberg agreed with a shiver.

"Doesn't surprise me, but do I remember right, in that his daughter, Sara, fell down the main staircase?"

"She did," said Knollenberg. "We've had many, many guests over the years call the front desk to report a little girl playing on the staircase with no sign of any parental supervision."

In the back of my mind I filed that away. I had every intention of helping poor Sara cross over, because it was my firm belief that no child ghost should be left to wander the confusing and often frightening grounded realms of the living. But there was no way I was going to mention this to the Duke's GM. I couldn't risk his saying no because he felt little Sara was best served up as some sort of morbid tourist attraction.

"You were asking me if any of our deceased residents were from Portugal," Knollenberg reminded me, shaking me out of my thoughts. "Was there a reason you wanted to know that particular fact?"

I nodded. "I'm not sure if you're aware, but I'm one of the mediums featured in that television show that's filming here tomorrow."

"Yes," said Knollenberg with a shy smile. "I spoke with Detective MacDonald after you'd given him your impressions about that horrible incident earlier this afternoon. He mentioned that you were quite talented."

I laughed. "Glad to know he found me credible. Anyway, the reason I asked you about one of your hotel ghosts being from Portugal is that I believe Dr. Sable and I were visited by this spirit here tonight."

Knollenberg's eyes widened and he opened his mouth to say something, but just then Steven came out of the bathroom, wearing a thin white bandage on his forehead. "All better," he said when he saw us.

"Can I get you anything?" I asked. "Ice? Pain reliever?"

"Both sound good," said Steven, walking over to lay his medical bag on the dresser.

"Be back in a flash," I said to the two of them, and darted out of the room. I figured the ice machine was likely located over by the elevators. I passed Gary out in the hall; he was still knocking on doors. "Any luck?" I asked.

"No one has answered the door," he said, glancing skeptically down the corridor. He was several rooms away from ours. "We're down to about a third of our capacity, due to all the construction. No one wants to stay in a hotel when there's the potential for a lot of noise."

"So we're the only two guests in this area?"

Gary shrugged, then glanced at his watch. "Looks like it. I've called downstairs to try to get a list of occupants, but they're pretty busy at the front desk. Many of our guests are checking out early."

"They are?"

Gary sighed heavily. "Dead bodies on the pavement and noisy construction seem to be motivating a lot of exits."

I shrugged my shoulders. "I can kinda see their point."

Gary winked conspiratorially. "Me too. Are you feeling better now that you've gotten some sugar?"

I smiled. He seemed like a nice guy. "I am, thanks.
I came out to look for the ice machine. Steven's
patched himself up, but the ice will help with the
swelling."

"That way," he said, pointing farther down the
hallway. "Next to the elevators."

I thanked him and gave him a pat on the back
before moving off in that direction. I reached the elevators and found the small nook where the vending and ice machines were. I took one of the plastic
buckets from the shelf and filled it with some ice
before turning to the vending machine, and was
relieved to see a small tube of Advil could be purchased for seventy-five cents.

While I was fishing around in my pockets for
loose change I heard the elevator ding and the doors
open. I didn't give it much thought—I was too busy
searching for quarters—but after a moment something odd happened. I heard the elevator doors shut;
then not two seconds later the bell dinged again,
and again they opened . . . but no sound of anyone
entering or exiting came to my ears.

I stuck my head out from the nook and glanced
curiously at the elevators. The double doors of the
two cars stared back: one set open and empty, the
other set closed. I looked down the corridor but
didn't see anyone who might have exited.

I shrugged my shoulders and went back to sifting
through the change in my hand. In the background
I heard the doors slide shut again, and just when
I'd found the third quarter the familiar *ding!* of the
elevator rang out again in the hallway.

I hesitated before placing the quarter into the coin
slot. I couldn't shake the unease that seemed to have

come over me. I stepped out into the hallway and faced the elevators again. This time the other set of doors stood open, no passengers on board and no one out in the hallway. "Weird," I whispered, and felt all six of my senses go on high alert. On the edge of my energy I could just feel the tiniest tickling sensation, and I knew there was spirit energy afoot— but whoever it was didn't particularly want me to contact them.

"Hello?" I said anyway. Nothing happened—well, except that the doors to the elevator closed again. I waited there for a moment, watching the lights at the top of the doors, and sure enough, after about fifteen seconds the right elevator's light lit up with a *ding!*

I waited, but the doors took a moment to open, and when they did my jaw dropped. Standing in front of me was five feet, seven inches of feathered, furry, and nearly unrecognizable gay man. "Nice getup," I said as Gilley stepped off the elevator wearing a bright pink feather boa, a black leather vest with fur trim, and leopard-print chaps over skintight jeans . . . and by skintight, I mean I had to avert my eyes.

"Oh, hey!" Gil said when he saw me. "I was just coming to find you. I was reporting something to the desk clerk downstairs, and I overheard that security had been called up to your room. You okay?"

"I'm fine," I said, turning back in to the nook to get the Advil for Steven. After retrieving it from the slot and grabbing the ice bucket, I walked with Gil toward my room. "There was a fight out in the hallway, and when Steven went to take a look, one of the guys slammed the door into his forehead."

"Oh, no!" said Gilley, stroking his feather boa like a beloved pet. "Is he okay?"

"He's fine," I assured him. "Just a scratch, but that's not the craziest part of the story."

"Do tell."

I opened my mouth to explain, but was distracted by all those feathers. "Where are you coming from, anyway?" I asked, looking pointedly at his wild outfit.

Gilley smiled. "I was just heading out, actually," he said. "There are some fabulous bars not far from here, and I wanted to look my best."

"Ah," I said.

Gilley seemed to notice my wide eyes looking at his getup, and he asked, "Too much?"

I smiled. "Naw. You're good."

"You really think so?" he said, stroking the boa again.

"We're in Frisco. Around here I'd count that as subtle."

Gil seemed to relax and flung the tail of the boa across his neck. "Anyway, while I was leaving the hotel I saw this little girl on the main staircase playing on the railing. I tried to get her to stop, but she said her father always let her play like that. So I looked around for the dad, but I didn't see anyone. I got her to tell me that her name was Sara, so I went to the front desk to report it. I mean, who leaves their kid out this late at night to wander unsupervised like that?"

I had stopped in my tracks as Gilley was telling me the story, and he'd walked on a few steps and was now looking curiously back at me over his shoulder. "What's the matter?" he asked.

I walked to him and handed him the ice bucket and the Advil. "Can you please take this back to my room, Gil? There's something that I need to check out."

"Uh . . ." he said, blinking in confusion.

"Thanks!" I replied without explanation, then dashed back to the elevators and punched the down button. The doors opened up and I pressed the G for ground, hopping from foot to foot. "Be there," I said, hoping the spirit of little Sara would still be at the main staircase. I knew better than to tell Gil that he'd actually had an entire conversation with a ghost. If Gil knew he'd just had a face-to-face encounter with a real ghost, he'd grow his own feathers and start clucking.

When the doors opened I hurried out and over to the main staircase, where I came up short. Heath was standing by the railing with his eyes closed and the most peaceful look on his face. I knew immediately that he was talking to Sara.

I approached cautiously; I didn't want to interrupt or intrude. When I got to within ten feet I stopped and waited. It took a little while, but eventually Heath opened his eyes and blinked a few times, and a moment later he focused on me in surprise. "Hey!" he said. "I didn't expect to see you here."

"Likewise," I said with my own smile. "Don't tell me; let me guess: You've been doing some ghost-busting for a certain spirit named Sara."

Heath looked taken aback. "You could hear us?" he asked.

I laughed. "No, I cheated. Gilley said that he was down here just a bit ago, and he was worried about a little girl playing around on the banister without any parental supervision."

· "And he didn't know Sara was a ghost?" he asked.

"I guess she appeared in full form," I replied. "He had no clue."

Heath nodded thoughtfully. "She's a cutie-pie," he said, and his chin lifted as he looked up toward the ceiling.

"You helped her over?" I said, thinking he'd done the right thing and assisted Sara in crossing over to the other side.

"I did," he confirmed. "She's a bit concerned about her father, though. I think he's grounded somewhere around these parts too."

"I have it on good authority that he is," I said with another smile. "Maybe tomorrow we can team up and search him out together."

Heath sighed tiredly but nodded. "Great idea. Let's hope this production shoot doesn't last all day and we'll have time to work that murder case and do some more spiritual hotel housekeeping."

Heath and I walked back to the elevators and he leaned in to push the up button, but before his finger could even touch it, the elevator bell dinged and we both looked at the double doors expectantly. "Huh," I said when the doors didn't seem to want to open. "That's weird."

Heath was looking up at the light above the doors, which clearly indicated that the car was on the ground floor. I watched as he leaned in again, and this time he pushed the button. "Hello," he said to the elevator. "Open sesame, people!"

I smiled, but my humor was short-lived, because in the very next instant the doors rocketed open and clanged loudly as they bounced back against the doorframe, and something gray and smoky shot right out of the elevator and into Heath so hard that he flew backward through the air and landed with a loud *whump!* on the floor.

I'll admit that I let out a yelp and ran to his side, but whatever had come out of the elevator car now seemed to turn on me. The gray smoke rose right next to Heath, who was trying to catch his breath after clearly having had it knocked out of him, and the violent presence reached a height of about seven feet, looming spookily above the young man.

I moved to my right, and the smoke wove eerily in that direction, resembling a cobra ready to strike if I got too close. "Heath!" I whispered. "Roll away from there!"

I kept my eyes on the smoke serpent and heard Heath gasp again for breath. A tiny moan came out of him, and I knew he was trying to do as I said. I moved to my left, and the head of the smoke serpent swiveled toward me. "Come on, ugly," I coaxed, opening up all my intuitive senses, trying to get a feel for exactly what I was dealing with.

"M.J.," I heard Heath groan.

"I'm right here," I said to him, crouching low and edging close to him so that I could pull him away from the hovering smoke.

"No!" he whispered, and I looked at him and saw that his eyes were clearly frightened. "Run!"

And then, almost as if it were in slow motion, I saw the smoke serpent shrink down right before darting straight at me! I had no time to react, and in the very next instant I felt something like a lightning bolt hit my chest, and a searing pain so sharp that I cried out even as I tumbled backward to land like Heath on the cold, hard ground.

In my ears there was something like the sound of a hiss, but also words were forming that I couldn't quite make out. I rolled around on the ground, trying to get away from the noise and the pain, and then I think I blacked out, because the next thing I knew I was blinking hard and looking up into Steven's concerned face.

"M.J.," he said softly. "Can you hear me?"

"What happened?" I said, staring first at him, then around at my surroundings. "Where am I?"

"You're in the lobby," he said, leaning in to put his arms underneath me and lift me up.

"Where's Heath?" I asked, putting a hand to my head, which felt as if it had been slammed against a wall.

"I'm right here," Heath said, and I squinted over Steven's shoulder to see him walking behind us, rubbing his chest.

"You okay?" I asked as Steven bent down to place me on an overstuffed chair.

"Yeah," he said, but by his pale cheeks and pinched eyes I knew he was feeling as bad as I was.

"What the freak *was* that?" I asked him.

He shrugged his shoulders and shook his head. "Hell if I know."

"Here's some water," said someone to my right. I looked over to see the manager, Murray Knollenberg, handing me a bottle of water. "I'm so sorry about this," he added. "My bellhop told me he saw the whole thing. He's having some sort of a meltdown in my office right now, and he wants to quit his job and walk off his shift immediately."

I gripped the side of the chair as I took a sip of water. I felt really queasy and out of sorts and was struggling just to keep up with the flow of the surrounding conversation. "Murray," I said after I'd had a few sips more and felt as if I could let go of the chair without falling out of it. "You've got a *big* problem on your hands."

Chapter 5

Heath and I explained to Knollenberg what we'd encountered, and the general manager kept insisting that to his knowledge, no incident like the one that had occurred by the elevators had ever happened before at the Duke. "We have our share of strange occurrences," he explained, "but no ghost has *ever* attacked our guests. Frightened them, maybe, but nothing close to the violent nature you're both describing."

I glanced over at all the scaffolding and orange cones marking areas off-limits due to the construction. Ghosties hate construction. They really take offense when you start tearing into walls and making a lot of racket.

"You think some of that might have awakened something and made it angry?" Heath asked, and I noticed he was glancing in that direction too.

"It's possible," I said. "But if the construction did provoke it . . . *what* did it provoke?"

"This is most distressing," muttered Knollenberg. "I should let the owner know about this." The GM looked over his shoulder at a man behind the front desk and called, "Oh, thank goodness you're back from your lunch, Anton. We'll need to close off the main elevator and direct our guests to the freight elevator for now. Will you help me set up some cones?"

Knollenberg left us to make his call and divert the traffic. Heath eyed the front desk and said, "Think I'm going to request a room on the ground floor so I don't have to use the elevator for a while." And he hurried off to make the arrangements.

Steven then looked at me and said, "Ready to go upstairs?"

"Am I ever," I said.

We walked over to the stairs—I wanted nothing to do with elevators for a little while either—when I heard Gilley's unmistakable, "Yoo-hoo!" Steven and I both stopped and looked back to see our partner trotting along in his leather pants, feather boa, and fur-trimmed vest. And wild though his outfit was, his face was deadly serious.

"I've checked the entire lobby," he said as he hurried to catch up to us. "There are no unusual readings coming off the electrostatic meter, M.J."

I closed my eyes and tried not to panic. "That means that whatever that thing was, it's on the move." I glanced at both Gilley and Steven, their expressions mirroring my own worry. "Gil, we need to start checking this place from top to bottom."

"*You* need to go to bed," ordered Steven, and the tone of his voice said he wasn't kidding. "The ghosties can wait until the morning," he added when I opened my mouth to protest.

"You don't understand," I insisted. "That thing . . . that . . . whatever it was, is no joke! I mean, if it could knock two trained mediums on our butts, imagine what it could do to the average layperson!"

"And what are you going to do if you find it?" Steven argued. "Right now you're in no shape to fight with it, M.J."

I rubbed my forehead again, and Gilley made a suggestion: "How about I go back to my room and get my sweatshirt? Then Steven and I can do a thorough check of all the floors, and if we find anything weird or any readings that are off the charts, we'll come get you and let you handle it, okay?"

I had to hand it to my partner—for how frightened he was of spooky things, this was really big of him to offer. After a moment's consideration, I sighed and nodded reluctantly. "Fine," I agreed. "But come get me if anything—and I do mean *anything*—weird buzzes the meter."

"I promise," said Gil.

I left Steven and Gilley at Gil's room to switch out of his party outfit and into his ghost-hunting uniform and then continued on to my room. The last thing I remember before my head hit the pillow was how grateful I was to have someone look after me for a change.

It was dark when I woke up, but my internal clock insisted that I'd slept long enough. I crept out of bed, trying not to wake Steven, (whom I had a very faint memory of coming back to the room earlier), and went to the curtain in front of the large sliding glass door to our balcony. Peeling back the curtain to see how dark it still was, I shrieked at the top of my lungs when I came face-to-face with a woman staring right back at me on the other side of the glass.

I heard Steven's voice behind me shout, "What is it? What's happened?" while I wheeled away from the curtain.

I backed myself against the wall as Steven hurried out of bed to my side. I tried to calm myself and told him, "There's a woman out on our balcony!"

Steven moved to the curtain and yanked it open, but no one was there. The balcony was empty.

"Son of a bitch!" I swore as I stared at the place where the woman had been.

Steven looked from me to the window, then back again. He then reached for the latch on the sliding door and opened it. Carefully he took a step out and looked around. With a shrug he said, "There is no one here."

I sat down on the bed and ran a hand through my hair, feeling my heart still thundering in my chest. "You know," I said to him as he came back into the room and shut the door, "it takes a lot to creep me out, but this place . . . well, this hotel may just do me in!"

"Maybe you were dreaming?" Steven suggested.

"I wasn't dreaming."

"Another ghost?"

"Yes," I said with a sigh as I got up and went back to the glass door and slid it open myself. I moved to the railing and peered down. Then something occurred to me, and I turned back to Steven. "I know who the woman was," I said after a bit.

"Who?"

"Carol Mustgrove. She committed suicide in the room right below us. I think she's taking a tour of the hotel and was attracted to my energy."

"Do you think that was who attacked you last night?"

I shook my head and shuddered, leaving the cool air of the balcony to go back inside. "No," I said as I latched the door again. "What came after Heath and me last night was more powerful than anything I've ever seen. And, Steven," I said, looking up at him nervously, "I'm not even sure it was ever human."

His mouth fell open slightly. "What else could it have been?" he asked.

I wrapped my arms around myself, feeling very cold all of a sudden. "I've heard stories from other ghost hunters about evil energies coming out of portals that aren't from this world."

"I am not understanding this," Steven said, scratching his head.

I headed over to my suitcase and rooted around for a sweater. Throwing it over my head I explained, "You know that portals connect the lower realms to our world and are easy pathways for some of the nastier ghosts to cross back and forth through, right?"

"Yes, you are talking about ghosts like Hatchet Jack," he said with a small shudder, referring to the particularly awful fellow we'd dealt with a few months back.

"Exactly," I said, going back to the suitcase for a pair of jeans. "Sometimes when a nasty ghost builds a portal, another entity can come with him."

"You mean," said Steven, searching for the right word, "like a *demon*?"

I nodded gravely. "Yes. I've never actually seen one—they're extremely rare—but I have a strong suspicion that something got through a portal somewhere here in the hotel and is now loose among the bricks and mortar."

"So which of these ghosts built the portal in the

first place?" Steven asked, saying aloud the thing that I was actually wondering myself.

"I have no idea," I confessed. "Did you and Gilley get anything off the meters last night?"

"No," Steven said. "It was very quiet, but there were several sections of the hotel that were closed off."

"Closed off? Oh, you mean because of the construction?"

Steven nodded. "But we checked everywhere we could."

"Well, the construction could definitely be kicking up this extra poltergeist activity. But from everything I've read in the hotel literature, none of the recorded ghosts at the hotel fit the profile for a spirit vile enough to create a portal to the lower realms. It certainly wasn't Sara, and I doubt her father is an evil guy. He seems to be solely concerned with finding his daughter. That leaves the bellhop who worked here for all those years—and again, I don't think he's our dark entity—and Carol Mustgrove, the woman who committed suicide in the eighties, unless there are a couple of other ghosties afoot that weren't in the literature."

Steven was silent for a bit before he asked, "What are you going to do?"

I sat down on the bed next to him and laid my head on his shoulder. "I have no idea," I admitted. "I mean, we're shooting this stupid show in a few hours, and then I guess I'll team up with Heath to see if we can't root around and locate a portal while we're also working on finding any clues about Sophie's murder, but I really feel like we're going to be searching for a needle in a haystack."

"Why would a needle be in a haystack?" Steven asked curiously.

"It wouldn't," I said. "Which is the point."

"Then why wouldn't you say you are looking for hay in a haystack?" he insisted. "I mean, that you would find. Looking for this needle, well, that would be a waste of time. But you could say that you are looking for the needle in the tailor shop. Now, that would make more sense, no?"

I resisted the urge to groan. Steven often struggled with the nuances of our American colloquialisms. "Good idea," I said, too tired to get into it. "We'll look for the needle in the tailor shop after the shoot."

Because it was early and we had some time to kill, Steven and I took showers, (okay, so we took one long one together), got dressed, and headed down to breakfast. We needed to report for duty by eight thirty a.m., but the time change was throwing me, and when we got to the hotel café I noticed it was only seven.

I ordered up a big plate of fruit and a Western omelet; Steven went for fruit and granola, and eyed my omelet when it arrived. "Do you want me to tell you what that is going to do to your arteries?" he asked. Steven's a heart surgeon by trade.

"Oh, please," I groaned with a wave of my hand. "All my grandparents lived well into their seventies or eighties, and my dad is still going strong. No heart disease in the family. I think I'll live."

Steven's eyebrows lifted a little, but he let it go. I dove in with earnest and was only on my second bite when I heard, "Morning, guys!"

I swiveled in my chair and noticed Heath behind us, looking a bit worse for wear too. "How'd you sleep?" I asked, while Steven pointed to a chair, motioning for Heath to join us.

"Not great," he admitted, taking the seat. "I've been in some creepy places before, but nothing like this hotel."

"Did something else happen?" I asked.

"Yeah," Heath said, smiling up at the waitress who was pouring him coffee. "About three a.m. the knocks started."

"Knocks?" Steven said.

I smiled. I knew what Heath was likely referring to. "Sometimes ghosts will make their presence known by making knocking sounds," I explained. Turning to Heath I asked, "Is that what you mean? Some spirit was trying to get your attention by knocking?"

Heath nodded. "And then the TV went on and off, on and off from about four to six a.m. I swear, I couldn't get a moment's peace."

"Did anyone give you a name?" I asked.

"Some woman named Carol," Heath answered, rubbing his eyes tiredly. "She kept saying someone was in her room or something."

I cocked my head and stared at him. "Freaky," I said. "Do you know that Carol came by my room early this morning too?"

"You're kidding!" Heath now eyed me with interest. "Did she knock and flip your television on?"

"No, she scared the crap out of me by appearing on my balcony," I admitted.

"Fully formed?"

"Like she was in the flesh," I said. "I think maybe

we should start with her after the shoot so that we'll have a chance at getting some sleep tonight."

"Great idea," Heath agreed. "And we're still going to work on Sophie's murder, right?"

I sighed wearily. This was turning into a heavily loaded working weekend. "Absolutely, but I think we should also try to find out what the hell that *thing* was that came out of the elevator," I added. "I'd hate to think what could happen if a regular hotel guest came up close and personal with something like that."

"Whatever it was, I'd prefer not to get too close to it," Heath said with a small shiver. "Frankly, that whole encounter freaked me out so much that I came really close to leaving here last night and heading back home."

"I feel ya," I said. "But if we don't do something about it, Heath, who will?"

He smiled wryly. "Let Angelica and Bernard have a turn."

I laughed. It was clear that we both shared a rather limited opinion of Captain Comb-over and Madam Hateful. "Now *that* I'd pay to watch," I said.

"It'll be interesting to see what they come up with at the shoot," Heath said.

I pushed my breakfast dishes away as I polished off the last bite of omelet. "Let's just hope the two of us get paired up, and not with one of them."

As it turned out, we weren't that lucky. When we had all gathered in the lobby at eight thirty a.m. and were directed into the only conference room not currently being renovated, called the Renaissance Room, where crew members were just finishing up arranging the set. Gopher pulled the four mediums aside and said, "For the first part of the shoot, I'll want girls against boys. M.J. and Angelica will start us off; then we'll switch it up and go with Heath and Bernard." Out of the corner of my eye I caught Angelica's reaction, and she looked less than pleased. "Then we'll break for lunch, and when we come back we can try a different grouping: Heath and M.J. against Angelica and Bernard."

Heath and I exchanged glances. At least we'd get paired up after lunch.

I was then directed by one of the stagehands over to a chair, where a woman with lots of brushes and powders got to work on my face while another woman began putting some curls into my hair.

Between the two of us, Gilley is more the girlie girl, and he looked on happily at the edge of my chair while I was made over.

"Steven tells me that you didn't have any unusual readings on the meters?" I asked him.

"None," he said. "There were a few blips around the revolving door leading into the mezzanine, but nothing spiky enough to warrant getting you out of bed. Still, we were up until three checking all the floors." Gilley yawned loudly for effect.

I noticed that Gil was wearing his magnetic sweatshirt. "You can't be near me when we're shooting if you're wearing that," I advised him.

Gil looked down. "But I want to watch," he complained.

"Well, then take off the sweatshirt," I said. "You're going to throw off any energy coming through these haunted possessions if you're nearby." From Gilley's exaggerated pout I could tell that he was struggling with the idea, but after a moment's hesitation he did remove the sweatshirt, folding it and placing it far away from the cameras. "Thanks," I said as I was allowed up from my chair and directed over to a small, well-lit area in the middle of the large conference room that held a round table covered by a black velvet cloth and a crystal ball in the center.

I took my seat and eyed the crystal ball skeptically. "You've seriously got to be kidding me," I mumbled as I thought about how goofy this whole thing was.

After a bit, Angelica took the seat next to me, but she avoided eye contact and seemed a bit stiff, so I didn't try to engage her. Instead I occupied myself with watching the crew at work as they looked through their cameras and monitored the lighting next to both Angelica and me. Some guy carrying a long pole with a furry-looking microphone on the end of it edged over to an X at the corner of the square mat put down for our little stage, and then someone with a clapboard walked in front of one of the cameras and held it up before he said, "*Haunted Possessions*, Angelica and M.J. Take one." Then he clapped it closed and we looked at our "host," a guy I hadn't met yet who introduced himself to the camera.

"Good evening," he said. "I'm Matt Duval, and this is *Haunted Possessions*. Tonight we're going to be looking into the lives of several everyday people who swear they own objects that are possessed by unseen forces. These folks have come to us for help, and we've acquired a top-notch team of psychics to determine whether these objects are in fact haunted, and if they are, what to do about it."

Matt then turned to Angelica and me. "Our psychic panel is made up of four psychics: M. J. Holliday from Massachusetts, Angelica Demarche of California, Heath Whitefeather of New Mexico, and Bernard Higgins, also of California."

As the camera passed over me I felt the urge to nod and smile, but internally I was feeling a bit like a fool. I think it was Matt's melodramatic voice as he narrated. This all just seemed silly to me.

After we'd each been introduced, Gopher yelled, "Cut," and we were divided into our groups, with Angelica and me at the table and Heath and Bernard watching off to the side. I caught Steven's eye as he stood out of the way at the back of the room, and smiled as he held up his thumb, giving me some encouragement.

After we'd taken our seats a woman holding a beautiful china bowl came into the room, and the crystal ball in the middle of the table was removed to make room for the bowl placed in the center. She smiled shyly at us, and I reached a hand across the table and said, "Hi, I'm M.J."

"Patty," she said, shaking my hand.

Patty turned and offered her hand to Angelica, but Madam Hateful simply scowled and said, "I do not want to interact with you before they begin shooting again."

Patty blushed and I rolled my eyes, irritated that I'd been paired with such an impolite bitch. One of the lighting guys held up a little meter next to Patty, then next to the bowl, made a slight adjustment, and gave a nod of approval before clearing out of the way. Matt came back to stand on his X, and the guy with the clapboard did his thing; then Matt introduced the scene.

"Patty Murphy from Ojai, California, has had this bowl in her family for four generations. Recently she noticed that the bowl was acting suspiciously; she claims to have witnessed it moving on its own. She suspects that it may be haunted, so let's check with our experts, M.J. and Angelica. Ladies, please give us your impressions."

Matt moved out of the way, and the cameraman closest to us moved in for a tighter shot. No one had really given us any instructions, so I focused on the bowl, letting my energy wrap around it to see what might be causing these strange occurrences. I got nothing from the bowl, but when I focused on the woman across the table, I noticed immediately that there was an energy standing right next to Patty and, for lack of a better word, hugging her fiercely. "I'm so sorry about your mother," I said to her as I realized in a quick flash who was standing next to Patty.

Patty gasped, and her eyes opened wide before filling with moisture. She was clearly too stunned to respond, so I added, "She's showing me an L, like Lynn."

"Her name was Linda," Patty confirmed.

I smiled in encouragement. "Was it cancer?" I asked gently, feeling that familiar nauseated feeling I always get when a spirit energy tells me he or she had cancer.

"Of the pancreas," she said, letting a tear drop. "She was diagnosed on May sixth, and she died on May twentieth. It was too fast for any of us to even digest."

On the edge of my energy I could feel the attention and focus of everyone in the room. They were riveted. I went back to the bowl and saw a wedding cake. My eyes darted to Patty's left ring finger, and I saw her engagement ring, and then I thought I could put it together. "You're planning a wedding, right?" I said, feeling out the message.

Patty opened her mouth to respond, but before she could speak, Angelica suddenly moaned loudly and fell forward headfirst onto the table. I was so startled that I lost focus and put my hand on Angelica's shoulder. "Are you all right?" I asked, bending to her ear.

That was when Angelica threw her arms in the air, clipping me in the mouth hard, and she began to moan and wail. "It's possessed!" she howled. "It's possessed by *evil*!" As if on cue the bowl in the middle of the table abruptly jumped. It literally hopped about an inch in the direction of Patty, and everyone in the room also jumped.

"It's not evil," I growled, holding my lip and feeling that throbbing sensation you get when you've been punched in a sensitive area. "It's her mother insisting she use the—" But I never got a chance to finish.

Angelica leaped to her feet and picked up the bowl, holding it high above her head with her eyes wide and crazy. She then threw the delicate china piece as hard as she could, and it smashed against the back wall into a bazillion pieces.

Patty screamed in horror, I gasped, and the entire camera crew seemed to react at once. Gopher yelled, "Cut!" and people rushed forward.

"*My bowl!*" Patty cried as she ran to the shards of porcelain littering the ground. "This was my *mother's* bowl!"

I stared in stunned horror at the poor woman sobbing on the ground while she gathered bits of porcelain; then my eyes cut back to Angelica, who looked like a cat that had just eaten the canary. It dawned on me in that instant that she knew she was facing away from the camera, and when she swiveled back around she flung her arm up onto her forehead and went down on the ground as melodramatically as she could muster.

Meanwhile, I rushed to Patty's side as she was crying uncontrollably, shaking and trembling while still trying to collect the pieces. "Honey, I'm so sorry," I said to her.

"How *could* she?!" she wept. "How could she *ruin* it?!"

Gopher came and crouched down next to us. "What the hell just happened?" he whispered to me.

"You hired a *freak* for this show!" I snapped at him. "The bowl moved because Patty's mother was trying to get her to use the heirloom in her wedding. There wasn't an evil thing about it!"

"Evil!" we heard Angelica moan from behind us. "The bowl was evil!"

"This is ridiculous!" I yelled, and got up, hoisting my hands firmly onto my hips to glare angrily down at Gopher. "That bowl was a family heirloom, for God's sake!"

Steven and Gilley had also come forward, and both of them were doing their best to help Patty pick up the broken pieces of her most treasured family possession. Gopher seemed completely at a loss about what to do. He bent down to the woman and apologized profusely, telling her that the insurance would cover the fair market value of the bowl.

That was when I threw up my hands and shouted, "I am *so* done with this!" and I stormed off in one of my better huffs.

I parted the crew like Moses at the Red Sea and shook my head as I passed Heath, who seemed to be on the edge of doing the same. "Good luck," I said to him, and shoved open the double doors leading out of the Renaissance Room. Behind me I could hear the quick steps of feet hurrying to catch up to me. "Don't even try to talk me out of it, Gilley," I growled, and the footsteps stopped.

"But, M.J.!" Gilley said, his voice high and pitchy. "The contract!"

I rounded on my partner, my fury bubbling over. "Did you not *see* what happened in there?" I roared. "Did you miss that a woman had her heart broken, as well as an heirloom that was *priceless* to her, because some jackass with the name of a rodent coaxed her onto this stupid show and handed her over to a *lunatic* posing as a medium? Do you think that any of those people in there care *anything* about presenting the truth, Gilley? Do you think they care about that woman and how she's just lost her mother to cancer? Do you think they care about *one goddamn thing* other than ratings?"

"M.J.," Gilley said calmly, and approached me the way a lion tamer approaches one of his more temperamental felines.

"Don't you 'M.J.,' me, Gilley Gillespie!" I shouted back at him. "This whole production is a load of crap! Anyone who would hire a fraud like Angelica isn't concerned with helping any of these people. This is bullshit, and I want no part of it!"

"You're right," said another voice, and my eyes

darted away from my pale-looking partner over to Gopher, who was coming out of the doorway I'd just exited.

I glared hard at him, still furious. "This is all your fault, you know," I said.

"Again," he said, looking irritatingly guilty, "you're right. I blew it. I had another medium lined up for this show with much better credentials, but she canceled at the last minute. The production company that bought the concept insisted that I have four mediums, two men and two women. I had twelve hours to come up with someone, and one of my stagehands found Angelica at a palm-reading shop along the highway."

I closed my eyes and shook my head, taking a few deep breaths while I was at it. After a bit I said, "I personally know two other choices who would have been perfect. If you had made one phone call, Gopher, *one* call to me or to Gilley, we could have handed you someone credible like *that*." And I snapped my fingers for effect.

"What can I say, M.J., other than I'm sorry? Angelica's fired, okay? She's done. Tell me what else you want, within reason, to come back onto the show, and I'll work on getting it for you."

Steven came through the double doors at that moment, and when he spotted me he looked relieved. "Patty is asking for you," he said. "She wants to tell her mother she's really sorry about the bowl."

And like that I softened. I sighed heavily and brushed a curl out of my eyes but stared hard at Gopher. "Here are my demands," I told him. "First, I'm going to take Patty shopping. I'll need to know where the closest Villeroy and Boch is, and I'll need a credit card. We're going to replace Patty's bowl with something her mom will approve of and that she can use in her wedding. Then you are going to pay for a full day at the spa for the poor woman so that she can relax after all this trauma."

"Done," said Gopher, and he was already pulling out his wallet to offer me his credit card.

"Hold on," I said to him. "I'm not finished." I heard Gilley gulp, but ignored him as I continued. "Next, if I come back onto your show, you are going to have me work with Heath, and Heath alone. I want nothing to do with Count Chocula in there."

"You mean Bernard?" Gopher asked. I nodded, and he said, "I can fire him too if you want. The truth is he was also a last-minute choice."

"Do whatever you want," I said tiredly, walking forward to snatch the credit card before adding, "but if *one* more thing gets damaged, smashed, or broken, I am outta here. *Capisce?*"

"*Capisce,*" Gopher agreed. "I'll tell the crew we're breaking for lunch early and wait for you and Patty to get back."

"Now you're thinking like a producer." I clucked and headed back with Gilley and Steven to find Patty.

About two hours later I had left Patty in the hands of the staff at the hotel spa for a complete head-to-toe workup and was feeling pretty good about myself. She'd been a little reluctant to go to the elegant china store with me, but when we found out it was just across Union Square and I'd convinced her that her mother was coming along for the ride to help us pick out something perfect to replace her bowl, she'd agreed.

I'd known immediately when we entered the store which bowl to go for, and as it turned out my intuition was right on the money, because Patty said that the one I pointed to and told her that her mom was jumping up and down about was exactly the same pattern that she'd selected for the fine china on her bridal registry.

As we'd had the bowl wrapped up, I'd told her again and again that her mother was fine with the heirloom's disastrous ending, and that she just wanted Patty to be happy on her special day. "Remember, when you're walking down that aisle, your mom is going to be right next to you," I'd said.

And it was times like that, when I was reminded about the power of my abilities, that the awesome nature of reuniting people with their deceased relatives was an amazing thing. I also thought that maybe, when we got back home, it might be time to do some professional readings again.

I'd done too many appointments for too long and finally gotten burned out nearly a year ago. That was how I'd gotten into ghostbusting. Gilley had bugged me ever since to get back to doing personal readings, but I'd been stubbornly reluctant until now.

When I arrived back at the hotel I saw Gilley, Steven, and Heath all having lunch together in the café. I strolled over to them and was greeted warmly. "How'd it go?" Steven asked as I took a seat.

"It went better than expected," I said, smiling and looking at Gilley. "Do me a favor when we get back home?" I said to him.

"Of course," said Gil. "You name it."

"Set me up some readings, if you can."

Gilley squealed like a girl and clapped his hands. "Really?" He giggled, fluttering his eyelashes as if he were dreaming.

I laughed. "Yeah. I think I'm ready."

"Wait a second," said Heath. "You mean you haven't done readings before?"

"Oh, she's done them," said Gil. "And I made the unfortunate mistake of overloading her schedule and working the poor girl into the ground. So she quit and went into ghostbusting. She hasn't let me set up an appointment for a one-on-one reading in a year!"

"I needed the break," I said, waving to a waitress. I ordered a club sandwich and Coke with lemon, then turned back to the group. "So what did I miss?" I asked.

"Count Chocolate is gone," said Steven. "Gopher fired him on the spot."

I looked at Heath to gauge his reaction, but he simply shrugged his shoulders. "I'm glad it'll be just you and me, M.J."

"What time are we due back at the shoot?" I asked.

Gilley looked at his watch. "We've got a half hour," he said. "Long enough for you to eat your lunch, at least."

"Cool," I said. I hate working on an empty stomach.

I polished off my sandwich and we put the entire bill on Gopher's credit card (I was seriously considering putting on a few more items from the fabulous shops around the hotel, just to teach the producer a lesson, but decided we might not have time), and we all wound our way back to the Renaissance Room for round two.

Heath and I endured more makeup and hair spray before taking our seats at the table and waiting for Matt to do his intros again. From the script he was following, it was clear that Angelica and Bernard would be completely edited out of the production.

I nudged Heath a little when an elderly man was shown into the room carrying a small urn that was carefully set down on the center of the table and checked for the right lighting.

I eyed the urn curiously and glanced at Heath. His brow was furrowed, and he glanced at me with a shrug. Matt then announced that the elderly man was Franco De La Torrez. He was bringing a small urn left to him by his brother, who had died mysteriously in the Amazon while on an archaeological expedition there some twenty years before. Franco knew nothing about the urn's origin, nor what might be inside it, but he was convinced that it was full of dark magic. Franco was also terrified of getting rid of the urn, lest it anger the evil energy filling it.

I'll admit, when Matt got through talking, it was difficult to keep from giggling. I noticed too that Heath was trying hard not to smirk. "Mr. De La Torrez," I said as soberly as I could muster, "why is it that you believe this urn to be haunted?"

"It feels bad," Franco answered, his voice cracked and flaky with age.

"Uh-huh," I said, turning to Heath. I was getting no read off the urn at all, and thought maybe he might pick up something.

"You say this urn came from your deceased

brother?" Heath asked. Franco nodded. "And your brother died in the jungle of the Amazon?" Again Franco nodded. "And in the twenty years you've had it, you've never opened it up to see what was inside?"

"I've been too afraid," Franco admitted timidly. "It might let out the dark magic!"

Carefully I reached forward and laid my fingers on the urn. Absolutely nothing was coming from it. Furthermore, Franco's brother wasn't coming through to me either, but I did get a female energy connected to the old man that gave me a name of Mary or Maria. "Do you know a woman who has passed with the first initial M, like Mary or Maria?" I asked him.

Franco pumped his head vigorously. "My sister, Maria," he said in wonder.

"And who's the male with the initial N?" asked Heath.

"My brother!" said Franco, his crackly voice filling in with a little bit of volume. "His name was Nico."

I was glad that Heath had gotten the brother and wanted to have him take the lead, but this Maria character was literally yelling at me and ordering me to open the urn. My fingers hovered over the top of it, and I glanced sideways at Heath, undecided. He seemed to know what I wanted to do and gave me a brief nod of encouragement. Carefully but quickly I opened up the urn, tensing as the lid came off.

For a moment, no one spoke and no one moved. Franco had let out a small gasp as he realized what I'd just done, but then he watched the top of the now opened urn with great attention. Finally, I tipped the

small piece of pottery upside down and out fell a
dried flower that was probably once white but now
appeared yellow and brown in its preserved state.

Franco reached for the flower with trembling
fingers and held it up, staring at it with moist eyes.
"Gardenia," he whispered. "It's a flower my family
grew in our greenhouses back home and sold at the
local markets. My brother's way of sending me a
peace offering."

"You and your brother were at odds?" I asked.

Franco again pumped his head. "I told him not to
go on that stupid expedition. I told him it was too
dangerous. The night before he left we got into a terrible fight. My sister tried to get us to make up, but
Nico wouldn't have it, and he left without saying
good-bye to me. That was the last time I ever saw or
spoke to him. Word came to us three months later
that he'd contracted malaria and died. They buried
him in the jungle, and as a last request from him, he
sent me this urn. I figured Nico was still so angry
at me that he'd sent a curse with the urn. I never
thought to open it and look inside."

I sat back in my chair and wondered how long
Franco had been held prisoner by believing the
worst of his brother. "See?" I said to him. "No
haunted urn, here, Mr. De La Torrez. Just a final gift
from your brother."

Franco's eyes leaked tears down his craggy face,
and I could tell the camera had moved in for a close-
up. "Thank you," he said hoarsely, holding the dried
flower with great care. "This is such a gift. Thank
you."

"And . . . cut!" yelled Gopher, intruding on the
sweetness of the moment. I sat back in the chair

and watched as the director strode forward with a big, confident grin. "That was fantastic!" he gushed, beaming at Heath and me, but his adoration was short-lived as he whipped back around to his crew and ordered, "Okay, people, let's move on to the next contestant. Someone help Franco back up to his room."

Before the next guest was shown in I leaned over to Heath. "We make a good team."

"We do." He beamed. "And if you didn't already have a boyfriend, I'd probably ask you out."

I felt like I blushed all the way down to my toes, and not just because Heath didn't look a day over twenty-one and I was . . . well . . . *older* by far. "That's the adrenaline talking," I said with a laugh.

"Yeah, well, can you blame me?" he said, still flirting.

"Honey," I said soberly, "I'm taken. But methinks there have to be loads of women closer to your age bracket who would be happy to go out with you."

"Yeah," he said with a grin, "but none of them *get* me, you know?"

"Oh." I laughed. "Trust me, I do understand." My eyes traveled over to Steven then, and I thought that I was really lucky to have found someone so willing to try to get me.

The afternoon moved on quickly, and Heath and I met with people from all different backgrounds with many different items and objects that they swore to be possessed or haunted, but none of them—as in, not a single one—had any kind of negative energy at all connected to it. In fact, in all cases the people sitting across from us had one thing in common, and that was a deceased relative with a strong connection to the object resting on the table. By moving the object or tapping on it or making it fall over, their relative was simply trying to get the attention of their loved one.

So Heath and I acted as true mediums, reuniting the person in front of us with their dead loved ones. And working with Heath felt really good. It gave my own intuitive abilities a nice boost, and it was really great to see these people let go of the fear of an object while embracing the love from their relatives who had passed on.

And when Gopher called, "Cut!" after a long afternoon of passing on these messages, I was really hoping that our producer would finally let us go for the day.

"I'm starting to fade," said Heath.

"I know what you mean," I said with a sigh. "Gopher?" I asked.

"Yes, M.J.?"

"Heath and I are whipped. Any chance we can call it a wrap for today?"

Gopher glanced at his clipboard, then back up at me, his look a little pleading. "Can you two hang in there for one more item?"

Heath shrugged his shoulders. "I guess," he said. "I mean, I can if M.J. can."

I rolled my head back and forth, feeling the glorious release of pressure as my neck cracked. "I suppose one more won't kill us," I relented.

"Awesome," said Gopher happily. "Mark! Bring in the last guest."

Heath and I glanced around the room as people bustled about. Throughout the afternoon we'd gathered quite a crowd as several of the off-duty hotel staff came to check out the production. I waved to a few of them who lined the back wall, curious expressions on their faces, and they waved back shyly.

Heath's attention, however, rested on the catering table, loaded with snacks that had been set up in between takes. "I'm hungry," he said, getting up. "Think I'll grab some crackers before we do the last guest." He then looked down at me and asked, "You want anything?"

I got up too and began stretching, trying to work some blood back into my stiff muscles. "Nah," I said. "Thanks, though."

Heath hurried away, and I continued to roll my head back and forth and arch my back, keeping my eyes closed and focusing on my breath, practicing a little yoga, while I tried to tune out the hustle and bustle of the crew around me.

I felt Heath return as I finished one final pose and opened my eyes. "Feel better?" he asked.

"Much." I smiled. He and I then turned back to our places and took our seats. That was when I noticed a long dagger that had been placed in the center of the table. Before I even realized what I'd done, I shoved myself out of my chair.

At my side I was stunned to see Heath react in exactly the same manner. "What the freak?" I whispered, feeling powerful waves of negative energy rolling out of the silver knife in all directions.

"What's the matter?" asked Gopher.

I gasped as a searing pain sliced along my skin and I literally sank to my knees. "Jesus!" I said, slapping my hand over my chest.

"M.J.?" I heard Steven shout from across the room. "What is happening?"

Before I could answer him, another hot slash sliced along my back and I cried out in pain. Beside me I could hear Heath suffering too. "Get it away!" he yelled, holding his arm and grimacing.

I pulled the hand on my chest away from my shirt. There was a thin red line appearing through the cotton fabric. "Take it out of here!" I shouted, and felt one more hot slice cut into my flesh, this time at the back of my neck.

The next thing I knew Steven was running toward me, but he wasn't coming fast enough. I began to crawl away from the table, as far from that knife as I could get.

And then something was thrown over my head that helped more than anything, and I realized that Gilley had rushed to my side and was covering my head with his sweatshirt.

Under the fabric I was gasping for breath, and all I could think about was that Heath was still too close to the table, and no one had moved the knife yet. I pulled the sweatshirt off me and said, "Gilley! Take this and throw it over the knife!"

"You're bleeding!" he said as he squatted next to me. "Ohmigod, M.J.! What the hell?"

Over by the table I heard Heath let loose another shout and looked in horror as a wide circle formed around the table. No one, it seemed, wanted to get too close to the knife. "Gil!" I yelled, trying to get my partner's attention. "Throw this over that knife, *now*!"

In the end it wasn't Gilley who reacted. It was Steven. He grabbed the sweatshirt and tossed it onto the center of the table, effectively covering the knife and putting an end to the torture that Heath and I were feeling.

"What the hell just happened?" Gopher asked in the silence that followed.

I looked up at him and said evenly, "We've just encountered a *real* haunted possession."

Chapter 6

It took a while for things to settle down, but when I look back on what happened right after Steven threw Gilley's sweatshirt over the knife on the table, it replays in my head like a silent movie. I remember snatches more than the events themselves: Steven crouching down next to me, a look of worry mingling slightly with a stoic medical assessment of my injuries. Gopher and his crew running around, keeping clear of the table in the middle, their faces stricken and pale. Matt Duval screaming into his cell phone at his agent to book him a plane back to Hollywood, that he was going back to rehab because he couldn't handle the hallucinations anymore. Gilley, helping Heath to his feet and coaxing him over to where I was on the floor so that Steven could have a look at him too. The thin line of red that trickled down Heath's cheek and another on his upper arm.

"Can you lean into me, M.J.?" I heard Steven ask gently.

I looked at him in a bit of a fog. "Huh?" I said.

"I need to see the wound on your back, *bebita*. Lean forward so I can see it, okay?"

I nodded dumbly and did what he asked as Steven pulled up the back of my shirt. I could feel his warm fingers touching my skin and it comforted me. I closed my eyes and let myself sigh.

"Does that hurt?" he asked.

I shook my head.

"It's not deep," he said.

I opened my eyes and saw Gilley also peering at my back. "Holy shit!" he squealed. "What the freak is *that*?"

I caught Steven's sharp glare at Gilley, and I sat up. "What's on my back?" I demanded.

"It's just a scratch," Steven replied simply, but I knew by the way he was avoiding my eyes that there was more.

"What else?" I asked, looking to Gilley, but my partner had also dropped his gaze.

It was Heath who spoke up. "It's the way you were cut," he said grimly. "It looks like it was made by three talons."

"Excuse me?" I said. "It was made by *what*?" It was then that I became aware that one of the cameramen was pointing his camera at me and recording what was happening. "Turn that damn thing off!" I shouted angrily, and he looked to Gopher, who was standing nearby.

Gopher nodded and made a shooing motion with his hand, and the cameraman lowered the lens.

"The cut on your back does look very much like it was made by something with claws," said Steven in the tense silence that followed.

"I agree with Heath," said Gilley. "M.J., I've never seen anything like it. It looks like a velociraptor took a swipe at your back."

I lifted the collar of my shirt away from me and peeked down at my chest. A long, curved cut swept from my right collarbone to just above my left breast. "That son of a bitch," I hissed. "If that leaves a scar I'm going to be so pissed!"

"I want to put a few butterfly bandages on the wounds on your back," said Steven. "The other cuts aren't as deep, but you'll need some antiseptic at the very least."

Heath pushed up the sleeve of his shirt and twisted his arm. Three claw marks raked along his shoulder. "Whoa," I whispered when I saw them. "What the hell attacked us?"

No one had an answer, and as I looked around the room every person in the space stared back, looking shocked and very scared. My eyes roved the crowd, and at the far end of the room I spotted a large mirror on the wall. "Hold on," I said to Steven, who was working on my back. "I want to see this for myself."

I got up and retrieved my purse, which was under a nearby chair. Digging through the contents I pulled out a compact and headed over to the mirror. Stopping in front of it, I briefly noted how beautiful the thing was, with its antique gold frame and intricate carvings. I turned around with my back to the mirror, then opened up the compact and aimed it over my shoulder. With my free hand I pulled up the back of my shirt—which is a tricky thing to do one-handed—and squinted into the round circle of my compact.

Three curved cuts curled up my back from just above my waistline to the top of my shoulders. Gilley was right: It did look like I'd been raked by a dinosaur. "Great," I grumbled, lowering the compact and turning to face the mirror. "Just great."

As I was about to head back to Steven so that he could bandage me up, out of the corner of my eye I caught the movement of someone coming in the door from the hallway. I glanced over at the door, but no one was anywhere near it. I turned back to the mirror and it reflected exactly what I'd just seen: The door was closed, and no one was nearby who might have just come in.

I would have thought longer on this, but I had other things on my mind—namely the claw marks, which were now stinging like crazy. Walking back to Steven, who was now inspecting Heath, I sat down in a chair and waited for him to tend to both of us.

When we were bandaged up I turned to Gopher for some answers. "Where'd that knife come from?" I demanded.

Gopher motioned to a nearby production assistant, whose name I think was Tracy, and asked, "What's the story on the knife?"

The girl, who couldn't have been over the age of twenty-one, pulled away the clipboard she'd been hugging to her chest and scanned her notes. "There's no knife on the list," she said. "We were supposed to do a teapot next."

I felt my eyebrows scrunch in confusion. "Come again?" I said.

Tracy was looking from Gopher to me with a look that suggested she'd be putting in her notice *really* soon, and she explained, "I have no idea how that knife ended up on the table. I was out in the hallway looking for Mrs. Stanton—that's the woman with the teapot who was supposed to be next—when I heard shouting coming from in here. When I got in the door, you all were on the ground."

"So who put the knife on the table?" I asked, looking around at every member of the crew.

Everyone I stared at simply shrugged. No one was claiming ownership of the knife. I turned to Gilley. "Did you maybe see who came in with it?"

Gil shook his head. "I was on the phone in the corner," he admitted. "I wasn't looking at you until you shouted."

"Steven?" I asked, turning to where he was packing up his doctor's kit.

"Sorry," he said. "I headed out for a Coke after that last take. When I got back in here, the knife was already on the table and you were just beginning to react to it."

"Heath?" I tried next. "Did you see who laid it on the table?"

"No," he said. "I was focused on the crackers, remember?"

"So *no one* saw anything?" I asked loudly. And apparently no one had, because as I looked around, absolutely everyone shrugged or shook their heads.

"What about you?" said Gopher. "Did you see who brought in the knife?"

I sighed heavily. "No," I admitted. "I was doing some yoga and stretching with my eyes closed. When I opened them again the knife was already in place, and I never saw who put it there."

Just then there was a knock on the door, and the production assistant standing next to it opened it up to reveal a small old woman with light gray hair. "Hello?" she said, holding up a teapot. "I'm sorry

I'm late, but I had to visit the powder room. Is it still my turn?"

"Mrs. Stanton?" said Gopher.

The woman nodded.

Gopher turned to me, a question clearly on his mind, but before asking it he glanced over at the sweatshirt covering the table. I knew what he was about to ask me, and said, "No way. I'm done with this stuff, Gopher. Heath may still be up for it, but I'm through for the day."

"Count me out too, pal," said Heath.

Gopher looked around at his crew. They too were shaking their heads, and I knew he'd have a mutiny on his hands if he asked them to work through one more take. "Okay," he said, running a hand through his hair. "Sorry, Mrs. Stanton, but we've wrapped for the day. Tracy will be in touch with you about tomorrow's schedule, okay?"

Mrs. Stanton was clearly disappointed, and she hugged her teapot to her chest and left in a bit of a huff.

After the door had closed behind her and Gopher gave the signal to his film crew to dismantle the equipment, Heath turned to me and said, "What're we going to do about the knife?"

I caught Gilley's eye and said, "We're going to bust it."

"You want to drive a spike through it?" Gilley asked.

"Nope," I said. "This calls for a more creative solution. What we'll need is a box large enough to hold the knife, but nothing flimsy. If we can find something made out of wood, that would be best.

We'll also need some magnets to line the box, and then . . ." My voice trailed off. I had no idea what to do with the knife after that.

"We throw it off the Golden Gate Bridge?" Gil offered.

That made me smile. "No, hon, I don't think that's the answer."

"Bury it?" Heath suggested.

"Whoa, whoa, whoa," said Gopher. "Hold on a minute here, everybody. From the quick shot I got of that knife it looked expensive. We can't just go burying a valuable artifact, especially when we don't know where it came from. What if the rightful owner came back in here and wanted his knife back?"

"He'd have some explaining to do," I said, feeling the tension settle into my shoulders.

"M.J.," said Gopher, and I could tell he was trying to use his persuasive voice. "I'm on the hook for one artifact already. We don't have the kind of budget to continue replacing these things."

"Fine," I said, crossing my arms. "What would you suggest then?"

Gopher thought for a moment and then offered, "The hotel safe? We could keep it locked up there and see if anyone comes along to claim it."

I looked at Heath, and he nodded. "Okay," I agreed. "We get it into a box lined with magnets first; then we lock it up in the hotel safe until the rightful owner shows up. But if it hasn't been claimed by the time we fly back home, I'm gonna press you to bury it and bury it deep, Gopher."

"Agreed," he said.

By now the crew had started to put away much

of the filming equipment and was storing it all in the corner of the room when I overheard Gopher telling one of the stagehands that they would shoot another few sequences tomorrow before calling it a complete wrap.

"I'm not going to be back tomorrow for more filming," I told him. "We've done our part, Gopher, and I doubt you'd find any judge in the land that would find us in breach of contract under the circumstances."

"Count me out too," said Heath.

Gopher waved nonchalantly at us as if it were no problem. "Tracy, see if you can't get Bernard to come back tomorrow. Try to smooth things over with him about having to let him go. We'll offer him an extra hundred dollars if he shows up tomorrow and does a few sequences. If they're really bad, we can always edit him out completely."

Heath and I shared a look, and I turned to Steven and Gilley. "Come on, guys. We've got some supplies to get so that we can stow the knife."

We left the crew to their work, and once we were out in the hallway Gilley had a great idea. "M.J., why don't Steven and I get the supplies we'll need, and you and Heath can take it easy for a little while?"

I think my partner was noticing the way I'd been walking—stiffly and with great care, as the cuts on my back and neck were still stinging something fierce. "I'd really love to take a power nap," I admitted wearily.

"God, that sounds good," Heath agreed. "You guys don't mind going to the store without us?"

"We can handle it," said Gilley.

"It's fine," added Steven, leaning in to give me a

quick kiss. "Go take your nap of power and we'll be back soon."

Heath and I watched Gilley and Steven head out, and then I asked him, "Feel like getting something to eat before we catch some Zs?"

"You mean, do I feel like talking over food about all the crazy stuff that's been happening here in the last twenty-four hours? Yes."

I chuckled, and we walked over to the café across the street and ordered a couple of sandwiches and some Cokes.

"So, have you ever seen or heard of anything like what happened back there?" Heath asked when our beverages arrived.

I shook my head. "Can't say as I have. And I would have doubted that it was even possible if it hadn't actually happened to us."

Heath pulled up his sleeve again to have another look at his wounded shoulder. "What kind of a spook does something like *this*?" he asked me.

I took a long time to answer, but the truth of it was staring us right in the face. "Heath," I said carefully, "I don't think it was a spook. I don't think it was a ghost. I don't think that anything that once walked this earth made that."

Heath eyed me critically. "Black magic?" he suggested.

I nodded solemnly. "You know what kinds of evil and unnatural things are said to have talons?"

"Demons," he whispered.

"Exactly." And even as I said that I was finding it really hard to get my head around the concept. I'd heard of demons, and I knew people—credible people—who believed in them, but to get swiped by one . . . well, that was an up-close-and-personal confrontation of the freaky kind, and it was making me a believer really quickly.

"Then the question that I have is," Heath said, pulling my shoulder back gently so the waitress behind me could set my sandwich down on my place mat, "who the hell summoned it?"

I knew then that Heath was under the same assumption I was: that demons were not something that roamed the earth freely, but had to be called up by some foolish and powerful soul in this world. "That's the sixty-five-thousand-dollar question, now, isn't it?" I asked. "I'll bet whoever did conjure it was the same person who laid that knife on the table."

"So what's the connection?" Heath asked. "How does the knife fit into all of this?"

I took a bite out of my sandwich and chewed for a bit before I replied. "I think it's a key."

"A key?"

I nodded. "I remember reading an article way back when about practitioners of black magic needing an object of power to open the gates to the lower realms and allow passage of a demon into our realm."

"Wait a minute." Heath gasped, setting down his sandwich. "You mean to tell me that that thing is now on the *loose*?"

I felt my eyebrows scrunch as I tried to recall the article that I'd read—but the details were elusive. "I want to say no," I said, remembering that the clawing had stopped as soon as Steven threw Gilley's sweatshirt over the knife. "But I think we should put Gilley on research and see what he comes up with. We definitely need to know what we're dealing with here."

"I just don't have any experience with this stuff," Heath admitted. "It's really blowing my mind."

"I hear ya," I agreed. "My main concern, however, is to put that knife somewhere safe, away from people. We need to contain it and whatever evil thing it's linked to. I mean, can you imagine if that thing had been let loose in the lobby here at the hotel?"

Heath scowled. "Maybe it already was."

I stared at him for a full three seconds before I realized what he was alluding to. "The serpent?"

Heath nodded. "Whatever attacked you and me in the lobby wasn't like anything I've ever seen before. It just didn't feel like a regular spook, you know? And that has me thinking that maybe our serpent's got claws."

"We've got to take care of that knife . . . and quick," I said grimly.

Heath glanced at his watch. "How about we pay the tab and try and get about forty-five minutes of nap time before Gilley and Steven get back?"

I reached for my purse. "Works for me."

"I'm in room one-twelve," Heath said as he laid some money on the table. "Call my room when you hear from your buddies and I'll come down to help you with the knife."

As it turned out I got only about a half hour for a quick nap before I heard Steven and Gil come into my hotel room. "Wakey, wakey," sang Gilley.

I groaned and rolled over. I'd been having such a nice dream about my mom, of all people, and being roused from visiting with her made me a little melancholy. "What time is it?" I asked groggily.

"It's nearly six," said Steven. "Did you want to sleep a little longer?"

I shook my head. "Nah." I sat up on the bed and yawned. "We've got work to do. Did you get a box for the knife?"

Gilley held up one of several bags. "We had trouble finding the right-size box that would hold the knife and still fit inside the hotel safe, when Steven came up with the great idea to get a cigar box." Gilley then set down the bags on the bed and fished around inside one of them, pulling out the perfect-size wooden box for our purposes.

"Nice," I said with a smile. "And the magnets?"

Gilley fished around inside another bag and came up with a handful of flat magnets. He then dumped the contents of yet another bag onto the bed and showed me some wood glue, metal spikes—in a smaller size than I was used to working with—a hammer, some nails, and a few sections of metal tubing with plastic caps on the end. "Looks like you two had fun at the hardware store," I said appreciatively.

Gilley and Steven beamed. "Did you want help putting this stuff together?" Gil asked.

"No, but thanks, doll," I said, getting all the way out of the bed and stretching. "You guys have done great. Oh, but, Gil, I do need some research if you have some time to spare."

"Always," he said.

"I need you to look up portal keys in relation to summoning demons."

Both Gilley and Steven looked at me as if I'd said something funny they couldn't quite catch. "Come again?" Gil said when I didn't offer more.

"I think the knife is a key that unlocks portals and allows demons to enter our world."

"*Real* demons?" Gil asked, his voice high and pitchy.

"Yes," I said. "Real demons. The kind that nightmares are made of."

"These things actually *exist*?" Steven asked incredulously.

I turned my back to him and lifted my shirt. "Do I need to say more?"

"No," they both said quietly. Gilley added, "How the hell do we lock up a demon if it's come through this open portal, M.J.?"

I let go of my shirt and turned back to face them. "We start by securing the knife. We then do a thorough search of the hotel, and if we find anything of the magnitude that attacked Heath and me, we give it all we've got with the spikes and the magnets."

"You think it's *loose*?" Gil gasped.

"I'm not sure," I admitted, reaching to retrieve my sweater off of a nearby chair. "I want to say no; I mean, when Steven threw your sweatshirt over the knife, whatever was attacking Heath and me stopped. So I'm hopeful that it's contained. Still, we've never dealt with anything like this before, which is why I need you to do some research and find out if any other ghost hunter has ever dealt with one of these things, and if they've managed to lock it down."

Gilley shivered, and his expression told me he really didn't want to stick around San Francisco much longer. " 'Kay," he said. "I'll look into it, but, M.J.?"

"Yeah?"

"Be careful."

I gave him a reassuring smile and squeezed his shoulder. "Trust me, after what went down this afternoon, we will be."

"I should come with you," offered Steven. "You may need me again."

"I don't think that's a good idea, sweetheart," I said patiently. Knowing Steven would worry, but not wanting to put someone inexperienced in the middle of things, I held firm on my decision to leave him behind. "I think it's best if Heath and I go it alone. We'll wear some of the magnets and do some protection work before we extract the knife, and I promise you, I'll play it safe."

"I am not liking that idea," Steven said, his dark brows furrowing. I couldn't help it; he just looked so damn cute that I leaned in and gave him a big, long kiss.

"I know," I whispered when I pulled away. "But that's the way it's gotta be for now."

"She'll be okay," Gilley reassured him, but he too looked a little worried.

I grabbed all of the magnets, the glue, and the box and walked to the door. Looking back at them before I left, I reminded Gilley, "You'll work on that research project?"

"I'll have something for you by the time you get back," Gil promised.

"Thanks, buddy," I said, and left the room.

I headed down to Heath's room and knocked on his door. There was no answer, so I knocked a little louder and heard a faint, "Coming!" from inside. A moment later the door opened and a bleary-eyed

Heath peeked out at me, squinting into the bright light of the hallway. "Is it time?" he asked, his voice husky with fatigue.

"It is," I said. Holding up the box and the magnets I added, "Can you help me configure this box for the knife?"

Heath opened the door wide. "Sure, come on in."

I walked into his room and moved over to the little side table by the window. Setting the articles down I took a seat and waited for Heath to flip on a few lights and come over to the table.

He joined me after he'd rubbed the sleep out of his eyes. "Man, I don't think I was out long, but while I was out, I was *really* out," he said as he sat down.

"I know. I was down pretty hard too before Gil and Steven came back from the store."

Heath reached forward to inspect the box. "A cigar box is perfect."

"Steven's idea," I said, laying out the magnets and the glue. "How about I glue the magnets and you hold them in place until they've dried a little?"

"That works."

We got to our task without speaking for a little while, and then Heath asked, "So, what's the game plan once we finish the box?"

"Well," I said, taking a moment to gather my thoughts. "The first thing I think we'll need to do is some psychic protection exercises."

Heath laughed softly. "Yeah, 'cause that worked so well for me last time."

"You were using protection?" I asked, then realized my double entendre and felt my cheeks blush.

Heath caught it too and he laughed. "I always use protection," he said with a wink.

"Sorry," I said, feeling even hotter. "You know what I mean."

Heath continued to chuckle, but he answered in between by saying, "Yeah. I encased myself in a gold orb and called in the big kahuna."

"Archangel Michael?" It was well-known in the spiritual community that archangel Michael was the go-to guy to help thwart negative energy when you were doing any kind of spiritual work.

"Yep," Heath said. "And maybe he went to lunch or something when whatever that thing was came out of the ether, 'cause I've never been bitch-slapped by something like that in all the time I've been doing this."

I thought back to my own protection in the morning, before the shoot began. I clearly remembered going through much the same ritual. "Okay, so we'll need to double up on the protection prayers and carry a few of these on us." I held up the loose magnets for emphasis.

Heath looked up from where he was holding down several pieces in the box and said, "Let's hope screwing with the electromagnetic field works."

About half an hour later, after some lengthy meditative preparation in which Heath and I had mentally covered our energy with reflective coating (this works really well for your average encounter with negativity) and called in archangel Michael to be our spiritual security guard, we were on our way back toward the conference room.

We passed the elevator and were traversing the

mezzanine when I saw Murray Knollenberg on the other side of the lobby. I waved to him and he came over to us. "Hi, you two," he said warmly. "How did your television shoot go this morning?"

Heath and I shared a look. "You mean you didn't hear?" I asked.

Immediately Murray's expression turned to worry. "Something else bad happened?"

" 'Fraid so," said Heath. "Mr. Knollenberg, I'm sorry to tell you this, but there might be a demon loose in your hotel."

I stifled the groan that wanted to bubble up from my insides, as that wasn't how I would have broken the news to the already beleaguered-looking GM. Sure enough, Murray turned as pale as one of the ghosties currently haunting his hotel. "A *demon*?" He gasped.

"We can't be sure," I said, giving Heath a pointed look. "But we were both attacked during the shoot—"

"What do you mean, you were *attacked*?!" Murray interrupted, and the poor guy looked as though he was ready to faint.

Heath pulled up the sleeve of his shirt and showed him the claw marks. Knollenberg's mouth dropped in horror. "How did that happen? I mean, how is that even *possible*?"

Again Heath and I shared a look. I said, "We're not sure, but we think it has something to do with one of the items brought to the set for Heath and me to give our impressions of. We're on our way back there to make sure that we encase the object so that it can't cause any more harm."

"Damage?" Murray nearly shouted, his head

swiveling back and forth between Heath and me. "What other damage did it cause?"

I held up my hand in a *take it easy* motion. "It's nothing," I said. "Everything is fine. The only damage was to us. We've got the knife temporarily contained under a covering that is holding the negative energy bound, and it should be fine until we can get it into this box." I held up the box to show Knollenberg that we had things under control, but he hardly looked convinced.

"Oh, my," he said, and, amazingly, his complexion seemed to lose even more color. Without another word he turned and began to trot off in the direction of the Renaissance Room.

"Great," I moaned, nudging Heath as we hurried after him. "That's all we need."

We arrived at the conference room's door just as Knollenberg was tugging it open, and before we could stop him he dashed into the room and we heard him shriek loud enough to wake the dead. (Sorry, but it was *that* loud!)

"Damn!" I swore, and leaped forward with Heath right next to me. We rushed in after the GM and stopped in our tracks, my mouth falling open far enough to expose my tonsils. "Holy mother of God!" I gasped, staring around the room in disbelief.

The place looked like someone with a machete had had himself a wild party. The curtains were torn into shreds of fabric; chairs were overturned and broken; shattered glass littered the floor; much of the camera crew's equipment had been thrown around and, I suspected, damaged; holes were punched in the walls; and a giant carved heart was drawn around the antique mirror across the room. But most disturbing of all was the table in the center of the room, where the knife had once been covered with Gilley's sweatshirt. All that remained of it were a few scraps of fabric and three long talon marks carved deeply into the tabletop.

While Heath and I took in the disarray of the room in silence, Knollenberg was holding his head in his hands and moaning about the cost of repairs.

Finally I turned to Heath and asked, "Why would Gopher leave all this expensive equipment here without posting a guard or locking the door?"

"Huh?" he said, pulling his eyes away from the table to look at me and focus on my question. "I'm sorry, what did you say?"

"I said that I don't understand why the producer on this shoot would leave all of this valuable equipment here to be vandalized without securing the room. You'd think that a member of the crew would have been left behind to watch over this stuff, or at least make sure no one got in here."

"You think a *person* did this?"

I glanced around at all the damage and felt my insides tighten at the prospect of facing something nonhuman that could cause so much destruction. "Well, someone human had to have come in here and removed the sweatshirt from the knife, at least," I reasoned. "I mean, we had it contained as long as the shirt covered the knife."

"But what if we didn't?" said Heath. "What if we only stunned it or something?"

I thought on that, and as I did I walked forward to the table where we'd sat for the shoot earlier in the day and looked down at the tabletop. Tentatively I ran my fingers over the three talon marks etched deeply into the wood's surface. Then I picked up the small shred of what was left of Gilley's sweatshirt and examined it. Something curious occurred to me, and it was that I could clearly see that the magnets had been ripped off the fabric.

I glanced around the area, looking for the little black squares, but none appeared to be mixed in with all the debris. I then peered under the table, and there were no flat black squares to be found.

"What is it?" Heath asked when I stood up again and scratched my head.

"The magnets," I said, lifting up the bit of fabric. "They're all gone."

Heath came over to me and inspected what was left of the sweatshirt. "Where'd they go?" he wondered.

"I don't know," I said. "But my theory is that someone knew about their power over spirit energy and ripped them off the sweatshirt, which likely gave the demon full rein to do whatever it wanted in here."

There was a little squeak behind us, and I turned to see Knollenberg with his wide eyes and pale complexion staring at us in horror. "You mean to tell me that whatever did this to this room is roaming free in my hotel?"

Neither Heath nor I answered him right away, and I think our silence told him more than words could have, because the poor man simply covered his mouth and shook his head. "This is awful!" he said. "We can't afford this! What am I supposed to tell our guests? I cannot expose them to this kind of danger!"

"I don't think it's time to panic just yet," I said,

surveying the room again and feeling a rather sick feeling settle into my stomach. "I know you're worried about your hotel guests, but if you'll give us just a few hours I think we can determine whether anyone is truly in danger. But first, we'll need to find Gopher and let him know what's happened. I'm sure he won't be very happy to learn that some of his equipment's been damaged, and I'll ask him about why he left this room unattended. Then Heath and I will conduct a thorough search of the hotel—if there's a violent poltergeist loose in this building, we're the ones who will attract it first."

"What will you do with it when you encounter it?" Knollenberg asked, and I saw how his eyes roved to the cigar box I held in my hands, which did seem a little pathetic against something powerful enough to destroy a large conference room.

"We'll cross that bridge when we get to it," I reassured him, and I really hoped I sounded confident . . . 'cause that wasn't at all how I felt. "For now, maybe you should have your staff alert you if anything out of the ordinary gets reported to the front desk. If anyone sees or hears anything unusual, come find one of us and we'll go investigate."

"But what if one of my guests is injured?" Knollenberg insisted, his eyes moving to Heath's shoulder, where he knew there were deep cut marks.

I contemplated his predicament for a moment or two. The poor GM was damned if he listened to us, and damned if he didn't. Finally, I shrugged my shoulders. "I understand this could put you in a very vulnerable situation. So I'll leave it up to you. If you want to go ahead and evacuate your guests, then do what you and the hotel attorneys would be comfortable with. In the meantime, we'll be on the hunt for this thing, and with any luck, we'll find it before anyone else does."

Knollenberg hardly looked reassured, and he muttered something about phoning the hotel's owner to get his take on it before hurrying out of the room.

"Do you think that was the right call?" I asked Heath as we took one last look around the rubble of the Renaissance Room.

"M.J.," Heath said soberly, "nothing about this thing feels right."

And as an unexpected chill went up the back of my spine, I had to agree.

Chapter 7

We didn't linger long in the Renaissance Room, deciding it was better to go find Gopher as soon as possible.

After stopping at the front desk to call the producer's room and discovering that he didn't answer the phone, I spotted Tracy, the production assistant, having a drink at the bar in the lobby.

I motioned to Heath and we walked over to her. "Hey, there," I said to get her attention. "Have you seen Gopher?"

Tracy looked up at me, and her eyes appeared to struggle to focus. From the cluster of shot glasses next to the nearly empty bottle of beer she was downing, I could easily guess why. "Oh, yeah," she said. "I've seen him."

I waited, but Tracy didn't seem as if she was going to put forth any more information unless I prodded her. "Can you tell me where?"

The young woman downed another shot of liquor before answering. "He's upstairs," she said with a sneer. "Humping his way through the production staff."

I decided not to tell Tracy that was a little too much information for my taste and kept my questions on track. "Do you happen to know what room he's in?"

Tracy swayed in her seat. "Why do you need to know, exactly?"

"Someone got into the Renaissance Room and vandalized some of the cameras and equipment. Gopher needs to be notified immediately."

Tracy's head wobbled on her thin neck as she swiveled to look in the direction of the conference room. "Where's Mike?" she said.

"Who?" I asked.

"The staff assistant," she said. "He was left to watch over the room."

I looked at Heath in alarm. We hadn't seen anyone else in the room. "I have no idea," I said, feeling a small pit of trepidation form in my stomach. "No one was in there when we looked."

Even through her drunken haze Tracy seemed to grasp the seriousness of the situation, and she blinked several times before digging through her purse to retrieve her cell phone. Clicking through what I assumed was her contact list, she settled on one and put the phone to her ear. After a few more seconds she said, "Yo, Mikey, where the hell are you? I got the ghost lady here telling me that the room's been wrecked. Call me back, pronto."

Tracy then scrolled back through the contacts on her phone and punched the send button with a bit of flourish and a heck of a sneer. Putting the phone to her ear, she waited out the rings while her fingers drummed the bar. "Yo, asshole," she said by way of a friendly greeting. "Maybe you can stop screwing

Leslie long enough to get down here. Your equipment's been vandalized and you're on the hook for it, so I guess there *is* justice in the world!" With that she punched the end button and snickered before dropping her phone on the bar.

"I'm assuming that was Gopher?"

Tracy picked up her beer and took the last long gulp before giving me a winning smile, which I assumed was an affirmative. She then got up and teetered on her high heels before she announced, "I gotta pee. Watch my stuff, will you?" And without waiting for an answer she trooped off in a zigzag toward the restrooms.

We watched her totter away, and no sooner had she pushed through the door to the ladies' room than her cell phone began to ring. I took the liberty of answering it, as the caller ID said it was Gopher. "What the hell kind of a message was that?!" yelled an angry voice the moment I said hello.

"If you're looking for Tracy, she's in the ladies' room," I replied calmly.

There was a pause, then, "Who is this?"

"M.J.," I said. "And we need you down here right away, Gopher. The Renaissance Room has been vandalized, and a lot of your equipment has been wrecked."

There was a flurry of profanity that followed, and I pulled the phone away from my ear. Placing my free hand over the receiver, I said quietly to Heath, "He seems upset."

"What happened?" I heard after the rain of profanity had stopped.

"I don't know," I admitted. "But you need to get down here and take a look."

"Where's Mike?"

"We don't know. When we went into the room no one was there."

"What happened to the knife?"

I thought that was a rather odd question to ask. It just seemed out of place, but I replied with what I knew, which wasn't much: "It's gone."

"Shit," he said. "I'll be right there."

I clicked off Tracy's cell and tucked it back into her purse. "He's coming down," I told Heath.

Heath and I waited by the bar for Tracy to get back and for Gopher to show up. The bartender asked us if we'd like anything, and I ordered a Coke and Heath ordered a cappuccino. We talked a little bit about the disarray of the conference room, and I could tell that Heath was as nervous about going after the demon as I was. "This is just so far beyond anything I've ever encountered," he was saying.

"I know," I said, looking over my shoulder as we sat at the bar to see if Tracy had managed to come out of the ladies' room yet. My eye fell instead on Gopher, who was just coming out of the elevator looking a bit rumpled, as though he'd dressed very quickly. Behind him and wearing a baseball cap was another young woman whom I thought I remembered being on the shoot that morning.

Gopher made a beeline for Heath and me, and when he got to us he said, "Did Mike show up?"

"No," I said. "Was he supposed to?"

"Goddamn it!" Gopher swore. "I've been calling his cell every thirty seconds since I got off the phone with you. I keep getting his voice mail."

"We haven't seen him," I said. "But the manager

of the hotel is calling the police to file a report on the vandalism."

"Is that thing still in there?" he asked, a bit nervously.

"You mean the demon?" I said.

"Yeah."

"We didn't see or feel anything in the room when we were there," I said. "I think that whatever it was that caused the damage—be it demon or person—has left the area."

"Okay, come on," he said to us. "You guys might as well show me what happened."

I looked down at Tracy's purse still on the bar. "Heath, you go with Gopher. I'm going to take Tracy her stuff and I'll join you in a minute."

"Got it," said Heath, and he, Gopher, and the other production assistant walked away.

I gathered up all Tracy's belongings and told the bartender that I was going to check on her in the ladies' room.

"Whoa," he said. "I can't let you leave without paying the tab."

"We already paid you for the Coke and the coffee," I reminded him before motioning to the clutter of shot glasses on the bar. "This was that other lady's tab."

"Yeah, well, I haven't seen her in the last ten minutes. I'll need something like a credit card to hold on to before I can let you take her purse."

I rolled my eyes and fished around in Tracy's handbag, coming up with a wallet and a credit card. "I don't feel right about digging through her stuff like this," I muttered.

"I won't charge the card unless she doesn't come

back," the bartender reassured me. "Just let her know that I'm holding on to it, okay?"

I nodded and got up from the bar stool, carrying Tracy's purse over to the ladies' room. She'd seemed drunk enough to have either gotten sick or passed out, and I was hoping that I didn't have to deal with a lot of that drama when I found her.

I pushed open the door to the ladies' room and called out, "Tracy?" No one replied. I then went inside and looked around.

The powder room was a peach tile with mint green accents. There were four stall doors, and over the four sinks was another mirror with a golden frame and intricate carvings, a twin to the one I'd seen in the conference room. As I was turning to the stalls, I caught movement out of the corner of my eye and glanced up at the reflection in the mirror. A woman was coming into the powder room, and I think she was the most beautiful woman I'd ever seen. She had long dark hair that fell in waves down her back, and her face was heart shaped, with full lips and large brown eyes. I smiled at her reflection and she nodded back.

I suddenly felt self-conscious about staring, so I turned to the stalls and bent down to check whether any of them were occupied. "Yoo-hoo," I called again as I walked along the stalls. "Tracy, are you in here?"

In the last stall I spotted a pair of legs wearing the same high heels I'd seen on the production assistant, and I knocked softly on the door. "Tracy, are you okay in there?"

She didn't answer, and I knocked a second time. "Tracy?" I said, pushing against the door to see if it would open. It was locked from the inside. "Come on, honey," I encouraged. "Wakey, wakey!" Still no reply, so I bent down again and tried to peer under the door. And that was when I saw Tracy's arm dangling at an odd position, and dripping down her arm and pooling in a small puddle was a thin line of red blood. "Ohmigod!" I shrieked, and stood up quickly.

Reflexively I turned toward the door to ask if the woman who had just come into the powder room could go for help . . . but there was no one else in the room. I then realized that I hadn't heard the woman enter any of the other stalls. Pushing that out of my mind for the moment, I shoved my shoulder into the door as hard as I could. It hurt like a bitch, but the lock on the other side held. "Tracy!" I yelled, backing up from the door. "Honey, hang on!" I then karate-kicked the door and it banged open, revealing the dead body of the production assistant covered in blood, her lifeless eyes open and horrified as a knife handle stuck straight out of her chest.

I reeled away from her and my back hit the sink hard, but I didn't feel it until later, when the police came. For the moment I was really finding it hard to breathe. I opened my mouth to scream, but the sound wouldn't form. All that I seemed to be able to manage was to take in large gulps of air. I turned and fled the powder room, crashing through the door out to the mezzanine. I must have looked as terrified and panic-stricken as I felt, because people were openly gaping at me, and one of those people was Gilley.

"M.J.?" he said, looking at me in alarm. "What's the matter?"

I pointed to the powder room and struggled to breathe. I knew in the back of my mind that I was hyperventilating, but I was powerless against it. Instinctively I doubled over, grabbing my knees and working to hold the intake of breath in my lungs for a few seconds before exhaling. In the background I heard Gilley shout, "Steven! Come quick! I think M.J.'s hurt!"

Gilley arrived at my side and bent down to peer up at my face. I shook my head and felt tears well and drop to the floor . . . just like Tracy's blood when it ran down her arm. I squeezed my eyes shut, but the horrific image just continued to play out in my mind's eye.

"Sweetheart," said Gilley, "what's happened to you?"

"Where does it hurt?" I heard Steven ask urgently.

I opened my eyes and looked up at my partner and pointed to the ladies' room. I fought to have my lips form the word *murder*, but all that came out was a "Mah . . . Mah . . . Mah!" sound.

"Man?" said Gilley. "A man did this to you?"

I shook my head and sank to my knees. The world was closing in around me, and I was dizzy and close to fainting. Tears continued to leak out of my eyes, and I felt a sob forming in the base of my throat. "Tray . . ." I said. "Hurt!" I finally managed.

"Someone hurt you with a tray?" Gilley tried, and I felt like swatting him.

I shook my head again and pointed back to the ladies' room. "Go . . . there!" I gasped just as Steven put something over my mouth and pushed my head forward.

"Breathe into this bag," he said calmly. "You're

hyperventilating, M.J. Just slow down for a second, okay?"

I took several breaths, squeezing my eyes closed and trying to concentrate on the regular exchange of air. When I felt a little less light-headed I pulled the bag away and pointed yet again to the powder room, saying, "Go there!"

I saw Steven and Gilley look sharply at each other; then they each turned to the ladies' room. Gilley got to his feet and quickly walked to the door, knocking loudly from outside. He looked over his shoulder at me, as if to ask permission to go in. I nodded vigorously.

Steven was rubbing my back gently and trying to get me to calm down. "It's all right," he said. "You're okay now, *cariña*; just keep breathing into the bag."

Steven didn't have a chance to say anything more, because not a second later everyone in the vicinity heard a high-pitched squeal that sounded like a howler monkey screaming for its life.

In the next instant, Gilley came crashing out of the powder room, shrieking and flailing his arms. "Murder!" he shouted. *"She's been murdered!"*

For the next hour the scene around us would have been comical if it weren't so tragic. The police arrived in short order, and my new friend Detective MacDonald was the first to take command of the situation. Crime-scene tape was set up in a large rectangle from the bar all the way to the ladies' room, forcing the hotel guests to find other ways in and out of the building.

A line slowly formed at the front desk, where guests demanded their money back and a quick checkout as word spread that the second fatality in two days had taken place at the hotel. Murray Knollenberg had gone from pale to ashen, and a light sweat dampened his brow. He teeter-tottered back and forth between his harried staff at the counter and the police investigators taking over the lobby.

Heath and Gopher had joined us on the couch in the lobby, where we were all ordered to sit and wait to be interviewed, and to his credit Gopher looked intensely upset over Tracy's tragic end. "She was such a good kid," he blubbered as a few leaky tears ran down his cheeks. "Why would anyone want to hurt her?"

Gopher also got a call from Mike, who phoned him from the airport to say that he had heard some strange noises coming from the room he'd been left to guard, and decided to hightail it out of there. He apparently didn't need the job that badly.

Gil was sitting next to me and not at all happy that I'd sent him into the powder room to discover the body. "You could have given me a little warning," he snipped irritably.

"So sorry my hyperventilating, shivering, and crying weren't big enough clues for you, Sherlock," I snapped back.

"Hey, now, you two," said Steven. "Let's not argue."

"I'm not arguing," I insisted, my nerves still on edge. "But I would just like to state for the record that this entire fiasco could have been avoided if a certain *someone* hadn't signed us up for a stay in Hotel Hell."

"Oh, like it's *my* fault," Gilley squealed, and I

rubbed my temples, remembering how his voice got very pitchy when he got indignant.

"I didn't say it was your fault . . . per se. I was just commenting on the fact that *normally* on a Saturday afternoon I am home watching television, and not so concerned with being attacked by demons and finding dead bodies in bathroom stalls."

Gilley crossed his arms and glared down at the floor. "Well, I am sorry!" he grumbled. "But you have been a real pill lately, and I thought a nice trip to fabulous San Francisco would do you some good. My apologies for trying to look out for you!"

"A pill?" I snapped, sitting up to stare hard at him. "*I've* been a pill? What the hell do you mean by *that*?"

"I mean that if I didn't know better I'd think you weren't getting laid," Gil said, and I heard more than one gasp from the people sitting around us. "But clearly that's not the case, so maybe it's an early case of perimenopause! Maybe you should think about having those hormones checked, hmmmm?"

"Oh . . . no . . . you . . . *didn't*!" I yelled, standing up, ready to literally swat my partner, when I heard the sound of someone loudly clearing his throat.

I whirled around, ready to tell whomever was trying to interject some reason into the conversation where to stuff it, when I realized that Detective Mac-Donald was looking at me with raised eyebrows and the smallest of smirks. "Mind if I interrupt this little love fest?" he asked casually.

I felt my cheeks burn as I plastered a rather strained smile onto my face while kicking Gilley in the shin with my foot. "Of course, Detective," I said. "Please join us."

MacDonald took a seat on the couch on the other side of Heath, who looked as though he wanted to be anywhere but here, and I knew exactly how he felt. "So," MacDonald said, flipping to a blank page in his notebook. "Tell me who found the body."

"I did," I said. And then I told him everything, from the last time I'd seen Tracy at the bar to finding her in the bathroom.

"And before you went into the restroom, did you see anyone else come out?"

"No."

"Did you see anyone else in there before you found Tracy?"

"No . . ." I said before remembering the woman I'd seen in the mirror. "Except there was a lady who came in right after me."

"And where is she now?" asked MacDonald, glancing around at those of us on the couch.

I stared blankly at him. "I have no idea," I admitted.

"Did she come out after you exited?" he probed.

I shook my head. "I don't think so, but I'll admit that I wasn't thinking very clearly right after seeing Tracy."

MacDonald's lips pursed as he looked over what he'd written. "What did this mystery woman look like?" he asked me.

I described her to him and noticed that as I did, Heath sat up straight and leaned forward, as if he were very interested in my description. "Okay, we'll interview the guests and see if we can spot her," he said. "Now tell me about this knife—the murder weapon. The general manager of the hotel says that you guys had it as part of the television show and that it's haunted by a demon or some sort of baloney?"

I looked at Heath and then over at Gopher. They were wearing the same shocked expressions. "The knife we've been looking for was the one used to murder Tracy?" Gopher asked me.

I was just as taken aback by the detective's question. It hadn't occurred to me that it was the same knife Heath and I were trying to find. "That I don't know," I said honestly. "I mean, Knollenberg is probably jumping to conclusions, although he was right to tell you that during our television shoot there was a knife that seemed to have some sort of unnatural power, but I hadn't considered it was the one used to kill Tracy."

MacDonald reached into his blazer and pulled out a small digital camera. Flipping through several shots, he arrived at one and showed it to me. "That the knife from your television show?"

I stared in horror at the viewfinder as the bloody blade with the intricate carvings was captured in the image. "Ohmigod," I whispered, showing the picture to Heath, Gilley, Steven, and Gopher, who all nodded grimly. "That *is* the same knife, Detective!"

MacDonald scribbled in his notebook before taking the camera back. "Talk to me about this unnatural power," he said. "What do you mean by that?"

Heath leaned forward and lifted up his shirt-sleeve, showing the detective the three claw marks on the top of his shoulder. "M.J. has the same pattern on her back," he told the detective. "Only the cuts on her back are a lot deeper and longer."

MacDonald's brows furrowed, and he looked

from Heath's arm to me, as if he were missing something. "Come again?" he demanded.

"That silver knife was introduced into the production," I explained. "We don't know who brought it in or laid it down on the table where we were sitting—I mean, we were both distracted and tired, and no one from the shoot remembers seeing who delivered it, but right after it was set in front of us Heath and I were both attacked and cut up by some sort of . . ." I paused, because I didn't know how to describe what it was that had clawed us. *Demon* just seemed ridiculous.

"Poltergeist," Heath filled in, obviously thinking the same thing.

MacDonald peered closely at Heath's wounds before asking me, "Can I see the ones on your back?"

I swiveled in my seat and pulled up the back of my shirt, hearing a long, low whistle behind me. "Ouch," he said.

I let go of the shirt and turned back around to face him. "It only stings a little," I said.

"So you're telling me a *ghost* picked up the knife and cut you two with it?"

Clearly MacDonald was having a hard time understanding what had taken place. "No," I said patiently. "The knife stayed on the table. An unseen force scratched us."

"Were you wearing the same clothes you are now?" MacDonald probed.

Heath and I both nodded. "We were," he said.

"So why aren't your clothes torn?"

I didn't have an explanation for that. "I couldn't say. It's the first time my skin's been punctured by an entity."

MacDonald scratched his chin thoughtfully. "And the whole television crew was witness to this?"

The question seemed to be directed at Gopher, and he nodded. "Yes," he said. "I remember hearing M.J. shout, like she was in pain, and when I looked over she was holding her chest, and a second later a cut appeared on Heath's cheek. It was freaky, like it just materialized out of thin air."

"I thought you said your back got tagged," MacDonald said to me.

I pulled the collar of my shirt down a little, thankful that I was wearing a sports bra and wasn't revealing too much of the ta-tas. "It got me here first."

The detective sat back on his cushion and regarded all of us for several long seconds. I had no idea what he was thinking, but I could guess that it wasn't anything flattering. "Tell me again how this knife plays into all this?"

Heath pointed at me, signaling that I should attempt to explain the unexplainable.

"We think the knife is some sort of key," I said.

"A key," MacDonald repeated.

"Yes," I said, choosing my words carefully. "We believe that someone very powerful and skilled in the art of black magic may have imbued it with the ability to open a portal."

"Portal?" MacDonald repeated again.

"Uh-huh," I said. "A portal is a gateway. It links our plane of existence, what you and I think of as the real world, with that of a lower plane of existence."

MacDonald's mouth fell open a little bit. "You mean . . . like hell?" he asked.

"Well, maybe not quite that far down," I said. "I mean, I'm still on the fence about whether or not hell actually exists, but I do know there is a lower realm where nasty energies can circulate and become more powerful. Often, when a really bad person dies, like a murderer or a rapist, they won't want to cross over into heaven because they can't handle the judgment they'll face. So they become grounded spirits, and they learn pretty quickly that because their energy is dark they can create a portal that allows them to enter this lower realm and learn about becoming powerful ghosts or poltergeists. These energies are never anything you'd want to fool with—you'll hear about how they learn to throw stones and slam doors and throw objects. Some even learn to start fires.

"Normally these dark energies will create this portal very near the site where they died, and in every single case that I've encountered, that portal is connected to something physically stationary, like the wall of a house or the side of a barn or even a headstone. And that's how we've been able to shut down the portals that we've encountered during our ghostbusts. By driving a magnetized stake through the physical object where the portal is connected, we can cause a collapse of the electromagnetic frequencies made at the portal's creation, and lock up any negative energies that are using it to go back and forth.

"But this knife thing, well . . . it's completely different. I think the knife represents something so rare that I've never encountered it. I think that it might not even be a key," I said, suddenly reconsidering my earlier premise. "No, this thing . . . this thing might actually be a *portable* portal, and I think that it's a portal that allows for something far uglier than just some dead murderer to come back and forth through it. I think that it allows for demons to come out of the lower realm and play havoc on our physical world."

"I did some research," said Gilley, speaking up for the first time since I'd yelled at him. "And I came across a ghost hunter from Europe who claims that some objects can retain such dark energy that they are essentially what M.J. is guessing at. This parapsychologist says that in very rare instances, an object can be a portable gateway to the lower realms."

"It's official," MacDonald said, slapping his notebook closed. "I'm in the Twilight Zone."

"I know it's a lot to take in," I agreed. "But you know by my work with you on Sophie's case that I'm not a wacko or a kook."

"And we have witnesses," said Heath. "M.J., remember the smoke serpent?"

"Smoke what?" asked MacDonald, and I knew we were pushing the envelope with this very open-minded cop.

Before I had a chance to explain, however, another detective came over and tapped MacDonald on the shoulder. "Ayden," he said, "you need to come in and see this."

"What?" said MacDonald, swiveling around to look up at the other detective.

"The ME's just arrived," said the man. "He's found these really weird marks on the vic's back. I know this is gonna sound crazy, but it looks like she's gone a round with Freddy Krueger."

MacDonald's face visibly paled, as did almost every other face gathered around the seating area. MacDonald swiveled back to me and ordered, "Show him your back."

I turned and lifted my shirt up and heard the other detective say, "Hey, that's exactly what they look like on our vic!"

I let my shirt drop and turned back around to see MacDonald getting up and pointing a finger directly at me. "Do not move!"

I held my hands up in surrender. "You got it," I said, feeling all eyes on me.

"Yikes," said Heath as MacDonald and the other man hurried away.

I sighed and rubbed my temples; it'd been a hell of a long day.

"Can I get you anything?" Steven asked me. "Something to eat, or drink, or a plane ticket for the first flight home?"

That got him a small smile. "I'm good," I said, reaching out to take his hand. "Thanks."

"M.J.?" said Heath.

"Yeah?"

"That woman you said you saw come into the bathroom—what did she look like again?"

I cocked my head. It seemed like a really odd question, but I indulged him by telling him, "She was really beautiful. Like, supermodel beautiful. She was a couple of inches taller than me, and she had long black wavy hair, kind of a heart-shaped face, and these big brown eyes. I think she walked in and walked back out again; I don't know, maybe she saw me in there knocking on stalls and decided to try another bathroom."

"Did she say anything to you?"

"No. Why are you asking about her?" I asked, curious why he was so interested.

"I saw her too," he admitted. "In that big gold

mirror with the scratched heart around it back in the Renaissance Room. And the same thing happened when I saw her. She came in through the door, smiled at me, and I was about to turn around to face her when Gopher found one of his cameras had been ruined, and that distracted me for a second or two. When I turned back around she was gone. I assumed the same thing you did, that she came in, saw the room or heard Gopher swearing about the camera, and turned on her heel and left."

I felt goose bumps rise along my arms. "About what time did that happen?"

"The best that I can figure it, it wasn't long after I left you, so probably about the time that you saw her too."

I felt as though someone had just given me a slap on the forehead. "Another spook?" I wondered.

Heath shrugged but then nodded. "I kinda think it might be."

Something dawned on me. "Ohmigod!" I said, staring at him as I put it together. "The mirror in the bathroom is identical to the mirror in the Renaissance Room!"

"So she's attached to the mirrors," said Heath.

"We'll have to ask Knollenberg about it," I concluded. "He should know if anyone has talked about seeing some phantom lady in the mirrors around here."

"What do you make of the heart carved into the wall around the one in the conference room?" Heath asked.

I shook my head. "I've no idea. But it's got to be significant," I reasoned. "I mean, the two mirrors seem to have some really odd coincidences connected to them, especially given that the knife used to kill Tracy was also the one used to bring out the demon in the room with the other mirror."

Just then MacDonald came back to our group. Pointing a finger at me, he said, "You. Come with me."

"Uh-oh," whispered Gilley. "You want me to come along, M.J.?" My partner was obviously feeling guilty about our little spat from a few minutes before, because I knew he wouldn't normally want to be anywhere near signs of trouble.

"I'll be okay," I reassured him. Steven squeezed my hand as I got up, and I gave him what I hoped was a confident smile. I didn't know what the detective wanted with me, and until I knew, it was pointless to worry about it.

I followed MacDonald across the mezzanine and over to the restroom. The door was propped open, and there were several people in the interior, including one man in a blue Windbreaker with the initials ME on the back of it. He was hovering over Tracy's body, and I averted my eyes quickly as I felt my stomach bunch.

"Jack," said MacDonald. "Can you show this woman the marks on our vic's back?"

I forced myself to look back at the ME as he was rolling Tracy over slightly and pulling up her shirt. As her shirt pulled away from her body I could see the three deep talon marks that mirrored those on my own back. I looked away again, and out of the corner of my eye I saw MacDonald nod to the ME. "Thanks, Jack," he said.

"I've never seen anything like it," said the medical examiner. "Her skin is cut but her clothes aren't, and, from the lack of blood, I'd say these were made postmortem, but why, I couldn't imagine."

"Where's the murder weapon?" asked MacDonald, and my eyes instinctively went back to Tracy, lying on the floor. With a bit of a shock I realized the knife had already been extracted from the middle of her chest.

"I assumed you'd want a rush on this, so I gave it to one of the techs. He's taking it back to the lab to have it dusted for prints ASAP."

"Lemme know the minute you get anything on it, okay?" said MacDonald.

"Will do," said the ME as he got up and moved past us. "I've got to get a body bag out of my van. I'll be back in a sec."

After the ME had gone MacDonald turned to the two techs dusting for prints and said, "Can you guys give us a minute?"

I felt a bit nervous as the men looked at MacDonald curiously but didn't question him, and they left the restroom. When we were alone, the detective closed the door and turned to me. "Can you do that thing you did with Sophie?"

I blinked in surprise. "Huh?" I asked, a little slow on the uptake.

"Can you talk to her, you know, help her cross over or whatever it is that you do?"

"Oh!" I said, looking from Tracy to MacDonald and back again. "Er . . . I guess."

"Good," said MacDonald. "And remember, ask her if she knows who attacked her before you send her away."

In any other situation the request from the detective would have made me laugh; it just seemed so ridiculous to have a street-smart cop be open to concepts of the metaphysical. But maybe they grew them a little less skeptical out here in California. I didn't linger over it, as I knew the ME would be returning with his body bag in a minute or two, and MacDonald was going to have to explain why he was in here with me while the door was shut.

I turned toward Tracy and closed my eyes, shutting out the pain and shock frozen on her once pretty face. Opening up my senses, I waited for a sign from her that she wanted to communicate. Seconds passed in which I was acutely aware that Mac-Donald was watching me closely, but no signal from Tracy wafted through the ether.

I called out to her in my mind, but got nothing back. There was no reply of any kind. I opened my eyes and looked at her lifeless body, willing some kind of psychic connection, but my intuitive receptors were silent.

"Well?" asked MacDonald. "What'd she say?"

I looked at him and frowned. "Nothing." I sighed.

"She doesn't know who attacked her?" he clarified.

"No," I said, shaking my head. "She's not here. I've been trying to connect with her since you asked, and there's no answer."

"What does that mean?"

"Well," I said, scratching my head. "It means either that she's crossed over and she's in transition or that she's grounded, but she's not grounded here."

MacDonald looked at me as though I'd just spoken Chinese. "Come again?"

I smiled. "Yeah, that probably wouldn't make

sense to you. What I mean is that Tracy could have already crossed over successfully, and, given the fact that she was very intoxicated when she died, that's a likely scenario. . . ."

"What does that have to do with it?" he said.

"It's something that's fairly common," I explained. "It's like the shock of what's happening to you doesn't impact you as intensely if you're inebriated, so a lot of drunks and drug addicts end up crossing over really easily. Anyway, if she has crossed over successfully, there's usually a transition period when they're not able to communicate with us, and sometimes this can take a while, like a few months even."

"Huh," he said. "Okay, I'm with you. And this other thing, that if she's on the ground she's not here?"

I hid a smirk at his interpretation. "What I meant was that if she is a ghost, what we in the biz refer to as grounded, then she might be grounded someplace other than where she died. She could actually be grounded at her home, and Gilley and I have run into this scenario a few times too. A person will die in one place, but haunt another. It happens a lot, actually."

"And neither scenario helps us with her murder," he said.

"Nope," I said. "Neither one does."

"So now what?" he asked me.

"Now I leave you to try to solve this case the old-fashioned way, Detective."

"But what about this demon thing that's clawing people?" he insisted. I could tell he was a little spooked by what he'd seen on my back and Tracy's.

I felt my shoulders droop. "That's where Heath—the other medium I've been hanging out with—and I go to work. The thing I'm worried about, though, is that your lab tech has the knife that we believe is the portable portal to the demon. You've got to let me know if anything weird happens when they go to dust it for prints, okay?"

MacDonald pulled out his cell phone and punched in a number. When the call connected he said, "Ben, it's me, Ayden. Can you tell me which one of your techs got physical custody of the knife from our vic?" There was a pause; then MacDonald's face flushed red with anger. "What the hell do you mean, you don't know?! Isn't it your job to assign these things?" MacDonald listened, then seemed to grow even madder. "How the hell does that happen, Ben? You tell me *how the hell does that happen*?"

I was growing increasingly alarmed. "They don't know where the knife is?" I whispered, but Mac-Donald was too furious to notice that I'd asked him something.

"Find that damn knife, Ben! You find it and find it quick!" he shouted.

From outside there was a knock. The door was pushed open and the ME stood there, looking a bit shocked to find us in here with his body and the detective yelling his head off. "Everything okay, Ayden?"

MacDonald slapped his cell phone closed and whirled on the ME. "Jack," he said tersely. "Who did you hand the knife off to?"

The ME looked a bit surprised by the question. "Uh," he said, "one of the techs."

"*Which* one of the techs?" demanded MacDonald.

"I don't know," said Jack, and I could tell he was beginning to see the reason to be alarmed. "One of the new guys, I think."

"Son of a bitch, Jack!" yelled MacDonald. "There *are* no new guys! We've had a hiring freeze for the past three months!"

"Oh, shit," whispered the ME. "Ayden, I'm really sorry—"

But MacDonald cut him off by holding up his hand in a *stop* motion. "Save it," he snapped, and yanked the door open, making a motion for me to exit the area pronto, which I did.

When we were out in the open again I realized that all eyes were now turned directly on us, everyone obviously alarmed by the yelling and swearing and such. "Did you still need me?" I asked as we walked toward the seating area.

"No," MacDonald growled. "But stick close; I may have more questions for you later."

"Will do," I agreed, and hurried over to Gilley, Steven, Heath, and Gopher.

"What happened?" Heath asked when I took my seat again.

"The knife has gone missing," I said. "Someone took it right out from under their noses."

"This is bad!" Gilley squeaked. "That means the portal is still open and the demon could be running loose anywhere."

"It does," I said soberly. "And it also means that anyone and everyone here could be in serious danger."

Chapter 8

"I think it's time we considered going back to Boston," Steven said reasonably. "This is too dangerous now. We should leave the police to solve this and not be like sitting geese."

I looked to Gilley, who was pumping his head up and down vigorously. "I agree," he said. "They don't pay us to put our lives on the line. Let's get the freak outta here, M.J.!"

"Hey, now," I said reasonably. "Let's not panic and bolt. If that knife is still somewhere in this hotel, lives could be at stake."

"Yes," agreed Gilley. "*Ours!* This is too much for us; we're in way over our heads. I say we get the heck out while we can, and leave this one to the police."

I stared at him and Steven for a long moment, weighing what they were telling me, but my conscience was having a tough time of it. "I don't know, Gil," I said. "I almost think we have an obligation to try."

"Obligation?" He gasped. "Are you *kidding* me, M.J.? When did you take some sort of public vow to hunt down dangerous poltergeists who could very well carve you up for dinner?"

"But that's the point, isn't it?" I threw back at him. "If someone like me is going to have a tough time with that thing, can you imagine some poor innocent encountering it?"

"Some poor innocent already did," said Steven, eyeing the ladies' room. "And she died. M.J., this is too big for even you. I think we should leave."

"Heath?" I asked, my voice a little pleading. "What do you think?"

Heath sighed and took his time replying. "I think Gilley's right," he said, and my eyes widened. I had expected him to take my side. "This is some heavy shit, and I'd prefer to duck out and leave it behind. Plus, we don't know for certain the knife and the demon are even still here. For all we know, the person responsible could have taken the knife and fled the area."

"Or," said Gilley ominously, "they could still be here . . . and watching us."

There was a long, tense moment of silence before all eyes seemed to fall on me, and I felt the weight of the responsibility. Before making up my mind I looked again at Heath, knowing I couldn't possibly attempt to take on a demon hunt without his help. But I didn't want to give up. These people needed us, and we were the only experts capable of helping. If the police did catch Tracy's killer—the person carrying the portal key—what then? How could a gun or a badge stop a demon?

I was about to argue the point when I heard a voice behind me say, "Pardon my interruption, but might I have a word with you two?"

I turned to face a tall, elegantly dressed older gentleman wearing a three-piece suit and a beautiful silk tie and carrying a walking cane with a silver handle. "With me?" I asked him, wondering if we'd ever met before.

"You and the young man on the couch," he replied, indicating Heath. It was then that I noticed Murray Knollenberg standing nervously behind the gentleman.

"M.J., Heath, this is Howard Beckworth," the GM said. "He is the owner of the Duke."

I cut my eyes to Heath, but he looked just as confused as I did. "Sure," I said when I saw him shrug his shoulders. "But we're trying to get on a flight, so can we make it quick?"

"Then quick it shall be," said Beckworth. "This way, if you please," he said, indicating that we should follow him.

"I'd like to bring my business partners along," I called as he turned to walk away.

Beckworth looked over his shoulder and gave me an agreeable smile. "Of course," he said.

Steven and Gilley jumped up, and so did Gopher. "Can I come?" he asked. "I've always wanted to meet *the* Howard Beckworth. He's worth a couple billion, you know."

I was about to tell him no, but Gilley said, "Sure, why not?"

"Whatever," I said, relenting, and trotted after our host and the nervous hotel manager.

We trekked along in a bit of a zigzag pattern through the crime-scene tape and exiting guests and police; past the check-in counter, which had clearly turned into the check*out* counter; down a corridor all the way to the end; and through a doorway leading us into a beautiful office with mahogany paneling, rich burgundy carpet, and a floor-to-ceiling set of bookshelves. The room was large enough to have a separate seating area, and Beckworth led us there, pointing to the two couches and four wing chairs arranged in a square. "If you will all please make yourselves comfortable," he said, taking ownership of the largest of the leather wing chairs.

I sat next to Heath, and on my other side Steven took up residence, placing a protective hand on my knee.

Gilley and Gopher took seats across from us, and Knollenberg perched uncomfortably on the edge of another wing chair.

Beckworth allowed a rather dramatic pause to extend after we had all settled, eyeing him expectantly, before he got to the point of this little gathering. "Mr. Knollenberg has informed me that along with these two unsettling fatalities, there is also some sort of dark occult activity of the hellish variety occurring in my hotel."

I noticed that the elderly gentleman spoke with a slight British accent, and wondered if he'd come from there or had just adopted it along the way to make himself sound more refined. "If by that you mean you've got a demon loose at the Duke, then yes, I would agree with that assessment," I said.

"This is most upsetting," said Beckworth. "Most upsetting indeed."

I couldn't be certain, but something told me that this guy wasn't all that surprised by this news. "Yeah, well, good luck with it," Heath said firmly. "We've decided to head home."

Beckworth smiled politely at Heath. "Yes, of course, and who could blame you?"

The question lingered in the air. No one commented, as no one really knew what to say. Instead we all waited to hear the old man out, and it was Knollenberg who actually piped up. After clearing his throat nervously, he said, "I have informed Mr. Beckworth that, by your profession, you two might be able to help us solve this problem."

"By our profession?" I said, curious about how much Knollenberg knew about Heath and me.

The fidgety manager tugged at his tie and said, "Yes. I've looked both of you up on the Internet, and your résumés are quiet impressive."

"You want to hire us," said Gilley, at last getting us to the point.

"We would," confirmed Beckworth. "As you can imagine, my hotel staff is ill prepared to deal with something of this . . . caliber. We've handled the rather passive spirits that have haunted this establishment over the years, but it is my understanding that the recent activity and force of destruction set loose in the Renaissance Room are unlike anything we've ever encountered here before."

"I'm sorry, no. It's too dangerous," said Gilley, and my jaw nearly fell open. Gilley *never* said no to a formal job proposal, especially when someone worth great gobs of money wanted to hire us. Usually I was the person trying to talk him out of putting my life on the line.

"Ah, Mr. Gillespie, is it?" said Beckworth, politely acknowledging him. Gilley flushed and nodded his head. "You seem to be a reasonable soul, and I must commend you for using caution; however, I am a man who is not easily swayed once his mind is made up. What figure might I offer you to change your mind?"

My head swiveled over to Gilley; I knew there was no way he could resist an open-ended offer like that. "There's no amount of money you could offer us," Gil insisted, and I was stunned. "It's too dangerous."

I held my breath and waited to see what Beckworth would say next, and was even more surprised when he frowned, nodded, and said to Knollenberg, "You said there were two other mediums in residence for the weekend?"

"Yes," said Knollenberg. "As I recall from our guest list they are Angelica Demarche and Bernard Higgins."

"Might you call up to their rooms and see if they would take a meeting with us?"

I held up my hands in a time-out. "Whoa, hold on there, Murray," I said, and turned to Gilley, who was staring at me curiously. "Gil," I reasoned, "we can't let those two frauds attempt to take this thing on. They'll be crucified!"

But Gilley's expression was firm. "M.J.," Gilley said softly, as if he were addressing a child, "you've already been severely injured. How could I ask you to put yourself at risk again? I mean, you're my best friend in the world! There's no way I could allow you to put yourself in harm's way for the sake of a job, no matter how much these people might need someone of your caliber and talent." And then Gil did something that made me want to either slap him or hug him fiercely: He actually winked his right eye at me—the one hidden from Beckworth and Knollenberg.

Gilley had been playing a game with Beckworth all along. He knew I really wanted to see this thing through and that there was no way I was going to allow two incompetents to go after something like this demon. I'd already changed my mind to accept the job, with or without Heath's help, and Gilley knew that. All this bravado was so that he could drive up the price.

So, in the split second that followed, I decided to let him work out the negotiations. "You're right," I said gravely. "It is too dangerous, but I think it might be even more dangerous to let Bernard and Angelica make a bad situation worse because they don't have a clue what they're doing."

Gilley sat back and shook his head resolutely. "It's your call, M.J. But I don't think any amount of money is worth this risk."

"What about ten thousand dollars?" offered Beckworth, and my stomach did a flip-flop.

Before I had a chance to say anything, Gilley chimed in with, "Each?" and indicated Heath, who was sitting on the couch, speechless but with big, interested eyes.

"Of course," Beckworth agreed easily.

Gilley took a moment to think on that, then slowly shook his head again. "No, I'm sorry, sir," he said, and I felt my heart beat hard in my chest. "We simply can't consider anything less than twenty . . . for each medium." I again glanced at Heath, who was biting his lip. His expression clearly said that not only had he changed his mind about joining the bust, but that he would have agreed to a far smaller price. I had a feeling that if Beckworth blanched, Heath was going to jump in with a lower counteroffer, but for now he looked like he was waiting Gilley's negotiations out, just in case he came out twenty grand richer.

There was an incredibly tense silence that followed, and I tried to look nonchalant when Beckworth's eyes fell on me as if to take my measure. Finally, though, he relented. "Agreed, Mr. Gillespie, but for that amount of money I shall want real results."

"Of course," Gil said with a smile. "We'll need to return to Boston and gather our ghost-hunting equipment, but we can be back here . . . the day after tomorrow, if you'd like."

"That would work perfectly," he said before turning to his general manager. "Mr. Knollenberg, I see that most of the hotel guests have either already left us or are in a hurry to do so?"

Knollenberg flushed bright red and pulled at his tie again. "I believe it's due to the fact that the police have been called here twice in two days, sir," he said.

"Of course it is," said Beckworth, and I was surprised that it didn't seem to bother him a bit that he was losing money. "I believe that, in the interests of retaining what good faith we have with our clientele, we should close the Duke for a few days and allow the police to finish the job of gathering their evidence, and let our paranormal team here have a chance to rid the hotel of any remaining spiritual activity without being hampered by our paying guests."

"Sir?" said Knollenberg, clearly surprised.

"The construction here at the Duke is causing us to run at one-third of our capacity anyway," continued Beckworth, as if he hadn't heard Murray's question. "So this situation isn't as financially costly to me as it could be. We have rooms to spare over at the Lark, in fact. Offer our remaining Duke customers a free night's stay and the same lower rate they were paying here for the rest of their visit if they are willing to pack their belongings and be transferred to the Lark. I'll send Conrad and his crew over here with a few limos to shuttle the guests between the hotels.

"Also, notify everyone who has a reservation with us between now and Thursday that the hotel will be closing due to an unforeseen plumbing problem or something similar. And give them a discount if they would like to transfer their reservations to the Lark."

"Sir," said Knollenberg, looking around at us a bit self-consciously. "Do you mean to say you actually want to *close* down this hotel?"

"Yes," said Beckworth easily. "At least for the next four days. I'd rather have this contained quickly, Murray, before it becomes a thing and we get smeared with a reputation for offering our guests an experience of something less than our fine standards."

Knollenberg's forehead looked glossy with sweat. "Of course, sir," he said. "I'll take care of it immediately."

"Thank you, Murray," said Beckworth. "And now, Mr. Gillespie and I shall iron out the details before I let him book his flight home to retrieve his equipment."

Knollenberg gave one curt nod, got up, and left the office, and Beckworth and Gilley hashed out the deal. When they were finished, Heath and I were tasked with ridding the hotel of any and all things going bump in the night, and that included this three-clawed demon, if it was still loose in the hotel.

Heath gave Gilley permission to negotiate on his behalf, so within the hour we all had a deal, and we left Beckworth's office with a mixture of moods. Gilley was, of course, elated; I was excited but nervous; Heath floated from stunned to exuberant; and Steven was pensive and uncommunicative. I had a feeling he didn't like this job one bit. Before I had a chance to ask him about it, however, I heard, "Uh, excuse me," and I glanced in surprise at Gopher, who was following us down the hallway. He'd been so quiet throughout the meeting that I'd forgotten he was even along. "Might I suggest one more idea?"

"Yes?" said Gilley, stopping in the hallway to listen to Gopher, and as he did I had a tickling sensation that Gilley had allowed Gopher into the meeting on purpose.

"What would you guys say to letting us film the exorcism?"

"It's not an exorcism," I snapped, hating that word and the thoughts of pea soup splattering everywhere that it always invoked for me.

"Okay, this *ghostbust*," said Gopher. "What would you guys say to letting me and one other crew member film it?"

I scowled in distaste. For a guy who had just had one of his lovers murdered he sure seemed like a shallow, insensitive opportunist to me.

"Talk numbers to me," said Gilley, who apparently wasn't nearly as put off as I was.

Gopher cleared his throat, obviously surprised by the suggestion that he would have to fork over some cash to film the bust. "Well," he said, "I was thinking it would just be a continuation of the same per diem we were already giving you guys for the *Haunted Possessions* shoot."

Gilley laughed as though Gopher had just told him a really good joke. "You're funny!" he exclaimed. "Which is why I'll thank you before I say, Not on your life."

Gopher appeared to squirm with frustration. "Okay," he reasoned, his eyes blinking rapidly as he thought about the alternatives. "Can I make a few calls and get back to you?"

Gilley waved his hand nonchalantly. "Yes, but you'll need to catch us before we leave for the airport, and FYI, there's no way we're allowing a film crew to interfere on a serious ghostbust like this for less than ten thousand dollars."

My eyes bulged, and next to me Steven actually coughed. It seemed we both had a *serious* new appreciation for Gilley's cojones.

To our surprise, however, Gopher didn't even flinch. "Lemme get back to you," he agreed, pulling his cell phone out of his back pocket as he dashed ahead down the hallway.

Gilley then turned to the rest of us and said, "You guys go pack while I call the airlines. Heath, you can stay here if you'd like. We'll catch a flight out first thing in the a.m. and be back in town by midmorning, day after tomorrow, with our equipment."

Heath nodded. "Sounds good," he said. "It'll give

me time to do a little sightseeing and go shopping for more clothes. I only brought enough for two days."

"I won't be able to come back," said Steven, and I looked at him curiously.

"Why not?" I asked.

"I have lectures to give, remember?" Steven said, reminding me about his lecturing gig for the University of Massachusetts Medical School on cardiothoracic surgical techniques.

"Crap," I said, and was a little surprised by how disappointed I was that he wouldn't be along for this ride.

"But may I just say," he said in a tone that was very serious, "that I don't like this idea one bit. I think it's dangerous and that you should not do it and we should all go home to stay."

I was aware that both Gilley and Heath were ready to argue with Steven, but I cut them off by saying, "I can't very well leave the general public to face this thing without giving it at least one try, honey."

"But you've already been hurt by this thing," he argued. "What if it did murder that girl? What if it decides that it likes murdering girls in general?"

"I'll be careful," I promised, raising my hand up as if I were taking a vow. "We'll come back armed with our equipment, and I'll have both Heath and Gilley to keep me out of harm's way. If it gets too dicey, then I'll quit and head back home."

Steven frowned, and I knew he didn't think much about my ability to determine when things might get too dicey. "We can't always take the easy jobs," I said to him. "Sometimes this occupation of mine gets a little freaky, and the more experience we have with this type of thing, the better prepared we'll be for anything else we might encounter down the road."

"I am not liking this," he groused, and pulled me in for a nice, tight hug. "Keep her safe, Gilley," I heard him say over my head.

"You got it, Doctor," Gil agreed.

Chapter 9

We arrived back at the hotel thirty-six hours and a whole lotta headache later, the major crisis being that the airline we booked with had lost Gilley's bag containing his magnetic sweatshirt. The airline had promised to track the bag and have it delivered to the hotel later. This did *nothing* to alleviate the panic attack Gilley was presently having. "What if it doesn't arrive in time?" he wailed.

"For the *eighteenth* time, Gil, we can always make you another one, or you can simply stay at the command center and lay out a bunch of magnetic grenades on your table. You'll be fine."

Gilley whimpered and looked at me with big puppy-dog eyes. "I want my sweatshirt," he whined.

"Jeez, Gil, you sound like you need a binkie and a baba too."

I waved at the security guard posted outside the hotel lobby, and he opened the door for us and helped us inside with our bags. The staff looked as though it had been cut back to the bare minimum, and as we were allowed entrance into the lobby by the security guard, we couldn't help but notice the large posters on the doors declaring that the hotel had been temporarily shut down due to construction. I felt a bit of unease enter the pit of my stomach.

The police crime-scene tape was still up across the ladies' room door to remind me of the awful things I'd seen in there, and I felt that tickle of unease intensify.

We found Heath sitting in the lobby reading a paper. "Hey, guys!" he said when he spotted us. He then glanced at his watch and declared, "When you say you'll be right back, you really mean it."

I yawned and set down the heavy duffel bag of equipment I was carrying to stretch. "I need a nap," I declared. My head felt as though it were in a fog, and my bones ached with fatigue.

"Didn't get much sleep on the plane, huh?" Gil said, and from the way he was looking at me I knew he was likely assessing the dark circles under my eyes.

"Nope," I said. "And I'll never know how you do it, Gil. You were asleep even before we took off from Boston."

Gilley smiled and bounced his eyebrows. "It's a gift," he said. "Go up to your room and get a little shut-eye. I'll talk to Knollenberg and find a central location to set up from; plus, I've got to find Gopher and his other crew member and coordinate with them."

This came as a surprise to me. "They're filming us? You didn't tell me that we agreed to that."

"They came up with the money," he said, smiling at both Heath and me. "How's an added five grand for your pocket, Heath?"

"Works for me!" he said happily. "Man, Gilley,

I can't thank you enough. My mom's getting up there in years, and I worry about her. She lives in this crappy trailer, and it's full of issues. I've had my eye on a house near my apartment building for a while, and with this money I'll actually be able to purchase it for me and Mom to live in. You're a lifesaver, buddy."

Gilley studied his nails nonchalantly, but the look on his face let me know he thought he was all that and a bag of chips. "I do what I can," he said with a sigh.

"Well, I for one am going to catch some Zs. Heath, why don't we meet back down here in a couple of hours and we'll come up with a plan of attack? Gil, when you go meet with Knollenberg, see if Heath and I can meet with him briefly, say around two-ish?"

"No sweat," Gil said. "Now go; you look dead on your feet."

I didn't linger but headed off, leaving the heavy duffel of equipment with Gil so that he could set it up when he found a spot for the base camp.

As I got into my room and glanced at the freshly made bed, I had a pang of sadness that I'd be sleeping in it all by my lonesome. I was going to miss Steven on this trip, and was quite surprised that I was developing such strong feelings for him. I wasn't known for letting men—other than Gilley, of course—get too close. Probably had a lot to do with my childhood, but it wasn't anything that I overanalyzed. No, Steven was the first guy I'd let in for a long time, and it both unsettled and thrilled me.

He was a good balance for me too. He was levelheaded, even-keeled, and logical. I was temperamental, prone to flying off the handle, and did things based solely on my gut feeling. Hey, maybe there was something to this opposites-attract thing after all?

Several hours later, and after a deliciously long shower, I was back downstairs and looking for Heath. Instead I found Gopher milling about the mezzanine with a light meter. I walked up to him from behind and said, "Hey," to get his attention.

He started and whipped around. "Oh!" he said, putting a hand over his heart. "Hi, M.J."

I smiled wickedly at him. "You seem a little jumpy, Gopher. Are you going to be able to handle this gig?"

Gopher laughed, but it sounded pretty forced. "Oh, sure. I just didn't hear you come up, that's all."

"Uh-huh," I said, not believing him for a second. "Have you seen Heath or Gilley?"

"Heath went out for takeout, but he should be back anytime, and Gilley is in the Twilight Room."

I pivoted in a half circle. "Where's that?" I asked.

"It's the smallest of the conference rooms," said Gopher. "You go down that hall and it's the second door on your left."

"Thanks," I called over my shoulder as I trotted away. "And if you see Heath, can you tell him I'm in with Gilley?"

"Will do," he said, and went back to his light meter.

I found Gil in the room that Gopher had indicated, and he had two long tables set up with monitors and computer screens, and magnetic spikes taped to his chair and the table. "Hey, girl," he said when I entered the room.

"Still no sign of your luggage?" I asked, looking pointedly at the spikes all about his area.

Gil made a face and said, "Stupid airlines! They've lost track of my bag, but they *assure* me they are devoting their best people to finding it. They mentioned something about its being routed to Thailand, and I hung up on them."

"Wow," I said. "Your bag is probably having more fun than you are right now."

Instead of answering me, Gilley lifted a walkie-talkie and spoke into it. "Great, Tony, I've got good reception. Let's move to the next floor." He then turned to me and explained, "That's Tony. He's the other cameraman from Gopher's team who's going to be following you guys around tonight."

"So you're almost set up?" I asked.

"Yep," said Gil, looking down at a clipboard that held his notes. "I know you wanted to skip the baselines and get right to the ghostbusting, but I thought it might not do us any harm to take a few readings on each floor anyway—that way we'll know if any spikes on the electrostatic meters are out of the ordinary or not."

I smiled. Gilley could never let go of his protocols. "That's cool," I said, then glanced at my own watch. "Did you get us a meeting with Knollenberg before we begin?"

"Sure did. He's expecting you in half an hour. Heath went out to bring us back some takeout, and I had him pick you up a club sandwich. He should be back anytime."

And just as Gilley finished speaking, the door behind me opened and Heath walked in loaded down with bags of takeout. "Who's hungry?" he asked.

We ate quickly; then Heath and I left Gilley to finish gathering his data and testing his equipment.

We found Knollenberg behind the front desk talking to three other men in ties. It was pretty obvious that these were the assistant managers, and Knollenberg was reassuring them that the hotel would be back open within three days' time and no one would be out of a job.

He also asked one of the men to return Detective MacDonald's phone call about security footage. "He left a voice mail on my phone," Knollenberg was saying. "Apparently the footage we forwarded to him cuts off immediately after the poor girl entered the restroom. It might be a malfunction of the cameras, but he wanted to know if perhaps the one above the door had captured anything. I took the liberty of reviewing the footage, and it's the oddest thing, but for a period of about two minutes all it recorded was snow. It then shows Miss Holliday coming out of the bathroom after discovering the young woman inside. So, Andrew, if you will kindly return the detective's phone call for me and make arrangements to get him a copy of the footage, maybe his lab techs can do something with it."

I cleared my throat at that point. Knollenberg turned around, and, upon seeing Heath and me, he said, "Is it four o'clock already?"

"Yes, sir," I said.

Knollenberg came out from behind the counter and said, "My apologies. I should be finished with my meeting here in a minute or two. May I show you into my office and have you wait there?"

"That'd be great."

Knollenberg took us down a hallway past a portrait of the hotel's first owner, Phineas Duke, and into his small but well-kept office. He pointed to two chairs in front of his desk and said, "I'll be back in just a few minutes," and he shut the door, leaving Heath and me alone, which gave us a chance to talk.

"You okay with all this?" I asked him.

Heath laughed heartily. "Am I okay with twenty-five thousand dollars? Shit, yeah!"

"You know this is probably going to get dicey, don't you?"

That sobered him. "I know," he said. "But there are two of us, and we seem to work pretty well together. And Gilley's already shown me your stash of magnet grenades, so I feel like we're well armed, at least. Plus, a lot of these spirits from the hotel seem to be pretty harmless—if you don't count that smoky, talon-wielding serpent demon, of course."

I smiled. "Yeah, if you don't count that."

"I think we should start with the easy stuff first," Heath suggested. "Let's get rid of the regular spooks that the Duke is known for before we tackle the heavy stuff."

I nodded. "That's a good idea. It'll give us a good chance to get familiar with the entire hotel too. That way we can work out a plan to deal with this demon when and if we encounter it."

"Do you think it actually killed Tracy?" Heath asked me after a small lull in our conversation.

I shrugged. "I just can't see it," I said. "I mean,

a knife-wielding demon? Doesn't that just sound a little too far-fetched?"

"Then what do you think happened to her?"

"I don't know," I admitted. "I mean, when Mac-Donald pulled me into the bathroom yesterday he asked me to make contact with her, but she wasn't around, so it's really hard to say."

"She crossed over?" he asked.

"Yep," I said, thinking that felt right. "And I'll bet she's currently in transition."

"So she's not going to be able to connect with any of us for a while," he said, and I was impressed that he was familiar with the state of transition for some souls.

"Looks like it," I agreed. "Then again, if my hunch is off and she's wandering around here, we might bump into her on our other detail."

The door opened at that point, and Knollenberg came in, looking drawn and tired. He forced a smile onto his face and sat down at his desk. "So sorry to keep you waiting," he said. "Where would you like to start?"

"Do you by chance have a blueprint or detailed map of the hotel?" I asked him. "We'll need to form a plan of attack, and it would really help to know what kind of structure we're dealing with."

"Of course," said Knollenberg, turning to a folder on his desk, which he opened and from it removed a packet of the hotel's plans, floor by floor. "I just had a few of these made up for our new assistant manager. They come in handy when we need to train incoming employees. How many copies would you need?" he asked us.

"Three should be good," I said, thinking that one copy each for me, Gilley, and Heath would be enough.

Knollenberg counted out three copies and handed them to us across his desk. Then he seemed to think of something and he rummaged around in his desk drawer before coming up with two key cards. "You'll need these, of course," he said, handing them to us. "They're master key cards which will give you access to any room in the hotel."

"Awesome, thank you," I said.

"What else do you need?" he asked us.

"We'll want a list of all the ghosts that have ever been known to haunt the Duke, and if you can provide us with the locations for the most common sightings, that would be great."

Knollenberg smiled and went back to the filing cabinet, pulling out one particularly thick folder and handing it to me. Opening it up, I realized that it was filled with dozens of complaints from both patrons and employees of paranormal disturbances going back some ninety-five years—which was almost as long as the Duke had been open.

"Whoa," I said as I sifted through the pages, and felt Heath lean in to look over my shoulder.

"You've kept track of each and every one?" he said.

"We have," said Knollenberg. "All of the previous owners, including Mr. Beckworth, insisted on it."

"Why?" I asked, looking up at him.

"Liability," said Knollenberg. "It's a litigious world, I'm afraid."

I didn't really know why it was important to catalog ghost sightings for liability reasons. I mean, what kind of lawsuit could be brought about by a ghost sighting? But I didn't question it. I was too happy to have found such a treasure trove of detail.

Lots of the complaints were eerily similar in both use of wording and description of the event. The most common one was about a small girl playing on the staircase, and concerned guests worrying over her safety.

Others referred to an older gentleman in "period costume" calling for his daughter, Sara.

Many of the accounts I had already heard or read about, beginning with a woman in a gray dress on the top floor knocking on doors at three a.m., asking if guests needed their beds turned down. A friendly bellhop who opened doors for guests, then promptly disappeared. A dark shadow appearing at the foot of the bed in room 518. Yet another complaint talked of the closet door constantly being opened and closed, along with faucets turning on and off by themselves, in room 420.

Still another set of accounts told of guests being touched by unseen hands in what used to be the dining hall and was now one of the largest conference halls, the Stargaze Room. And, of course, the suicidal woman I'd seen on my balcony, Carol Mustgrove from room 321.

I looked down at the list in front of us and said, "The woman on the top floor who knocks on doors hasn't been seen since 1984?"

"That's correct. No one has reported her since then," he confirmed.

"She's probably gotten across, then," said Heath.

I nodded in agreement. "We'll do a spot check just in case." I then frowned as I thought about that friendly bellhop. "Mr. Knollenberg," I said, regarding the manager thoughtfully, "didn't you say you knew this bellhop who died and appears to be sticking around?"

Knollenberg nodded, his eyes taking on a faraway cast. "Mickey O'Reilly," he said. "He was a sweet old guy. He worked here into his eighties, you know. He loved the Duke, and we all knew something had happened when he didn't show up for his shift right before Christmas. Mickey never missed work."

"Have *you* seen his ghost?"

Knollenberg shook his head. "No. But not a week goes by that one of my other bellhops doesn't tell me Mickey's at it again. He's especially known for holding the door open for pretty ladies. We had Brad and Angelina here recently, and we're pretty sure Mickey held the door open for Miss Jolie, because one of the check-in clerks told me that she wanted to tip the sweet old man out front, but she couldn't seem to find him to give him her thanks. At that time no one over the age of twenty-five was working the door."

I smiled and asked delicately, "Is it all right with you if, as long as he isn't scaring anyone, we leave him as he is to open the doors? It just seems to me that Mickey got a lot of enjoyment out of his job, and I don't think he's here because he doesn't know he's died so much as he's formed a very strong attachment to the Duke, and I'd hate to force him to give that up."

"Er . . ." said Knollenberg. "I guess. As long as you don't think he's suffering or anything."

"I really don't," I said gently. "Still, I'll try to check in with him just to be sure."

"Okay," Knollenberg agreed.

Heath was also studying the list, and he asked the general manager, "What about the lady in the mirror?"

I'd forgotten about the woman whom both Heath and I had seen in the mirrors of the Renaissance Room and the bathroom.

"What lady in what mirror?" Murray asked.

Heath and I exchanged a glance, and I explained. "We both saw a beautiful young woman with long black hair in two of the mirrors you have here at the hotel."

Knollenberg looked completely puzzled. "What mirrors?"

"The one in the Renaissance Room and the one above the sink in the ladies' restroom," I told him.

Knollenberg continued to look at me blankly. "Those mirrors are new," he said. "Mr. Beckworth purchased a set of four of them at auction. We've put them in several areas of the hotel."

"Well, there seems to be a spirit who's very attached to them," I said.

"Do you mean to tell me that we've acquired yet *another* ghost here that we haven't heard of before?" He gasped.

" 'Fraid so," I said. "Can you tell me where the other two mirrors are?"

"One is by the elevators on the ground floor, and the last one I believe is on the third floor."

A chill went up my spine, and I looked at Heath. "The vestibule with the elevator is where we encountered that wicked powerful serpent, remember?" I said to Heath.

He nodded gravely. "I'm seeing a pattern," he said.

"A pattern?" asked Knollenberg.

But I ignored his question and asked him instead, "Where did you say those mirrors came from?"

"Mr. Beckworth brought them back from his most recent trip to Europe. He said he bought them at an auction and thought they would go perfectly here at the Duke."

"Do you know anything more about them? Where they originated? Who might have owned them previously?" I asked.

"No," he said. "But I can certainly ask Mr. Beckworth."

"Please do," I encouraged. I knew it was more than a mere coincidence that the mirrors were new and so was all of this violent poltergeist activity. I strongly suspected that there was a link.

We left the general manager's office shortly thereafter armed with a list of the spooks we'd have to tackle and our floor plans. Heath and I decided to get a drink and talk strategy. I texted Gilley to see if he wanted to join us, but he sent back a message that he, Tony, and Gopher were still testing out the reception of the monitors, cameras, electrostatic meters, and walkie-talkies, and that Heath and I should just fill him in later about how we planned to tackle the bust.

So Heath and I headed next door to the restaurant again. After we'd taken a seat at the bar and given our drink orders to the bartender, I pulled out the list, along with copies of the hotel's floor plans, and spread them out on the bar. I then began to cross-reference with the sightings documented in Knollenberg's files and came up with the areas within the hotel where we'd need to concentrate. "If we focus on these hot spots and take care of the easier ghosties first, we'll have more time to deal with the more negative energies."

"Okay," Heath said, "I'll go with that. Where did you want to start?"

I circled the top floor. "Here," I said.

"The woman in gray?"

I nodded. "And I think we should split up." Heath looked at me doubtfully, so I explained. "With these easier spirits we might as well tackle them on our own, and you did such a great job getting little Sara across, I'm confident you can do the same for a few of these other ones."

"And if the gray lady has already gotten herself across?" he asked, likely remembering that the last sighting had been well over twenty years ago.

"Then you can move to room five-eighteen."

"What's in there again?"

"A dark shadow hovering at the foot of the bed."

"Great, a dark shadow. Those spirits always creep me out," he admitted. "I mean, what's up with the shadow form anyway?"

"It's easier to maintain," I said with a smile. "Full form is much more difficult and uses up a ton of energy."

"Ah," said Heath. "Okay, then. I'll tackle the lady in gray, then the shadow guy. Where're you going to be?"

"If you're working from the top down, I'll work from the bottom up. My first target is going to be Mr. Duke; I want to get him to his daughter pronto. Then I'll tackle the handsy ghost in the Stargaze Room."

Heath was quiet, so I glanced over at him and

saw that he looked a bit apprehensive. "What's up?" I asked.

"I don't know that I'm in love with the idea of going it alone," he said. "I mean, that demon thing could be anywhere."

I smiled, really understanding how hard it was for even a medium to tackle ghost hunting alone. "I forgot to mention that we'll both be connected to Gilley via our cameras, walkie-talkies and instruments, and we'll both have a cameraman in tow."

"How is that going to help me?" he asked, arching a skeptical eyebrow.

I laughed wickedly and told him, "If anything big and smoky jumps out at you, throw the cameraman at it and run like hell!"

Heath chuckled heartily and winked at me. "Now, *there's* a plan!"

"Seriously, though," I said, getting back to the business at hand. "You'll be carrying a couple of our magnet grenades, and the moment you pull the cap off one of those babies no poltergeist is going to want to come near you."

"Are you sure they work?" he asked me.

I pumped my head up and down. "Absolutely positive," I said. "I've used them against one of the nastiest spooks I've ever dealt with, and it shut his ass down but good."

"Something as bad as that demon from the knife?"

"Okay," I said, conceding his point. "Maybe not *that* bad, but still, it was enough to convince me that in a pinch they really work."

Heath and I worked out the rest of the details for the ghost hunt, agreeing that we'd take the first night to work on getting rid of the easier ghosts, which would leave us with the next two nights free to work on the more difficult ones.

We also both agreed that if any of the ghosts on our personal lists refused to move on, we would join up later and tackle them together. "What if even as a team we can't get them across?" Heath asked. "I mean, have you ever tried to convince a suicide victim that they need to cross over? They usually put up a really good fight."

I knew he was talking about Carol Mustgrove. "You're right," I agreed. "Let's tackle Carol together."

Heath then looked over at my paper and put a hand on my arm. "How are we going to work on her if we can't get into her room?" he asked.

I gave him a puzzled look, and he explained. "It's a crime scene. I'm sure it's still sealed."

"Oh, crap!" I said, slapping my forehead. "You're right." I thought on that for a beat or two, then said, "You know, she did come onto my balcony the other night. I'll bet she's been rattled by the mess that's become of her room. As long as that room is sealed off by the police, no one's allowed in to straighten things up." I remembered the chaos of the crime scene in room 321 after Sophie had been murdered. "Which means that if Carol is upset about the mess, she's going to be on the move, and maybe we can access her from my balcony or someplace else she might be hiding out."

"It's worth a shot," he agreed.

"And if we can't get to her, we can't get to her. Technically Beckworth shouldn't fault us if we're unable to clear out Mustgrove. I mean, if we're barred from access to the room she haunts there's not much we can do."

"Right," he said. "When do you want to start?"

I glanced at my watch. It was half past five. "I think we should start right at midnight," I said. "That'll leave us with about five and a half to six hours of really good ghost hunting before dawn breaks and things get quiet again."

"Cool. What should we do until then?"

I reached into my pocket and pulled out some money. Laying it on the bar I said, "I'm going to go back to the hotel and fill Gilley in on our plan and give him a copy of the floor plans. Then I'm going to try to catch some shut-eye. If I were you I'd do the same, 'cause it's going to be a long night and we'll need to be fresh."

"Great," Heath agreed. "I'll meet you in the Twilight Room about eleven thirty, then?"

"Perfect," I said, and we left the restaurant.

I found Gil back at the conference room talking to Gopher and Tony. From the looks of it, my partner was giving them each a lesson in using the thermal imager and electrostatic meters, and also from the looks of it, both men seemed to have caught on long before and were now suffering through Gilley's extended lecture.

"Your needle is going to bounce around a lot," he was saying. "It doesn't necessarily mean that there's something metaphysical happening. The trick is not to overanalyze it. You just need to keep your eye on the meter and your medium, and see if there are any weird measurements on your meters when M.J. or Heath gets a blip on their internal radar."

"Hi, guys!" I said from behind Gilley. "How's it going?"

"Swell," said Gopher, but his voice couldn't have been more monotone.

"Hey, M.J.," said Gilley. "Did you guys come up with a plan?"

"We did," I said, spreading our list of ghosts and the floor plans out on the table. "While Heath works from the top down, I'm going to work from the bottom up. We're tackling the easier ghosts tonight and the tougher energies tomorrow."

"Super," said Gil. "Tony's going to follow you with the night-vision camera, and Gopher's going to tag along behind Heath."

"That works," I said, smiling at Tony, who looked really nervous about what he'd gotten himself into. "I'm going to catch some more Zs, and I told Heath that we'd start around midnight. Does that work for everyone?"

Three heads nodded back at me, and Gilley said, "That's about perfect."

I turned and headed for the door. "Great, I'll see you all back here around eleven thirty."

I was just coming out of the hallway when I heard someone call my name. I looked over and saw Detective MacDonald entering from outside and waving at me. "Holliday!" he said, his voice echoing around the empty lobby. "Can I talk to you a sec?"

"Sure," I called back, and trotted over to him. We met in the seating area by the bar, and he and I sat down.

"I hear you're doing some sort of séance thing tonight," he began.

I laughed. "Not quite. We've been hired by the owner to do a ghostbust of the hotel."

"How many ghosts does this place have?" Mac-Donald asked, looking around as though he expected to see something jump out at him at any minute.

"More than you might think," I told him. "Are you here about Tracy's murder?"

"I think so," he said, reaching into a folder he was carrying and holding out a picture to me. "Do you get anything off this?"

I eyeballed the photo of a very pretty blonde with big green eyes and high cheekbones. She looked to be in her twenties, and radiating happiness, but I felt immediately that she was deceased. "She's dead," I said, staring at the photo intently.

"She is," he confirmed. "Can you tell me anything more?"

"She died violently," I said, and then a sound crept into my head and I said, "Does her name have a *sh* sound in it?"

"Her last name does," he said. "This is Faline Schufthauser. She was murdered two months ago in Strasburg, Germany. A knife matching the description of the one that killed Tracy was found in her chest, but was later lost or stolen out of evidence."

"The poor girl," I said, staring down at her image and filtering through the impressions that I was getting off of her picture. Then something quite unusual floated through the ether to me, and I stared up at MacDonald in surprise. "Detective?" I said.

"Yes?"

"This is going to sound really weird," I prefaced, "but was this girl a criminal?"

MacDonald broke into a grin and shook his head

back and forth in appreciation. "She was," he said. "You're looking at one of Europe's best and most elusive art thieves."

"Whoa," I said. "She looks so innocent, doesn't she?"

"Which is why she was so good at it for so long," said MacDonald. He then reached into the folder and pulled out a piece of paper. "Faline Schufthauser was born in Austria, educated in a Parisian art school, and, as far as Interpol can determine, began stealing expensive works of art right out of college. She spoke several languages, and because her parents were affluent she knew how to fit into the social scene of the rich and famous. She's credited, or should I say suspected, in sixteen different robberies, but was never caught. She'd probably still be on the run if she hadn't been murdered."

"How can you tell that she was killed by the same knife?" I asked.

"Because luckily the Strasburg police got a few pictures of it before it went missing. When we plugged our own photos of the knife that killed Tracy into our database we got a possible international connection. I'm waiting on my techs to blow up the images from Germany, but so far, it really looks like they're a match."

"So how does a knife from a murder in Europe find its way over here?" I asked.

"It comes along with the murderer," said MacDonald, and I felt my skin prickle with goose bumps.

"Ah," I said after a pause. "Yeah. That would work. Are there any leads on who might have killed Faline?"

"Her ex-boyfriend was suspected at one point but

was later cleared. Another theory is that one of the people she stole something from managed to track her down and get their revenge, but no one in any of the suspected robberies was anywhere near her at the time she was killed."

I handed the photo back to MacDonald. "This just gets weirder and weirder," I said. "I mean, you've got two dead girls, both with international connections."

"Tracy has an international connection?" said MacDonald.

I shook my head. "No, not her. I was talking about Sophie. You're still working her case too, aren't you?"

MacDonald blinked at me as if I'd said something that stunned him. He then got up off the couch and abruptly announced, "I've got to get back to the station. I'll talk to you later." And with that he hurried out of the hotel.

I shrugged and got up myself, then headed back to my room to read a little and try to get some sleep. I had a feeling that even though we were starting with the "easy" ghosts, it was still going to be a long night.

Chapter 10

At ten minutes to midnight I was back down in the Twilight Room with Gilley, Heath, Gopher, and Tony, and we were going over things one more time. "We'll all be connected via these headpieces," Gilley was saying as he handed out the headgear he and I used to keep in contact during our ghostbusts, while Tony held a camera to record the footage for the TV show.

"How do these work exactly?" asked Heath, and I showed him how to put it on. By clicking a small button on the side of the earpiece he could both hear what everyone else was saying and open his mike up for communication, while the small box that he clipped onto his belt would control the channels. "Channel one will be for you, Gopher and Gilley, to keep in touch with each other," I said. "Channel two will be for me, Tony, and Gilley; and channel three will be for everyone. We'll have five people on that line, so use it only if you need me to hear your status or if you need my help. Because we'll all be connected to that channel, it can get a bit jumbled if everyone's talking at once."

"It's a good idea to say 'over' when you're finished speaking," instructed Gilley, and I thought he looked really excited to be doing his commando thing in front of an audience. "Gopher, I'll be recording all the sound down here to the wave file I told you about. You can have a copy to use in your broadcast when you need it."

"Great," said Gopher, putting on his headpiece, and through my own gear I heard him blow into the microphone and whisper, "Testing, testing, one, two, three, testing."

"I can hear you," I said, giving him a thumbs-up. He blushed slightly and was quiet again.

"Mediums," said Gil, addressing Heath and me, "we're going to follow your lead. The camerapeople are here only to observe, so if you get into a tricky situation and need backup, don't look to them; look to me. And each of you should be ready to run to the aid of the other if something goes wrong or the demon reappears."

"Or just push your camera guy in front of it and run," whispered Heath, not realizing that his mike was on and that both Tony and Gopher could hear him. I laughed, but those two *really* didn't look amused.

Gilley cleared his throat and continued. "Now, I've given each one of you two magnetic grenades. Inside those lead tubes is a magnetic spike. By uncapping the top and tipping out the spike you have a powerful weapon at your disposal against any ghost that comes within a ten-foot radius of you.

"Cameramen, it is *imperative* that you not play with the spikes or take the caps off the grenades unless something really bad happens. If the magnetic spikes inside are exposed too soon, we will lose the spirit that your medium is trying to cross over, so even if you're scared, you can't use them unless either Heath or M.J. gives the okay."

Gopher and Tony shared a look, and I distinctly caught Tony giving a small shudder. "It'll be fine," I reassured him. "You probably won't see anything at all. I'm going to do all the work."

Tony nodded, but he didn't really look convinced. "Now," Gil continued, "I've asked the staff to cut the lights throughout the hotel, as it's much better for ghost hunting to have relative darkness. You are each equipped with flashlights should it be too dark to see, and you can also just look through the viewfinders of the night-vision cameras."

I looked at my watch. "Gil," I said.

"Yeah?"

"It's time."

"All right," Gilley relented. "Remember, I'm here if you need me," he added dramatically.

I turned my head so that I could roll my eyes without Gilley noticing and gathered up my equipment. I was armed with two of the grenades, which I put into the nylon tool belt I'd started wearing on these busts, along with my flashlight, a granola bar, a bottle of water, an electrostatic meter, and one of the thermal imagers. When I was loaded up I turned my headset to channel two and motioned to Tony. "Let's roll."

We headed first to the hallway leading to Knollenberg's office, giving a nod to the lone assistant manager, looking tired and bored behind the front desk. "He 'as gone home for ze evening," the man called, and I noticed that he had a lovely French accent. I stopped midway down the hall to poke my head back out and look at him.

"I know," I said. "We're working to locate the ghost of Mr. Duke. You haven't seen him, have you?"

The assistant manager, whom I remembered from the other night, when Heath and I were attacked by the serpent, and whom Knollenberg had called Anton, said, "Er . . . *non*."

"Cool. If his ghost comes out this way, would you try to stall him?"

"Stall 'eem?" Anton squeaked.

"Yeah," I said, as if I were asking the easiest thing in the world. "You know, strike up a conversation with him, and try not to let him move through you or disappear until we come back out."

Even in the dim light Anton seemed to pale. "I must go work on my reports," he announced. "I shall be in ze office if you need me." And with that I watched with a giddy smile as he ducked into the small office right behind the counter area.

"You're mean," Tony admonished, but there was humor in his voice.

"Hey, you gotta get your giggles in where you can," I said cheerily. "Come on, I think there's a hot spot near Duke's portrait." We moved farther down the hallway, and I opened up all my senses. When we came to the painting displaying Phineas Duke's image, I stood still and closed my eyes. In the background I heard a slight humming sound and knew that Tony had started filming.

"M.J.?" Gilley's voice blared into my ear. "What's your twenty? Over."

I held back a heavy sigh at Gilley's wanting to

overplay this whole commando thing and said, "We've arrived at the Duke portrait. I'll contact you as soon as something happens. Over."

"Copy that," Gil said. "Over."

I closed my eyes again and concentrated, feeling out the ether. It took a little while, but soon I had the smallest thread of energy, which felt male, and then a picture formed in my head of a man in his midforties with thinning hair and a big, bold mustache. His clothing was refined, and in his hands he carried a top hat. Then, very faintly, I heard a sound that wasn't in my head, and I also heard Tony gasp and ask, "What was *that*?"

I opened one eye. "You heard it too?" I asked.

"Yeah," he said. "It sounded like someone said, 'Sara.' "

I smiled and opened the other eye. "It did," I agreed. "Come on." I moved away from the portrait and followed the slight tugging sensation back down the hallway and out onto the mezzanine, already knowing where the energy was that was pulling me toward it.

Again I heard a noise, but this one was different, and Tony gasped again behind me. "What was *that*?" he said.

"Horses' hooves," I said. "Out on the street."

There was a pause, and I had the sense that Tony was aiming the camera outside. Then he said, "There aren't any horses out there!"

"I know," I said calmly. "If you've read your history, you'll know that Mr. Duke was tragically killed two months after his daughter died when a horse-drawn carriage overturned and crushed him."

"Shit," Tony hissed nervously. "Aren't you scared?"

I stopped in front of the large window overlooking the street outside. "Not at all." Then I closed my eyes again and reached out in my mind. *Mr. Duke,* I called. *Mr. Duke, can you hear me?*

Right next to me and in a clear, crisp voice, a man asked, "I say, have you seen my daughter?" That was followed by a small shriek in front of me, and my eyes snapped open.

Glaring hard at Tony the shrieker, I warned, "Listen, pal, either get it together here or go home. I've got to focus, and I can't do that if you're squealing like a little girl."

"M.J.? Your meter readings are off the charts. What's your twenty? Over," called Gilley into my ear.

Tony was shaking head to toe, and I clicked on the microphone and said, "I've just made contact with Mr. Duke." In my mind I could feel the spirit of Duke getting agitated. *Have you seen my daughter?* he repeated, his tone sharp in my head.

"Yes, Mr. Duke," I said aloud. "Your daughter is safe and sound and waiting for you. Would you like to join her?"

Where is she? he said in my mind.

I looked into the camera and said, "He's just asked me where his daughter is."

Who's that you're speaking to? asked Duke.

"No one, Mr. Duke. Getting back to your daughter. She's been waiting for you, and I'd like to take you to her, if I may."

"Lead the way," the disembodied voice said softly.

I walked over to the staircase and looked up to the

top step. For the sake of the television and knowing Mr. Duke would find it difficult to continue a verbal conversation loud enough for the microphones to pick up clearly, I decided to improvise a little. "Mr. Duke, if you can hear me all right, would you please make a sound, like a tap or a knock?"

Right next to Tony there was a loud *thonk*, and I swear the cameraman looked as though he were ready to bolt.

I smiled winningly into the camera, as if this were all a bit of fun. "Marvelous, Mr. Duke! That's really good. Now, sir, if we could communicate through knocks, that would be wonderful. Do you remember the last time you saw your daughter here?" I asked, pointing up to the staircase. "Please knock once for no and twice for yes." There were two distinct knocks right near my feet.

"Excellent," I said. "And do you remember that little Sara was playing on the banister when you last saw her?" Again two knocks thudded on the floor. "Great, Mr. Duke, you're doing really well. Now, however, I'm afraid I might upset you, because I'm going to ask you to remember what happened next. Do you remember?"

There was a long pause, followed by one solid knock for no.

I took a deep breath and went for it. "Yes, well, I'm not surprised, sir, because what happened next was most upsetting. But, little Sara fell from the banister and hit her head. And I'm so sorry to remind you of this, Mr. Duke, but her body did not survive."

Without warning a knock so loud that it trembled the floor sounded, and a vase on one of the tables tipped over and crashed to the ground. "Holy shit!"

squealed Tony, but followed that quickly by saying, "Sorry!" when I glared at him.

"Mr. Duke," I called into the pregnant silence that followed. "I know this is most distressing to you, and I'm so incredibly sorry for your loss, but, you see, a good friend of mine has recently been in contact with the spirit of your daughter, and Sara is safe and well where she is, and really hoping that you'll join her soon. Would you like to join her, Mr. Duke?"

I waited several beats for an answer, but nothing came. "Is he gone?" whispered Tony.

I ignored him and called out again, "Mr. Duke! I need you to listen to me, because your daughter needs you, sir! She misses you terribly, and she needs her father. Won't you please let me know that you're here by tapping for us again?"

Two small but solid taps sounded near my feet, and I felt a flood of relief. "Awesome!" I said, and clapped my hands. "I knew you could do it, Mr. Duke. Now, I must remind you of something else very unsettling, and that is a time shortly after you lost your Sara. You were outside and a horse reared up, and when it did something fell on you. Do you remember?"

There was another pause, and finally two taps sounded.

"So you remember that the carriage fell on top of you, Mr. Duke? You remember that you were trapped beneath it, and the next time you woke up things were really different, correct?"

Two knocks.

"Yes, that's it," I coaxed. "And the reason they were different, Mr. Duke, was because you did not survive the coach falling on top of you. Like Sara, your body did not recover. But this is the most magical and wonderful thing, Mr. Duke. Because of that, you can rejoin Sara! You two can be reunited and never lose track of each other again!"

I paused to see if Duke would respond, and was thrilled when I heard two more knocks.

"Good for you, sir!" I encouraged. "Now, let's get started sending you home to your daughter."

For the next few minutes I talked Duke into crossing over, which he did with relative calm and ease. Tony told me a little later that on camera he'd seen a twinkling light rise up along the staircase and then flash brightly twice before going out altogether, which I thought was a really good visualization for what actually happens.

After we were finished with Duke I clicked on my microphone again and said, "Gil, we've successfully gotten Mr. Duke across. Over."

"Awesome, M.J.," said Gil. "Heath is working on the shadow figure in room five-eighteen. Over."

"No luck finding the lady in gray on the top floor?" I asked. When Gil didn't immediately reply I sighed and gave a weary, "Over."

"Nope," he said. "Heath thinks she must have crossed on her own twenty years ago. Over."

"Cool," I said. "We're on our way to the handsy guy in the old dining hall. Over."

Clicking off my microphone again I motioned to Tony to follow me, but he hesitated and said, "I don't know that I want to keep going."

Great, I thought. *I get saddled with the big baby in the group.* "I get it," I said to him. "I mean, this stuff isn't for everyone. And I'm sure that Gopher won't mind if you bail. I mean, it's not like you really need this gig anyway. He probably doesn't throw you a ton of work or anything, right?"

Tony seemed to hop from foot to foot, the camera now off and in the dim light a very worried expression crossed his face. "It's just that, well, I wasn't expecting it to be like this, you know?"

"Sure, sure," I reassured him. "This stuff requires some strong nerves. I understand if you don't really have what it takes. I'm sure everyone will understand; like, your friends and family will really get how scared you were, and no one will even *think* to make fun of you or anything, right?"

Tony's eyes narrowed. He was clearly suspicious that I might be doing just that. "Hey," he said, but before he could say more I turned and began to walk away.

"Give my best to the wife and kids," I called over my shoulder. "I'm sure you'll find another, better-paying gig soon!"

Behind me I heard the soft padding of sneakered feet hurrying across the marble floor. "Fine," he growled. "But if anything else crazy happens, I'm outta here!"

I regarded him with a level look. "Sugar," I said, in my best Georgian drawl, "you better gird those loins, 'cause, trust me, you ain't seen jack yet."

Tony and I headed to the largest of the conference rooms, located at the end of the same hall where Gil had set up his command center. I stopped briefly at Gilley's door and poked my head in to say hi. "Hey, guy, just stopping by for a wave. We'll be right next door."

Gil looked up from his monitors and gave me a smile as he pushed his earpiece in with his finger and said, "Come again, Heath? I didn't hear that. Over."

I was closing the door when I heard Gilley's voice spike as he said, "What's his position?"

I hesitated and stuck my head back through the opening. "What's going on?" Tony asked from behind me.

"Heath!" Gilley shouted into his microphone. "Heath, do you copy? Over?"

I opened the door fully and stepped inside the room while reaching to turn the channel for my headgear to three. Immediately my ear filled with shouting and commotion, and I gasped. "Christ!" I said, staring wide-eyed at Gil, who was mirroring my own reaction. "Where are they?" I demanded.

"I don't know!" Gilley cried. "They were in room five-eighteen, and then Heath said they were coming down a few floors, and all of a sudden I heard Gopher scream and Heath started yelling, and now I can't get either of them to respond!"

I whirled around and began running as a terrible commotion sounded in my ear. Behind me Tony was calling to me to wait up, but there was no way I was going to slow down. I got to the stairs and churned up the steps. Pulling the microphone close to my mouth I shouted, "Gil! Can you get a bead on their monitors?"

In my ear I could still hear shouting and what sounded like furniture being tossed around. Through all that I heard Gil say, "I think they're on the third floor!"

"Heath!" I yelled as I reached the top landing

and dashed in the direction of the interior stairwell. "Heath, can you hear me? Over?"

But Heath didn't or couldn't respond. *"Heath!"* I screamed. *"Use your grenade!"*

Still the commotion continued even while I tugged open the stairwell door and began running up the steps. I reached the second-floor landing and tried again. "Gopher!" I yelled. "Pull off the cap on your grenade!" But no one was responding to my pleas.

From way behind me I heard the stairwell door open and Tony shout, "M.J.!"

My arms were pumping as I urged my aching thighs to keep moving quickly up the stairs. "Get up here!" I called down to him. "And have your grenades ready to launch!"

Finally I reached the third floor and burst through the door. I could hear pounding and shouting from down the corridor, and worse, I could also feel the presence of something dark and terrible.

I was hit with a wall of awful foreboding and immediately knew I was being watched. There were no lights on, so I yelled down to base camp, "Gilley! Have them turn the lights on!"

"What?" he said. "M.J., you're breaking up. I did not copy that. Over!"

I clicked on my flashlight and moved stealthily down the hall in the direction of the muffled shouting. "Have the manager turn on the lights!" I tried again.

"Copy that!" Gil said. "Give me a few minutes; I've got to go find him!"

"He's in the office right behind the front desk," I said, still moving carefully down the corridor, my free hand resting on the cap of my grenade. "Heath?" I called. "Gopher?"

The pounding and muffled shouts got louder the farther down the hallway I moved. I picked up my pace and made it to the end, which left me the choice of turning right or left. I chose left and walked with care as my eyes, ears, and sixth sense opened up wide.

On the edge of my energy I could feel something vile, like a snake or a serpent slithering in the ether. My heart was thumping loudly in my chest when suddenly, from behind me, there was a loud bang. I froze in my tracks and stepped to the side with my back to the wall, pointing my flashlight behind me.

I could hear thumping, and the ground seemed to tremble slightly under my feet. It was then that I caught Tony, panting hard and sweating up a storm, around the corner as he came directly into my flashlight beam. "I . . . told . . . you . . . to wait," he said in a gasp, completely out of breath.

"Right," I said to him with little sympathy. "Do you have your grenades?"

Tony held up one of the metal tubes while he aimed his camera in my direction, and I noticed that both of his arms were trembling with either fatigue or fear, but probably a little of both. "Where are they?" he asked me.

"I think they're down this way," I said, noticing for the first time that the pounding and muffled shouting had stopped, and that worried me greatly. "Come on," I said, moving farther down the passageway.

We walked for about ten yards, my beam bouncing back and forth along the corridor and that slithery negative energy becoming more and more acute. "Heath!" I yelled again, but nothing came back to me. "Gopher!"

"Where are they?" Tony asked, his voice quivering with fear.

"I don't know!" I admitted worriedly. "I heard them before, but now they're both quiet. Gil!" I shouted into the mike. "What's the status on those lights?"

"I can't find the manager!" Gilley squealed. "But I'm looking for the master control switch. It's got to be around here somewhere."

I motioned to Tony, and we'd continued for a few paces when I felt something under my feet. I pointed the beam down to the ground and saw that it was a headset. Picking it up I held it out for Tony to see and asked, "Whose is it?"

"Not sure. But it means at least one of them was here."

I folded the headset and was tucking it into my utility belt when I heard Tony shriek in fear. My head snapped up, and I saw him pointing over my shoulder, his mouth open in horror. I turned and took a step back. In front of us and in the dim light being cast from my flashlight was a shadow that was at least eight feet high. It loomed in front of a doorway and swayed back and forth like a cobra. "Holy shit!" I swore. It was just like the thing that had attacked Heath and me down in the lobby.

Tony and I pressed our backs against the opposite wall, and for a brief moment I found it hard to breathe. Then two things happened simultaneously:

The first was a terrific pounding from right behind me; the second was that the lights came on.

Both Tony and I jumped and dashed down the hallway, away from the serpent thingy, when I realized I hadn't used my grenade. Pulling it out of my utility belt, I popped the cap, dropping the magnetic spike into my hand.

I looked over my shoulder and, in what felt like slow motion, I saw the shadow serpent crouch low and chase after us. I tossed the spike over my shoulder and pulled out my second grenade.

Tony was slightly ahead of me, and he was screaming bloody murder. He dropped the camera and his grenade without pulling off the cap; then he tossed his other one over his shoulder without looking back or pulling off the cap. I had to duck to avoid getting hit in the face with it, and barely managed to hold on to my one remaining grenade. I glanced back one last time and saw the shadowy serpent rear up as it came to my magnetic spike, twisting and turning, and a sound echoed down the hallway that was very much like a hiss.

I gripped my last grenade tightly, and, gathering every last bit of courage I had, I whirled around, changed direction, and started running *at* the serpent. I'd gotten only a few feet when something hot seared my shin. "Ah!" I yelled, but kept going. The serpent swayed as I approached, and it got taller.

I pulled out my spike, holding it firmly, and ran full-tilt right at the ugly thing in the center of the hallway. "You're going back to hell!" I shouted, and threw my spike at the center of the serpent.

The spike sailed through the air, slicing into the

shadowy serpent before it seemed to shiver, and then, in an instant, it disappeared. I stopped just short of where it had vanished, my chest heaving and my shin feeling as if it were on fire. I pulled up my pant leg and inspected my wound. There was one long, curved cut that was bleeding freely. "Bastard!" I yelled at the empty hallway.

"M.J.!" I heard Gilley's faint voice coming from somewhere in the distance, and I realized my headgear had come off and was on the ground just down the hall. I went to retrieve it and put it on.

"I'm okay," I said, still panting for air.

"Did you find Heath and Gopher?"

As if in answer the pounding and muffled cries picked up again, and I headed back down the hallway. Near the room where Tony and I had seen the serpent I found a narrow door. Using the master key card that Knollenberg had given to Heath and me, I swiped the lock and it opened. Gopher and Heath tumbled out.

"Oh, thank God!" said Heath. Getting to his feet, he tugged on Gopher's arm. "He's unconscious," he said.

I realized that Heath and Gopher had been trapped inside a small utility closet and wondered how the hell that'd happened. "You okay?" I asked, bending down to help him with Gopher.

"Yeah, yeah," Heath said. "I'm fine. Just a little woozy. Hey, you're bleeding!" he added, looking at my hand, which had the blood from my shin on it.

"I'm fine," I said. "Come on. Let's see if we can get Gopher down to the elevators and the hell out of here."

*   *   *

With a whole lot of effort we managed to get the producer down to the first floor, where Gilley and a still terrified Tony were waiting for us. By this time Gopher had come to, and was blinking at us rather stupidly. "Wha . . . wha happen?" he asked as the elevator doors opened and Gilley rushed in to help.

"You fainted," said Heath.

Gopher shook his head vigorously as if to clear it. "I did?"

"Yep. But you're all right now. Come on, guy, help us out here; can you get to your feet?"

Gopher looked from Heath to me to Gilley as if he were seeing us for the first time, but then it must have dawned on him that we were trying to lift him up, because he did manage to get his legs to work, and with only a little wobbling he was back on his feet.

We eased him out of the elevator and over to the couch in the lobby area. "How're you feeling?" I asked when we got him to sit down.

"Okay," he muttered, taking the bottled water that Gilley was trying to hand him. "God, what the hell happened up there?"

I glanced at Heath and noticed that his face was really pale and his eyebrows were pushed together as if he were in pain. "Are *you* all right?" I asked him, and motioned to Gilley to get another bottle of water.

"I think so," Heath said, rubbing his temples. "I've just never been attacked like that before."

"What happened?"

Heath edged away from Gopher and sat on the other side of the couch. "It was creepy," he said.

"Granted," I allowed. "If you two saw anything

like what Tony and I did, I'll give you that, right, Tony?" I looked over my shoulder to see my cameraman behind the bar unscrewing the top of a whiskey bottle and proceeding to pour much of its contents into a large highball glass.

Realizing that I had asked him a question, he ignored me and directed his gaze to Gopher. "I quit, man," he said.

He then gulped down the whiskey and poured himself a second glass without saying another word.

I turned my attention back to Heath and said, "Tell us what went down up there."

Heath took a sip of water and began. "We couldn't get the guy in room five-eighteen to accept his death. Turns out he's another suicide. The best I could get out of him was that his name is Gus and he'd lost his entire life savings in a poker game. He shot himself in that bed later on."

"Did he give you a time period?" I asked, hoping to research these facts in the city's newspaper records and maybe find a personal detail about Gus that we could use to get him to cross over.

"Early nineteen hundreds."

"Cool," I said, then waved my hand for him to continue with his story.

Heath took another sip of water. "We left Gus's room, and the next spirit on the list was Carol Mustgrove. I know you said we should tackle her together, but when I checked in with Gilley, he said that you had just finished up with Duke and were on your way to the dining hall, so I thought I could at least give Carol a shot and see if maybe we'd get lucky."

"How were you going to get into her room?" I asked, thinking about how it had been sealed off by the police.

"I wasn't," said Heath. "I planned on trying to pull her out of the room and talk to her in the hallway. And for a minute or two, M.J., it worked."

"It did?"

"Yes," Heath affirmed. "I was standing in front of her door, and she actually came out into the hallway. She thought I was her ex-fiancé, and, man, was she ready to tear me a new one."

I smiled. Carol struck me as the uppity type too. "I think that was the right way to play it to get her to come out and talk," I said, thinking Heath was a natural at this ghostbusting thing.

"Yeah, well, it didn't last long." Heath sighed. "Anyway, Carol comes out into the hallway and she's calling me Brian—I'm assuming that was her ex's name—and then she starts yelling at me that I'm having an affair with another woman, and she even knows the other woman's name."

"She's got a good memory, for a spirit," I mused. Usually grounded spirits become so foggy and confused that some of the finer details and names of people they only had an acquaintance with become lost.

"I don't think the name came from memory," said Heath with a bit of excitement. "She said she knew the other woman's name was Sophie."

I gasped. "No *way*!"

Heath nodded. "I don't think she was talking about the *actual* woman Brian had an affair with," he said.

"Me either," I agreed. "Sophie was murdered in

Carol's room," I said. "Do you think Carol could have witnessed it and was confused about who Sophie was?"

"I really do," said Heath.

"What else did she say?"

Heath's face fell. "Not a lot," he admitted. "It was right after Carol said the name Sophie that . . ." Heath's voice trailed off, and I noticed that he was looking at Gopher oddly.

"And then what?" I asked, switching my gaze from Heath to Gopher and back again.

"Well," Heath said, fiddling with the bottle cap from his water, "I heard Gopher say something."

I noticed that Gopher's expression had turned troubled and his gaze dropped to the floor. Heath didn't appear to be comfortable continuing, so I asked Gopher, "What did you say?"

Gopher didn't answer me right away; he just continued to stare down at the floor with a faraway look. Finally, however, he muttered softly, "I don't remember."

"You weren't speaking English," said Heath. "And I don't know what the hell you were saying, but it was supercreepy."

Something clicked in my head at that. "Did it sound like Spanish or Portuguese?"

Heath looked up at me in surprise. "Yeah," he said. "It did sound like that."

"Gopher, what do you remember about the moments leading up to then?"

Gopher shrugged but managed to make eye contact. "I don't speak Spanish," he insisted. "Or Portuguese."

"I believe you," I coaxed. "But I really need to know what you remember."

Gopher's jaw clenched and unclenched. "I remember filming Heath," he said. "I remember getting a tight shot of room three-twenty-one. I remember feeling this *really* intense blast of cold air hit the back of my neck, and then . . . and then . . ." Gopher didn't seem to be able to finish the thought.

"Let me guess," I said. "You don't remember anything else after that?"

"No," he said with a shake of his head. "I kinda do. I mean, I remember feeling like I'd been drugged or something. I guess it was that I felt really disconnected and far away, and I remember words coming out of my mouth, and in the back of my mind I couldn't figure out what I was saying, and then I remember running a little and opening a door, but it was so weird because *I* didn't want to open the door, and then I remember Heath being right behind me, and I shoved him into this small room or something, and he was fighting with me, but I pushed him in, and in my mind I knew I shouted at him that I was going to kill him. . . ."

"You wouldn't let me out of that closet," said Heath. "I tried to get you to move so that I could get out of there, but you wouldn't budge, and then you just fainted right on top of me, and all I could do was kick at the door with my feet and hope someone heard me. I'm really claustrophobic, and I get sick to my stomach and find it hard to breathe when I'm confined."

Gopher stared at Heath in amazement. "I didn't mean it, man!" he said. "You've got to believe me, Heath: I didn't mean anything that I said or did!"

"You're right," I said, trying to calm him down. "Gopher, you had no control over that period of time."

"M.J.," interjected Gilley. "What do you know that the rest of us don't?"

"It happened to me too."

Gilley looked at me curiously. "What happened to you?"

I ran a hand through my hair and gathered my thoughts. "The night we first arrived," I began, "Steven and I were in our room, and I felt a foreign energy take hold of me, and Steven said that my features changed and that I started speaking Portuguese."

"Whoa," said Gil. "A body snatcher!"

"Yeah," I said to him. "I've heard of this phenomenon before, and it can only be done by one hell of a powerful spirit, usually someone incredibly dark, and even then they can't sustain it for long."

"I'm confused," said Tony from behind us, and I realized that he was trying to follow our conversation, even though he looked about two sheets to the wind by now.

"Gopher's body was taken over by a very negative entity."

Tony blinked dumbly at me, and I heard Gopher say, "I was *possessed*?"

I turned back to face him. "In the strictest sense of the term, yes."

Gopher's face turned ashen. "Oh, my God," he whispered. "Do you think it's still *in me*?"

"No," I said with conviction. "I think that the spirit that took you over is gone. But there's another thing that I'm even more worried about." The faces all around me looked like they couldn't take much more, so I decided to get right to the point. "If I was clawed again," I said, pulling up the pant leg of my jeans to reveal the cut there, "then the knife that killed Tracy was somewhere close by."

"Shit," said Gil. "Shit, shit, *shit*!"

"We've got to call the police!" Heath insisted.

"Great idea," I agreed, then glanced at my watch. It was two a.m. "MacDonald sure isn't going to like me waking him up at this hour."

"He'll like it even less if we wait till morning," argued Gilley. "And one more thing, M.J.," he said, looking toward the front desk.

"What's that?"

"You should know that the night manager is missing."

"Anton?" I said.

Gilley nodded. "I saw him right before we started, but I haven't been able to find him since I went looking to turn the lights on."

I felt a chill spread up my spine. Pulling out my cell phone from my back pocket, I hit 911.

Chapter 11

They found Anton in the men's room. He'd been knocked unconscious, and there was a nice-size gash on the back of his head. MacDonald said the night manager had gone in there, heard the door open behind him, and was just turning his head to see who had entered when he got a good knock on the noggin.

EMS took him away by ambulance to the hospital, and Knollenberg was notified. He showed up not long afterward looking like hell.

"Hi, Murray," I said, waving at him when he came running in the door just as the ambulance with Anton pulled away.

"What happened?" he asked me, pivoting his head around like one of those bobble toys you see on dashboards.

"Anton was konked on the head," I told him. "We think by the same guy who's been running around here letting demons out and causing general mischief."

"Is he all right?"

"We think he'll be fine," I reassured him. "But . . . er . . . he wanted me to tell you that he's quitting, effective immediately. He'll be back later in the week to collect his things."

Knollenberg sat down heavily on a bar stool. "Damn," he said. "And he had such great credentials. I was really hoping he would work out."

Tony, who was still standing behind the bar, got out a highball glass and shared some whiskey with him. "Here ya goes," he slurred, pouring a generous portion. "To take the hedge hoff."

Knollenberg looked at the amber liquid in the glass, and I knew he really wanted to down it, but instead he turned back to me and asked, "What else happened?"

I told him everything. How we'd managed to cross Duke over and were working on the other ghosts when Heath and Gopher were tackled by one powerful spook, and how, when I went to help, I got knocked around a little too.

"And you called the police when you discovered Anton?" said Knollenberg.

"No, we called the police when we realized that the only way I could have been slashed by that demon was because the knife that acts as the portal key was close by. The police are scouring the third floor, looking for it."

"Are *they* safe up there?" asked Knollenberg, eyeing me critically.

"I hope so," I said. "They wouldn't let me tag along. MacDonald wants me to stay put."

"We'll know if things go bad," Gilley said dryly. "The screaming, running, and general pandemonium should alert us."

Knollenberg sank back wearily against the bar and eyed the stairs nervously.

"Gil," I said in an even tone. "Lay off, okay?"

Gilley rolled his eyes and muttered, "I'm just saying we'll know."

Heath got up from the couch and walked over to the bar. "I take it we're through with the ghost hunting for the evening?"

"Have a drink," I urged. "And pass me one while you're at it."

"What's your poison?" asked Tony, wobbling on his feet.

"I'll take a beer. M.J.?"

"Ditto," I said.

"Gimme a scotch," said Gopher, getting up from the couch.

About the time that everyone had downed their drink, MacDonald and a few guys in uniform came down from the third floor. "Any luck?" I asked the detective.

"Nada," he said. "We searched every single room and got squat."

"I was afraid of that." I was beginning to feel that familiar chill along my spine.

"So I guess you were wrong about the knife being nearby," said MacDonald as he rubbed his face tiredly.

"No," I said quickly. "That knife was there, Detective, I swear. It's just that whoever has it was on the move and likely has it hidden somewhere else by now."

MacDonald eyed me critically. "Someone besides you guys and the skeleton crew is here in the hotel?"

"I believe so," I said. "Which means that someone else has access to the hotel and is able to get in through the locked doors."

"Knollenberg," MacDonald barked.

"Yes, Detective?"

"I'll want a list of all your employees, current and recent past."

"How far back would you like to pull from?"

"Two years should do it," he said.

Knollenberg got up from his bar stool. "I'll be back in a few minutes." And he hurried away in the direction of his office.

MacDonald eyed me after he'd gone. "Got a minute?"

"I've got all night," I said, motioning for Tony, the drunken bartender, to round me up another beer.

"Cool," said MacDonald. "Come over here and talk to me."

I grabbed the fresh beer and walked with Mac-Donald over to the steps on the other side of the mezzanine. "I know that Beckworth is probably paying you a lot of money to get rid of these ghosts," he began.

"He is," I confirmed.

"And I know that you take your work seriously," he added.

"I do."

"But I want you to consider pulling out and going home."

That surprised me. "Come again?"

MacDonald looked around warily. "I've never liked this old hotel," he confessed. "I came here once for a wedding and ended up getting a room. I swear something or someone stared at me the entire night."

"Do you know if you were on the fifth floor?" I asked.

MacDonald blinked. "You know," he said, "I think I was!"

I shrugged my shoulders and took a pull from the beer. "Gus," I said.

"Who?"

"Gus. He's a ghostie in residence here. He was watching you."

MacDonald shivered. "Anyway," he said, squaring his shoulders, "when we were upstairs looking through all the rooms on the third floor, we all felt this really nasty vibe. I think this hotel is bad news, M.J. I think that you guys should forget about this place and go home."

"Can't," I said with a sigh. "We made a deal with Beckworth, and it was for a *lot* of money, Detective. Besides, I've never walked away from a job where innocent people stood to get hurt if I didn't do something. And I won't let this hotel be my first."

MacDonald pointed to my shin. "What if that keeps happening?"

"Well," I said, also looking down, "there's not much I can do about it until someone recovers that knife."

"Yeah," said MacDonald, "about that. I may know something that could give us some answers."

"What?"

"Do you remember when you told me that you thought it was weird that there were two women with international connections that I was investigating?"

I scratched my forehead and said, "Vaguely."

"Turns out there was more of a connection than we first thought. I'd read in Sophie's profile that she worked for an insurance company in London. Do you want to know which one?"

"It's going to mean something to me?"

"It might," he replied. "She worked for Lloyd's of London, and you'll never guess what her title was."

I stared at him blankly. "Adjuster?" I couldn't figure out what he was getting at.

"Investigator," he said, bouncing his eyebrows.

I swirled this information around in my head, but I wasn't picking up what MacDonald was trying to lay down. "Huh?"

"Sophie was an investigator with Lloyd's of London. She specialized in stolen art and artifacts, often posing as a fence to recover the fleeced property."

My brain latched onto the meaning now. "Whoa," I said. "That woman in Germany . . . what was her name?"

"Faline Schufthauser."

"Yeah, her . . . she was an art thief, right?"

"Now you're getting it."

"So Sophie was . . . what? Here looking for Faline? Or something she'd stolen?"

MacDonald rubbed his face again. "Hopefully I'll know that tomorrow," he said. "I've requested from her boss a list of the items assigned to her. I'm just waiting on them to e-mail it to me."

"So maybe this knife was stolen by Faline," I said, continuing to follow the thought. "Maybe whoever used it found it lying around her place and used it to kill her!"

"It might have gone down that way," he said.

"And maybe Sophie was trying to recover the knife for someone's collection!"

"Could be."

"Did Sophie know that Faline was dead?" I asked, finding the flaw in my argument.

"If that's who she was investigating, she sure as hell should have. I mean, it made national headlines in Germany."

"And what does all this have to do with Tracy?" I asked, failing to see how things linked back to her.

"That's what I'd like to know," said MacDonald, getting up to stretch his back.

I sighed. "Your work is a bitch," I told him.

"And yours is a piece of cake, right?" he said with a smile as he held out his hand to give me a lift from the stair I was sitting on.

"Good point."

"What do you guys plan to do now?" he asked.

I held the half-empty beer up in front of him. "We're calling it a night for now, but we'll go back at it tomorrow as soon as it's dark."

MacDonald eyed me the way your dad does when he really wants to forbid you to do something, but knows that he'll lose that battle. "Be careful, okay?"

I saluted him. "Yes, sir."

He rolled his eyes and left it at that.

The sun was just coming up when we finally wrapped up our drinking binge. I was feeling mighty good when Gil suggested we all go out for breakfast. We invited Knollenberg along—the poor guy had been holed up in his office since he'd arrived at three a.m.—but he declined.

We found a taxi and asked the driver to take us to the best greasy spoon around, and were dropped off at Curly's Coffee House. We trooped in like drunken sailors and plopped down in a big booth.

After ordering a plate of corned-beef hash and

eggs (which I crave only when I'm tipsy), I began a discussion with the rest of the group to see where their heads were as far as continuing the hunt.

"I'm in," said Heath.

"You know I'm in, M.J.," said Gil, and I knew that as long as he could wear his commando outfit with all its pockets full of magnets he'd be okay.

"I'm in," said Gopher, which surprised the hell out of me, and I began to have a little more respect for our producer.

"I'm out," said Tony.

No surprise there.

"Aw, come on, buddy," pleaded Gopher. "Stay on with us."

"No way, no how, Goph," Tony said, holding up the backpack he'd brought with him, which held all his stuff, and I knew there was no changing his mind, especially now that he was beginning to sober up a bit. "I only stuck around until now because it was the middle of the night. But after breakfast I'm heading straight to the airport. I never want to set foot in that hotel again!"

Gopher opened his mouth to argue, but I cut him off. "Let it go," I said softly. "This stuff isn't for everybody, Gopher, and Tony came up against something really terrifying last night. I don't blame him for wanting out."

Gopher scowled but let it go.

When it looked like the argument had been dropped, I continued with, "We'll need to talk strategy. Gil, we're through with teams. From now on the three of us will stick together like glue. Gopher, you can continue to film, and I'm going to give you a crystal to carry in your pocket. It should help if anyone tries to take you over again."

"Shouldn't I just wear some magnets, like Gilley?" he said.

I shook my head. "That's going to screw with our ability to talk to these ghosts," I said. "The crystal will do the trick; don't worry."

"And how should we try to protect ourselves?" asked Heath. "Clearly what we're doing isn't working very well."

"I think that one of us should be on point with the entity we're trying to contact. And what I mean by that is that while you're focused on talking to, say, Gus, I'm going to be feeling out the ether for any nasties so that we'll have ample warning and can get to our grenades quickly."

"That works," Heath agreed. "As long as someone's got my back, I'm all for continuing on."

"I think we should also put some of the extra meters in those areas where you'll be continuing the bust," suggested Gilley. "That way I'll be able to warn you ahead of time if you're about to walk into a hot zone."

"Great," I said. "We can lay those out today before we crash."

"And what do we do if I'm unable to get Gus and the other ghosts across to the other side?" Heath asked.

"We tag the other partner and let them have a crack," I replied with a smile as my eggs and hash arrived. "Just like wrestling."

"So we start with Gus on the fifth floor then?" Heath said.

I pulled out from my pocket the list of spirits we

were tackling and eyeballed it. "Yep. We start with him; then I say we move down to the dining hall. Let's check out that woman in the mirror too while we're there, and that'll put Carol Mustgrove last."

Gilley was jotting this down on a pad of paper he'd brought with him. Looking up after scribbling, he said, "Which mirror are we going to focus on?"

"The one in the Renaissance Room. We can't get into the one located in the ladies' room— remember?"

Gilley looked at me blankly.

"It's sealed off by the crime-scene tape," Heath reminded him.

"Oh, yeah," he said. "Cool."

We all ate in silence for a bit before Gopher asked, "Do you think you'll be able to get all the spirits over in one night?"

I chewed my food before I answered. The hash was delightfully salty, just the way my tipsy self liked it. "I hope so. That's the aim, at least, and if we can manage it, that will leave us with one final night to deal with the demon."

"How are we even going to find it?" Gopher said. "I mean, if that thing is on the move, isn't it going to be tough to pin down?"

I looked at my plate and didn't answer him right away, and I could feel all eyes focus on me. Finally I said, "We'll catch it the same way you catch any predator."

"How's that?" Heath wondered.

"By setting up some bait."

The boys all looked around the table at one another as if to say, *Not it!*

I held back a smile and said, "I'll be the bait. But, Heath, I'll need you nearby."

Gilley didn't look happy. "Is that your entire plan? You're going to set yourself up as a lure and hope that this thing comes after you?"

"Pretty much," I told him. "I mean, I'm still working out the logistics and all, but it's about the only thing we can do."

"But how are you going to fight it when it shows up?" Gil complained. "M.J., that thing is tied to a portable portal! We'll need to find the key, and by key I mean knife, and by knife I mean murder weapon, and by murder weapon I mean murder*er*; and by that I mean, *Are you insane*?!"

I flung my hands up in surrender. "Then what would you suggest, Gil?"

Gilley opened his mouth to say something, but nothing other than, "eh . . . ah . . . er . . ." came out.

"That's what I thought," I said. "We've got no choice, when you think about it. We've got to try, and hope for the best."

I noticed then that most of the men had stopped eating. It appeared I'd ruined their appetites. "Anyway," I continued, "we've still got a day to work it out. Maybe another idea will come to me, and we can go with that instead."

"Oh, if only," said Gilley dryly.

I polished off the last of my breakfast and pushed my plate away, giving in to the huge yawn that indicated I was more tired than I'd thought. Reaching for my purse and pulling out some cash, I said, "Let's all head back to the hotel, set up those gauges, and get some decent shut-eye. This feels like it's going to be a long night, fellas."

*   .   *   *

Back at the hotel Gopher asked Knollenberg if he
could change rooms to something a little closer to
the ground floor and was given the key card to a
room on the first floor. Gilley and I thought that was
a brilliant idea, as it would keep us all close to the
action and less spread out, so we also asked for new
rooms near Heath and Gopher and got them.

As I was waiting for Knollenberg to assign me a
new room, I had the chance to ask him about the
mirrors that Beckworth had purchased at auction.
"I'm so sorry," he said while his fingers tapped on
the computer. "I haven't had a chance to ask Mr.
Beckworth about that yet."

"It's okay," I reassured him. Wanting to take it
easy on the guy, but needing that information, I
pressed, "Can you please remember to ask him the
very next time you speak to him?"

"Of course," said Knollenberg with a blush.

"Oh!" I said, thinking of something else. "And
would you happen to know about a man who committed suicide here in the early nineteen hundreds?"

Knollenberg hit one final key on his computer
and gave me a small smile. "No, that was a little bit
before my time."

I laughed. He'd said it so dryly that it was un-
expectedly funny. "I understand that," I said, still
giggling. "Do any of your hotel records go that far
back?"

"I can check," he offered. "But you might also
find some information in the archives of the local
newspaper."

"That's a great idea," I said. "I'll get Gilley right
on it."

Once Knollenberg assigned me my new room, I went up to my room to pack and move my stuff down a few floors. I saw Gilley just coming out of his new room as I was making my way down the first-floor hallway. "Hey," I said.

"What room are you in?" he asked me.

"The one right next to yours," I said, stopping to eyeball the brass plates. "By the way, I have an assignment for you, and I need you to look it up before tonight."

Gilley yawned dramatically. "Oh, yippee," he said drolly.

I ignored his sarcasm. "Can you look into the online archival records of the local newspapers to see if there's an account of a man with the first name of Gus who committed suicide here at the hotel in the early nineteen hundreds?"

"That shouldn't be too hard. Sure," he said. "I'll look it up."

"Great!" I gave him a pat on the back. "Print off anything you can find."

"What time will you be rising and shining?" he asked as I made my way through my door.

I glanced down at my watch. "I'll probably get up around two and go for a run. Want to grab a bite to eat around four?"

"We'll need to set out the extra electrostatic meters," he reminded me.

"Oh, crap," I said, pausing in the doorway. "I forgot. Okay, then we'll place the meters at four and eat around five."

"Did you want to get started before midnight?"

"Might as well," I said. "That sky looks like rain,

and if it starts pouring, then we can start anytime we're ready."

"Thank God for rainy days," said Gil. (Ghost hunting is best when the atmosphere is damp.)

"Cool, see you at four."

I slept until about two thirty, then went for a run, which was tougher than I thought on the slopes and hills of San Francisco. I made it back to the hotel by three fifteen, showered, and met Gil in the mezzanine by four to set up the electrostatic meters—which, thank God, we had plenty of.

"Do we want to put these only on the floors we're going to be working?" Gil asked me.

"How many do we have?"

Gilley looked into his duffel bag. "Eight," he said.

"We have that many?"

"You know how fritzy they can be," he reminded me, referring to how easily the meters tended to short out. "I wanted to make sure we were well stocked for this gig."

"I think it's a good idea to put them in all the places we'll be working, plus maybe a few in the higher-traffic areas, like down here on the ground floor."

My partner and I went through our plan for that evening and placed all the meters in their strategic locations. Gil then wanted to go back down to his command center and make sure he was getting a reading off each meter. I joined him, as we were going to get something to eat afterward.

Sitting next to him and taking up the clipboard

with the numbered meters and their corresponding locations, I went through them with him.

"Number one reads slightly above normal," Gilley said, starting to go through the meters one by one.

I glanced at the sheet on the clipboard that documented each meter assignment and said, "Checkmark for fifth-floor meter. Next?"

"Meter two readings are normal."

I scrolled down the sheet again and found meter two's assignment. "Check for dining hall meter," I called.

"Meter three readings are normal."

"Check for lobby meter."

"Meter four readings are slightly elevated," Gil said.

"Check for ground-floor elevator."

"Meter five readings are . . ." I looked up from my clipboard as Gilley paused, only to see his eyes widen with alarm before he shouted, "Off the freaking charts!"

I leaned in and glanced at his laptop and noticed that the electromagnetic meter on the third floor next to room 321 was in the red zone. "Jesus!" I gasped. "Have you ever seen them so high?"

Gilley shook his head. "Never! It's got to be a faulty gadget," he determined, but his face looked worried.

"Come on," I said, setting the clipboard down. "Let's go check it out."

I hurried to the door and pushed it open, holding it for Gilley, whom I expected to be right behind me. When I glanced back, however, he was still in his seat, looking at me skeptically. "You coming?"

"I don't wanna," he said feebly. "What if that *thing* is up there, and it's causing the meter to jump?"

I rolled my eyes. "Okay, grab some grenades and let's go!"

"But . . ." Gil said, looking from his laptop screen to me and back again as if he were searching for another excuse.

"Oh, *fine!*" I snapped. "Stay here then!" And I let the door close. I walked down the hallway in an aggravated huff and nearly slammed right into Heath, who was likely coming to look for us.

"What's up?" he asked me.

"We've got a meter spiking on the third floor, and Gilley the Girl has decided he's too scared to come with me to check it out."

"I'll go with you," Heath offered.

"Thanks," I said, feeling better immediately. I hadn't wanted to go up there alone, and I was glad that he was willing to tag along with me.

We hurried to the elevators and rode up to the third floor. I handed Heath one of the grenades from my tool belt, which I'd luckily strapped on before I left my room. "Just in case," I told him.

"How high was the meter spiking?" he asked.

"High enough to proceed with caution," I warned, gripping the cap on the grenade firmly as I watched the floor count on the control panel of the elevator. "But it might be a false alarm. I mean, the thing was spiking way beyond anything we've ever seen before, so it could just as easily be a faulty meter."

"How often do you get a false reading?"

"Often enough," I said as the boxcar stopped and the doors began to open.

We moved out of the elevator and proceeded

down the hallway with caution. I was in the lead, and Heath had my back. We got to the first corner without incident, and I had my senses wide-open, but nothing much was hitting me.

"You feel cold?" I asked Heath, thinking that the telltale sign that indicated ghosties were about might give us an early warning.

"No. You?"

"No," I said. I paused before turning the corner and reached into my tool belt for one of the last three electrostatic meters that we'd each be carrying that night. The readings were normal.

"What's it say?" Heath asked.

"It's normal. No unusual hits at all."

My cell phone rang at that moment, and both Heath and I jumped. I took a breath and answered it. "What?" I barked, seeing that it was Gilley calling.

"The meter's gone back to normal," he told me.

"Are you getting a bead on the one I'm holding or the one down the hall?" I asked.

"The one we planted outside room three-twenty-one," he confirmed.

I began moving forward again. "Okay," I said. "We're almost to it, and we can check it out."

"I have a good reading on your meter, by the way," said Gilley. "I think we can cross it off the list too."

We came to a stop outside room 321; and I looked down. The electrostatic meter was resting peacefully right up against the door. It hadn't been moved or touched that I could tell. I bent down to pick it up and examined it. "It looks fine. Gil, what do you want me to do with it? Do you want to replace it with the one I brought along?"

"I don't know, M.J. I mean, it seems to be working now."

"It does," I agreed.

"Is there a light socket nearby?" Gilley asked me. "You know how those things can spike when they get near a hot outlet."

I looked up and down the hallway, and I finally spotted an outlet about ten yards away. "There's no way it could have gotten a buzz off the plug in the hallway, Gil. It's too far away."

"Okay, well, let's switch it out with the one you've got; that way we'll know if we get big spikes again that it's not that particular meter."

I clicked off the phone and swapped the gadgets, then motioned for Heath to head back down to the main floor. But before we took even two steps we both froze. "You feel that?" I asked as a cool breeze seemed to blow across the back of my neck."

"Cold air?" he said, pivoting on his heel to look back.

"Yep," I whispered. I held my hands up and closed my eyes, concentrating. It was then that I heard the familiar clicks and blips coming from the electrostatic meters. My cell rang again and I flipped it open. "We've got action," I said to Gil.

"On both meters," he confirmed. "What's your location, M.J.?"

"We're standing in front of room three-nineteen."

"So you're next to three-twenty-one?" he asked.

"We are," I said, holding my hand up and feeling the air in front of the door.

"I've got a female," said Heath. "I think this might be Carol."

"Gotta go, Gil. I'll call you back in a few." I clicked

off the phone and focused all of my intuitive radar on picking up what was in the ether. Meanwhile, the cold around us intensified, and the electrostatic meters continued to blip noisily.

"It's definitely Carol," Heath said after a moment, and on the edge of my energy I was just starting to feel her too.

In my mind I saw a woman in her mid- to late forties, with frosted hair and nails perfectly manicured. Her clothing was preppy, a high collar and a blazer with shoulder pads. Her slacks were navy and finely creased, and her shoes were brown leather loafers, no socks. Her features appeared too sharp, her nose thin, her chin a bit long, and her lips pursed in a permanent pout.

Her eyes, however, appeared narrow and suspicious. "She wants to know who we are," said Heath.

"Hi, Carol," I said directly to her, and I felt her energy point toward me. "My name is M. J. Holliday, and this is Heath Whitefeather. We'd really like to talk to you, if you're open to it. We think that something very bad happened in your room the other day. Something that turned your living area into a mess. A woman was attacked, and you might have seen what happened. We really need to ask you if you might be able to describe who the woman was fighting with."

I could feel a sense of immediate dismissal. Carol didn't seem to think much of me or my line of questions, and she turned her energy back toward room 319.

"Wait, don't go!" Heath pleaded, and I was both surprised and relieved that he had such acute senses.

"Carol, we know what happened to you. How your fiancé left you right before your wedding. He was a total jackass, and I'm really sorry about that."

For a moment nothing happened, other than Carol's energy seemed to hover in front of us while she considered what Heath had said. He turned to me and whispered, "We need to try a different angle here; she's not interested in telling us about Sophie."

I nodded. "I think your fiancé really regrets what he did to you," I told her. "I mean, you're obviously a beautiful woman, and I think he likely just had a really bad lapse in judgment."

Heath smiled as Carol's energy came toward us again. "I hear you got even by running up his credit cards," he said. "The rat bastard. I'll bet that bill hurt when it showed up in his mailbox, huh?"

In my mind's eye I really felt as though Carol's spirit were wickedly delighted by that. She was lapping up what we were putting down. "And I hear the woman he left you for later cheated on him," I said, taking a huge chance.

In the hallway Heath and I actually heard a woman's gasp. "It's true," said Heath, looking at me encouragingly. "I hear she slept with his best friend, in fact."

Carol was now radiating satisfaction. "He's devastated, you know," I said. "He really wanted you to come back to him, but now it's too late."

And in that instant I felt Carol's energy pull back—it felt like I'd just said something really upsetting to her.

"She wants to know why," whispered Heath.

I realized then that Carol didn't realize she was

dead. "Remember?" I asked her. "You came back from your shopping, and then you took out your pistol . . . do you remember that, Carol?"

The ether seemed to vibrate as if a shiver ran through it, and the cold around us intensified and my teeth began to chatter. "She says she remembers," whispered Heath. "But go easy, M.J.; I don't think she's going to like this next part."

I nodded. "And you were so upset, Carol. Do you remember how upset you were?"

"She says yes," Heath interpreted, and I was grateful she was communicating directly with him, because I was able only to sense her feelings and emotions.

"And when you looked at all those packages and those pretty new things, you realized that the spending on your fiancé's dime was going to upset him, but it didn't seem like enough to you. You wanted him to really regret his decision, right?"

"Yes again," said Heath.

"And when you looked at the situation, you realized the *only* way to truly get even with him was to take your own life. That was the one way to send a powerful, lasting message to him, right?"

I looked at Heath to see what Carol would say, but he remained silent for so long that I finally asked, "What's she saying?"

"Nothing," he said. "She's just sort of stunned, and she's not saying any . . . Oh, wait a second; she just said, 'Come back later; I need to think.' "

"She needs to *think*?" I repeated, looking at the spot in the hallway where I felt Carol was hovering. "Carol!" I said. "Wait; don't go away. We really do want to help you."

But even as I said those words I could feel the ghostly woman fading back through the door of 319. Out of the corner of my eye I caught Heath's head snap in that direction, and he said, "She just asked if we could keep the staff out of her room unless someone is willing to clean up the mess. She doesn't want to be disturbed."

"Well, crap," I said, frustrated that we'd been so close to getting through to her.

"We can come back tonight after we've given her some time," Heath reasoned. "Maybe when we try to make contact again she'll be more open to letting us help her, and maybe she'll be willing to share some details about what she might have seen when Sophie was murdered."

I nodded reluctantly and motioned to the hallway. "Feel like getting something to eat?"

"I do," he said.

We started walking back down the hallway when my cell rang again. "Hey, Gil," I said without even looking at the caller ID.

"What happened?" he demanded. "The meters went back to normal about a minute ago."

"We made contact with Carol Mustgrove."

"Did you get her across?"

"Nope," I said with a sigh. "She seems to need some time to think things through, and she told us to come back later."

"Well, that sucks," Gil grumbled. "We've only got tonight and tomorrow. How much time did she want you to give her?"

"We're going to try again later on tonight. Heath and I are on our way back downstairs. We'll swing by to pick you up so that we can catch some dinner."

"I'll call Gopher and see if he wants to join us."

I frowned. I didn't really want him along, but then I figured that if he was going to continue with the shoot, it might be good to talk strategy with him over dinner. "See you in a minute," I said as the elevator doors opened.

"Meet me at the front desk," said Gil.

We rode the elevator down and went over to the check-in counter, where we saw Gilley chatting with Anton, the night manager who'd been attacked the night before. "Hi, Anton," I said cordially. "How's the head?"

Anton turned around so that I could see the small white bandage on the back of his head. "Eet still hurts," he admitted.

"I'm surprised to see you behind the counter," I said. "We thought you were quitting."

"*Oui*," he said, blushing. "But Monsieur Knollenberg and Monsieur Beckworth, zey can be very persuasive. Zey like my résumé, and zey promised no more night shifts."

"That was nice of them," I said, then caught something he'd said. "Did you meet with Mr. Beckworth personally?" I asked.

"*Oui*. He came here an hour ago, and he's been talking with Monsieur Knollenberg in ze office."

I looked at Gilley. "Is Gopher coming to dinner?"

"He's on his way down. He said to give him ten minutes."

"Perfect," I said, then gave my attention back to Anton. "Would it be possible," I asked him, "for you to ring into Mr. Beckworth's office and see whether I could ask him a few questions?"

"Questions? May I tell heem to what zis is about?"

"I want to ask him about the mirrors he bought at auction." Anton gave me a blank look, so I said quickly, "It's my understanding that Mr. Beckworth bought four mirrors at an auction recently and that he's placed them in several locations around the hotel. Heath and I have both seen a figure in the mirrors' reflection, and I believe that they might be linked to a woman's spirit. I believe she might have a close affiliation to the mirrors and may also need to be assisted in crossing over. I just want to ask him where he purchased them, and if he knows anything about their history."

Anton blanched—I could tell he didn't like the idea of haunted mirrors much. "One moment," he said. "I will go ask him about ze mirrors." He hurried away down the hall toward the offices.

"Where did you want to eat?" Gilley asked me.

"We could go next door," I suggested. "Or there's Biscuits and Blues just down the street."

"Yeah, I've heard good things about that place. Let's go there," said Heath.

"Hello!" came a voice across the lobby. We all looked up and saw Gopher hurrying over to us. "Where're we eating?"

I felt a tap on my shoulder and turned around. Anton was back at the counter, and he didn't look like he had good news to share. "I'm very sorry, mademoiselle, but Monsieur Beckworth eez about to leave shortly, and he still has some things to go over with Monsieur Knollenberg. When I told him ze details and how urgent your mission was, he said he didn't know zat ze mirrors were going to be a problem. He said not to bahzer with zem. He will have zem removed and disposed of. Apparently zey are not valuable."

"Er . . ." I said, surprised by Beckworth's reaction.

"What's up?" said Gilley, just tuning in to my conversation with Anton.

"Beckworth doesn't want us to bust the woman in the mirrors."

"Why not?" said Heath.

"He's going to remove and dispose of them."

"Less work for us to do, then!" Gilley said happily.

"Yeah," said Heath, "good point, Gil."

"So you're okay with just leaving that poor woman grounded?" I asked the two of them.

"M.J., we can't very well get rid of *every* ghost in San Francisco. Besides, we've got two more grounded spirits to work on and a demon to hunt down, all in the next day and a half. And we'll still get paid the same, so let's just put our energies where we need to, okay?"

"Fine," I said, not really agreeing with them. "But when we get back from dinner I'm just going to poke my head into the Renaissance Room and see if I can't make contact." Gilley gave me look of exasperation. "I can't just leave her stuck there without some kind of effort, Gil!" I said.

He shook his head ruefully. "Oh, M.J., such a softie for the ghosties. Come on, girl; let's get some eats."

Chapter 12

By the time we finished with our meal it had begun to rain, and darker clouds appeared on the horizon that looked like they had the potential to be really nasty. "Might get some lightning and thunder out of those," said Gilley as we hovered under the restaurant's awning, waiting for a cab to take us back to the hotel.

"Good ghost-hunting weather, though," I said. The more damp and electrostatically charged the atmosphere, the easier it was for spirits to show up and work their mischief.

A cab finally stopped and we quickly piled in. We made it back inside the hotel in short order, and everyone shook off the rain. Gilley looked at his watch and asked me, "When do you want to start?"

I looked back out at the rain. "Anytime is good. Why don't we meet in the command center in twenty minutes and get to it?"

"Sounds good," agreed Heath.

"I'm in," said Gopher.

"Great. See you back in twenty," said Gilley.

The boys headed to their rooms, but I still intended to check in with the mirror lady, so I hurried off in the direction of the Renaissance Room. As I passed the front desk I noticed a new manager sitting at the computer. "Hey," I said with a wave.

"Mmmmph," he mumbled moodily, barely glancing up as I passed him. I figured that this was the guy who'd been working days until Anton threatened to quit, and he was now stuck with the night shift.

I got to the Renaissance Room and opened the door slowly. I took out my electrostatic meter and checked the gauge. Readings were normal.

I entered the room cautiously and noticed that the area was already undergoing some repair. The shredded curtains had been removed, the glass swept up, and all of the camera equipment was gone—probably packed up and shipped off by Gopher's crew.

As for the repairs, I had seen a few guys in overalls come into the hotel right before Gilley, Steven, and I had headed back to Boston, so maybe this was what they'd been called in to do.

I flipped on the light and looked around at the spackle on the wall and the cans of paint nearby. But what struck me was that across the room was the outline in spackle of the big heart carved by the demon—but no mirror.

I quickly traversed the room and squinted at where the mirror had been. The mountings that had held it to the wall were still in place, but the mirror itself was gone. "Well, shit," I muttered.

Then I remembered that there was another mirror that I could access by the elevators. No one had reported seeing the woman in that one, but I was barred from the ladies' room, so I thought I might as well give it a shot.

I left the Renaissance Room and headed to the elevators, passing the happy guy behind the desk again. I rounded the corner and looked on the opposite side of the double doors to see if there was a mirror there, but a blank wall stared back.

I spun in a three-sixty, looking for another place where a mirror of that size might have been hung—and got zippo.

I growled in frustration and turned back to the wall where I thought the mirror would have been placed, and noticed for the first time against the busy wallpaper that the mounting brackets for something long and rectangular were still embedded in the wall.

I moved closer and reached my hand up to touch them, convinced that this mirror had been recently taken down too.

There were footsteps behind me, and I swiveled to see Gilley and Heath coming toward me. "Whatcha doin'?" said Gil.

"Looking for the mirrors," I said. "But the one in the Renaissance Room and this one have already been taken down."

"Did you try the one on the third floor?" asked Heath.

"Oh, yeah! I forgot about that one. Gil, do we still have a little time before we need to meet?"

"You've got ten minutes," he said, checking his watch.

"You in?" I asked Heath.

He smiled and waved lazily back to the elevator. "Lead the way."

We got off on the third floor. I'd forgotten my tool belt in the command center but Heath produced an electrostatic meter, which he handed to me in the elevator. As the doors opened I pointed it forward. I wanted to make sure that if Carol was willing to come out and play, we'd know she was around. "Is the mirror down this way?" I asked, pointing in the direction of Carol's room.

"I thought it was this way," said Heath, pointing to the other end of the hallway.

"Okay, let's go your way first."

We proceeded down the hall, our senses on high alert, and even before we got to the end of the hallway I knew that the mirror had once been mounted there but had recently been removed. The brackets on the wall glinted in the overhead light.

As we got within a few feet there was a terrific clap of thunder, and the lights dimmed. "Ooh," said Heath with humor in his voice. "Spooky!"

I smiled. "I love thunderstorms."

Heath opened his mouth to reply, but at that moment there was yet another tremendously loud clap that shook the walls, and the lights dimmed again, then went out, leaving us totally in the dark.

We waited for a few heartbeats in silence, probably both thinking the same thing, that the generator was going to kick the lights back on, but nothing happened and we stayed in the dark. "Okay," I said, reaching out to touch Heath, but when I did he made a sound that was in a deeper octave and really weird.

"You okay?" I asked, pushing my hand out to try to find his shoulder. Again he made a sound that was deep and guttural and sent chills all the way up my spine. It was then that I heard my electrostatic meter begin to click and buzz and whine.

"Heath," I said, growing increasingly uncomfortable. "Heath, what's going on?"

Before I even had a chance to assess what was happening I felt him shove me hard against the wall and grip my throat. In my ear he whispered something in Spanish, but as my brain worked to catch up I realized he wasn't speaking Spanish, but Portuguese.

His tone was lethal—it didn't even sound like him—and I clawed at his hands, which were slowly squeezing my windpipe closed. All the while he continued in that awful, sickly, seductive tone of voice, and I truly believed that whatever fiend had just taken over Heath's body was having some vile fun.

Meanwhile I couldn't breathe, and I felt as if I were sinking as my strength faded. In that rather absurd moment I remembered a boy I'd dated in high school who'd been a tae kwon do champion in the junior leagues. He'd shown me several of his best self-defense moves and suggested that by learning them I could always take care of myself. One of them involved using my arms to jam down on the elbows of any frontal attacker, and that was what I did now as I karate-chopped Heath at the elbows.

He let go immediately and we both fell to the floor. I gasped for breath and instinctively began crawling away. My cell phone rang then, and in the dark I fumbled for it while still trying to get away.

"M.J.?" Gilley said when I'd flipped it open. "Hello?"

"Gil . . ." I managed in between ragged breaths.

"We've lost power," he said. "The command center is down. I won't be able to monitor if we start now, so we're thinking that we should wait a few before—"

"Gil!" I wheezed.

"What?"

"Help!" At that moment someone or something grabbed my leg and squeezed hard. I felt nails dig in through the fabric and I screamed, kicking and pulling away from the viselike grip on my shin.

I dropped the phone and tried to stand up, but the grip intensified. "Lemme go!" I yelled, and struggled to hop down the hall. In the background I could hear the faint but panicked voice of my partner shouting through the cell phone I'd left behind that he was on his way. I was terrified to think that he wouldn't get here in time. Heath was obviously possessed and was gripping my leg hard enough for me to yelp in pain.

But then I heard a moan coming from just ahead of me, and I realized with *real* alarm that Heath wasn't behind me. Somehow he'd managed to get ahead of me, and he too was inching forward in the darkness.

That meant that whatever was holding on to me wasn't human. I screamed again and kicked and crawled forward, and finally the thing gripping my shin let go. I scratched at the wall, trying to stand up, but in the dark I was disoriented and dizzy.

I felt something brush past me, and down the hall I heard a dragging noise, and it felt as if I were surrounded by unseen danger. I stopped trying to move forward and sat down with my back against the wall. Curling my legs up close to my body and breathing heavily, I ducked my chin and began praying.

The dragging noise continued, a sort of lurching

forward, then a pause, another lurching forward, then a pause, and the whole thing was so unsettling that I squeezed my eyes closed as tightly as possible and whispered Hail Marys over and over.

I'm not sure when the dragging noise stopped, but in the distance I heard a door slam, and the next thing I knew a hand was laid flat on my head. By now I was sobbing, and I screamed at the top of my lungs, kicking out and trying to get away again.

But then I realized that someone was yelling my name, and in the next moment a beam of light appeared at the end of the hall, illuminating things a fraction. I saw then that I was staring at Heath, who was on the floor, holding his head and staring at me with wide, terrified eyes.

"What the hell happened?" he whispered.

"M.J.!" I heard from the direction of the beam; then pounding feet came racing toward us.

I squinted as I looked up into the light while I tried to collect myself, but it was hard, because I was shaking all over. "Gilley!" I cried when he got close, and I could see that Gopher was right behind him.

Gil dropped down next to me and repeated Heath's question: "What happened?"

But I couldn't seem to talk articulately. Instead a bunch of burbling came out of my mouth, and I managed only to frighten everyone more. "Come on, honey," said Gil, handing off to Gopher a magnetic spike he'd brought along, so that he could reach under my arm and help me to my feet.

"I don't want to be here right now," I said, irritated that I couldn't stop shaking or crying.

"So let's get out of here," said Gil. "Gopher, you help Heath. Let's get them back downstairs."

With Gilley's help I made it to the stairwell, and, one step at a time, we found our way down to the mezzanine. Outside the storm was raging, and the walls reverberated almost continuously with the sounds of thunder as lightning flashed brightly.

Gilley and Gopher pointed Heath and me to the lobby sitting area, and by that time I'd collected myself and was able to catch a glimpse of the manager on duty having an animated conversation on his cell phone.

I sat down on the sofa, and Heath plopped down next to me. I couldn't help it: I scooted away from him a little. He looked wounded and asked, "What did I *do*?"

Gilley crouched at my feet and took hold of my hand. He dabbed at my wet cheeks and soothed, "There, there, M.J., you're okay. Now stop crying, because your mascara's getting all runny."

That made me smile just a bit. "Thanks," I said to him.

It was then that he seemed to notice something on my neck, and his hand moved to my throat as he sucked in air. "Sweetie!" he said in alarm. "There are bruises all around your neck! Who did this to you?"

My eyes roved over to Heath, and he reacted like he'd been punched: His eyes bugged out and his jaw dropped and he looked pained. "No way!" he said. "I didn't do that to you, did I?"

I nodded.

"Oh, man," said Gopher. "Oh, man, that's bad!"

Gilley wheeled on Heath. "Why did you do that to her!?" Gilley demanded, standing to his full height and putting his hands on his hips. I couldn't be certain, but I swore Gil was ready to slap Heath.

"I didn't!" Heath said, cowering back on the couch. "I swear, dude! I . . . I . . . I don't know what came over me! I barely remember anything beyond the lights going out!"

I laid a hand on Gil's arm. "It wasn't him," I said.

Gilley looked from my hand on his arm to Heath to me, and I could tell I had confused him. "Wait," he said. "What?"

"It was our Portuguese guy," I said. "He nabbed Heath."

"The same guy that got into me?" said Gopher.

I nodded. "We had no warning," I said. "It happened just like that." I snapped my fingers for emphasis.

"Why did you go up there without one of these?" Gopher asked as he held out one of the magnetic spikes.

A huge flash of lightning outside and an immediate thunderclap made me jump, and I put my hand over my heart, willing myself to chill. After taking a few calming breaths I said, "I just wanted to get a quick look at that mirror, but because we were pressed for time I didn't think to grab my tool belt. It never occurred to me that we'd be hijacked like that."

"What mirror?" Gopher asked.

"The twin to the one in the Renaissance Room," I explained.

"The one with the girl in it?"

Gopher had my full attention. "What do you know about it?"

"When I was helping to pack up the camera equipment I happened to glance in the mirror, and

I saw this *really* beautiful girl walk into the room, but when I turned around, she wasn't there. I looked back at the mirror—there she was. And I'll admit it really freaked me out."

I looked pointedly at Gilley. "We need to see one of those mirrors."

"But, sweetheart," he said, still fussing over me, "they've all been taken down, and this bust is clearly showing signs that it's time to quit. Whatever keeps attacking you guys is just too powerful. I say we cut our losses and catch the next flight home."

"I agree," said Heath. "M.J., I swear, I had no control over what I did to you!"

"I know you didn't, Heath," I said, trying to cut him some slack. "It's okay."

"I'm so sorry," he said again, and I could tell he felt terrible over what had happened.

"Come on, M.J.," said Gilley. "Let's go pack our gear and get out of here while we're all still in one piece, okay?"

I got up from the couch without answering him and began to pace back and forth. Something about those mirrors was really irking me. And the thing I kept coming back to was that giant scratched-out heart that had encircled the one in the Renaissance Room. The more I thought about the woman in the mirror, the more it occurred to me that her ethnicity could easily have been Spanish—with her long black hair, fine white skin, and dark eyes. I wondered suddenly if she could have been Portuguese.

I stopped my pacing and reached for my cell, only to realize that I'd left it up on the third floor. "Gil," I said.

"Yeah?"

"Can I borrow your cell?"

Gilley pulled his phone out of his pocket. "Who did you want to call?" he asked.

"Detective MacDonald," I said.

"Why, honey?"

"Because I *need* to see that mirror, and the only one that couldn't have been dismantled yet is the one in the women's restroom."

"You want to have him come down here and un-seal a crime scene so that you can go looking for the ghost in the mirror?" Gilley asked incredulously. "M.J., he'll never agree to that."

I pulled out MacDonald's card from my back pocket and punched in his number. While it rang I said, "Fine, then I'll just have to lie."

"Okay, I'm here," said a rather wet and foul-humored detective about half an hour later. "What is so urgent that it couldn't wait until morning?"

I'd suggested to MacDonald that I had received intuitive information on the murder of Tracy, and for reasons I couldn't say on the phone, I had to tell him in person. "I need to get into the restroom," I said, pointing to the women's lavatory, which was covered in yellow crime-scene tape, the door locked with a padlock.

MacDonald's eyes darted over to that side of the room. "I can't unseal a crime scene without a damn good reason," he said.

"Oh, I have one," I insisted. There was a long, pregnant pause while my mind raced to make one up.

"And that would be . . . ?" MacDonald said help-fully.

"I think Tracy is in the mirror of the bathroom," I said, improvising like hell.

"In the *mirror*?" MacDonald asked.

"Yes."

"Like Alice in Wonderland?" he said skeptically.

I tried to look confident and assured as I told him, "I know it sounds a bit wacky, but it can happen. And I won't know for sure unless you allow me in there and give me some time with that mirror."

MacDonald swiveled on his feet to look at Gilley, Heath, and Gopher, who were all sitting mute on the couch, watching us intently. "This for real?" he asked Gil.

"There have been confirmed sightings of this phenomenon," said Gilley. "And if M.J. says she thinks some grounded spirit is caught in a mirror, then I'm not about to question her."

MacDonald scratched his head and scowled. I could tell that he'd be taking a big chance if he allowed us in there. "Fine," he said, reaching into his pocket to pull out a set of keys. "But I'm going in with you."

"Great," I said. "I'll need someone to hold the light for me."

"Hey," said Heath as MacDonald and I began walking to the door. "Be careful, okay?"

I nodded to him and pulled the collar of my shirt up a little more around my neck. Gilley said I had some faint bruises there, and I didn't want the detective to see them and start asking questions.

I waited for MacDonald to cut the paper across the crack of the door, which would indicate that the seal had been broken, and then unlock the padlock.

As he held the door open for me he said, "Just please don't touch anything."

"Got it," I agreed, entering the dark interior, which smelled dank and metallic and made me wrinkle my nose.

MacDonald switched on the flashlight (the hotel power was still out, and we'd learned that the backup generator had failed completely) and followed me in. I stepped carefully around the litter of latex gloves and paper on the floor, avoiding the bloodstain in the center where Tracy's body had been moved once they got her out of the stall, and walked over to stand in front of the mirror.

My reflection looked stark and spooky in the dimness of the room. "So, what do we do here?" MacDonald asked. "Say the words 'Bloody Mary' three times and wait for her to show up?"

I smiled. "Yes," I said. "You say it three times, and I'll wait outside. Lemme know if anyone shows up." I made a show of trying to walk past MacDonald, but he gripped my arm tightly.

"Oh, no, you don't," he said, but there was a smile on his face. "Okay, do your thing so we can get out of here. This place is giving me the willies."

I turned to the mirror and focused all of my attention on it.

Nothing happened.

I closed my eyes and reached out with my intuitive sense for any sign from beyond the grave.

Nothing happened.

I opened my eyes again and stared at the mirror, willing the woman who'd shown up so frequently to appear.

Nothing happened.

"What's happening?" MacDonald whispered.

I sighed. "Not a damn thing." I reached up then and touched the frame, running my fingers down the beautiful carvings. I remembered what Anton had said—that Mr. Beckworth hadn't paid a lot of money for them—which surprised me, because the frame alone looked as if it were worth a fortune.

I closed my eyes again and concentrated, all of my senses acutely open. I heard a sound from behind, like a door squeaking open, and MacDonald barked, "This restroom's closed, lady; try another one."

My eyes snapped open and I stared into the mirror. In the reflection I could see MacDonald's shadowy, irritated face, and over to the right of him a beautiful woman with long black hair half in the door and half out, but the light behind me in my peripheral vision was all wrong.

The woman, however, appeared unsettled by MacDonald's angry tone and was backing out when I called, "Wait! Don't go!"

MacDonald's face registered surprise. "M.J., she can't come in here," he said, and I saw him turn toward the door. Then I saw his jaw drop when he realized the *actual* door was closed, but the one reflected in the mirror was partially open. "What the . . ." he said, his head swiveling back and forth between the door and the mirror.

"I need to talk to you!" I said to her. *"Please!"*

The woman shook her head, and in my mind I heard her say something that sounded like gibberish.

"Damn it!" I swore under my breath. "You don't speak English, do you?"

The woman in the mirror scrunched up her face—
she had no idea what I was saying.

I closed my eyes and concentrated. *I know you can
understand my thoughts, however, right?*

I felt a mental nod.

Please show me in pictures what happened to you.

My mind immediately filled with the image of an
enormous sailing vessel, and the smell of salt and
sea wafted under my nose. The ground beneath my
feet felt as if it were rocking rhythmically, and my
stomach was seriously regretting my earlier meal.

I also felt panicked. The view changed as the eyes
I was looking out of turned in a one-eighty, and I
saw a huge, sleek black ship right alongside the one
I was on.

There was shouting and the clanging of metal,
and all around me utter chaos reigned as men with
swords attacked the men from my ship. There was
nowhere to run, nowhere to hide, and I felt rough
hands on my arms, and my terror increased.

I was dragged roughly over to the black ship, and
I faced a man who was formidable in height, with
cruel black eyes. He seemed to look lustfully down
at me, and the meaning of his words was impressed
in my mind. This man knew me. This man had recognized my ship from my father's fleet, and he'd
hunted us down like prey.

I knew then that I would never reach the shores
of my destination—Spain, and my beloved fiancé,
whom I'd been sailing to wed. I also knew that I
would likely end up as this man's enslaved concu-
bine, and my skin crawled at the very thought.

The pirate in front of me whispered my own
name, "Odolina." He stroked my cheek, and I spit

in his face. He slapped me so hard that my vision clouded with stars; then he leaned in again to whisper in my ear. I could feel his hot, foul breath on my cheek and noted that his accent was thick but his Portuguese perfect, the meaning of his words filling my mind with understanding. He planned to rape me that very evening.

I was hauled away to a dark, smelly cell belowdecks and thrown inside before the door slammed shut. Time passed, but I wasn't sure how much; then the door to my cell opened and I was hauled out and up. The deck was covered in blood, and the bodies of my father's crew were being tossed overboard.

My heart ached for those men, as they had always been good to me and had fought the pirates bravely.

I was brought to stand before the cruel pirate captain, and he lifted my chin, looked into my eyes, and licked his wicked lips. I recoiled and felt as though I wanted to vomit. He laughed and pointed behind me and shouted in a foreign tongue I did not recognize to the men holding me.

I was dragged kicking and screaming to a door, which was opened, and I was tossed inside. It was his cabin. I turned to flee, but the door was slammed shut and promptly locked. I pounded on it, but to no avail. After a time I took stock of my surroundings. The room was littered with the treasure of my dowry, and already leaning against the walls were the special gift I'd commissioned for my betrothed. Four large mirrors with frames of solid gold reflected my terrified image back at me. But the face in the mirror wasn't one I fully recognized. The woman standing there, pale and terrified, had long black hair, deep brown eyes, and alabaster white skin, and while I noted this in the back of my own mind, I was too distracted by the sounds from outside as the wicked man's voice moved closer and closer.

My eyes darted about the room for a possible escape. I ran to the porthole, but feet visible on the other side of the glass told me I'd surely be caught. Then I looked for a weapon and in desperation dug through the drawers of the bureau. There, just as the pirate captain's footfalls sounded outside the door, I found a long silver dagger.

Metal keys rattled outside the door, and I braced myself against the far wall, where the mirrors were propped. The door opened, and there stood my captor and soon-to-be rapist, and something in that moment moved me to do the unthinkable: I raised the dagger, intending to stab the pirate, but as if the knife had a mind of its own, it turned in my hand, and I plunged it with all of my might into my own chest.

The pain was intense, and it caught me totally off guard. "Uh!" I moaned, reeling back to the present and fully into myself as I crashed into MacDonald.

"Whoa!" he said as he caught me. "What's going on?"

"Out," I said, clutching my chest. "I need to get out of here!"

MacDonald half carried, half pulled me out of the ladies' room. Gilley rushed over when he saw us emerge. "What happened to her?" he demanded.

"I don't know," said MacDonald. "This woman appeared in the mirror, just like M.J. said she would, but it wasn't Tracy; it was someone else. And then she disappeared, but M.J. had her eyes closed, like she was in some sort of trance or something, and she wouldn't respond when I tried talking to her. Then she made this weird grunt like someone punched her, and next thing I know I'm carrying her out of there."

"Put her over on the couch," Gil ordered, before running around to the other side of the bar.

Heath helped MacDonald get me to the sofa, and I sat down and shook my head. It was still spinning a little from the intensity of that vision. Gil handed me a bottle of water from the bar, and I took a sip.

"Take your time," Heath said gently, and I knew he understood more than anyone else how discombobulated I was feeling.

"I'm okay," I said after another minute. "That was just a powerful experience."

"So what happened?" asked MacDonald. "What'd she tell you?"

I told them all about what I'd experienced, and when I was finished Gilley said, "So she killed herself with the knife?"

I nodded. "She did. But, Gil, I swear that wasn't her intention. It just sort of happened at the last minute—and I don't know if she saw the pirate in the doorway and decided it was futile to try to fight, or if the knife had a mind of its own."

"Mind of its own?" repeated Heath. "You don't mean . . ."

I nodded. "I do," I said. "The dagger she used was the same one that we've been searching for. It's the portal key, and the knife that killed Tracy."

"Whoa." Gil gasped, then asked, "By any chance did you get a time period from her?"

"I'd say it was the early sixteenth century," I said.

MacDonald looked curiously at me. "How could you possibly know *that*?"

"It's one of the things that gets imprinted on you when you do this work. Time translates with the imagery. I can't pin it down to a specific year, but when I tell you this was the early fifteen hundreds, that just feels right."

"This stuff is so cool," said MacDonald, the corners of his mouth lifting appreciatively.

"So the mirrors and the knife go together," said Heath. "Isn't it freaky how they would both show up here together five hundred years later too?"

"Too much of a coincidence, if you ask me," I said. "And, Gil, there's something else about the mirrors."

"What?"

"They're gold."

Gilley nodded. "Yes," he said. "I remember the frame is painted gold."

"No," I said, shaking my head. "They're not just *painted* gold; underneath the antique-looking paint, they're *real* gold."

"I don't get it," MacDonald said. "If that frame in there were real gold, do you know how much that'd be worth?"

"No," I said. "But whatever figure that is, multiply it times four." When MacDonald looked at me blankly I told him how Mr. Beckworth had recently purchased four of those mirrors at auction, and when told that they might be haunted, he had suggested that he would have them removed and disposed of.

"So where are the other mirrors?" the detective asked.

"It looks like Beckworth has already started taking them down," I said. "But what I want to know is, does he have any clue about how much they're *really* worth, and does he know that there's a connection between the mirrors and the knife?"

At that moment the lights came on, and we all squinted in the now brightly lit room. Across the lobby we heard the assistant manager shout, "Finally!"

"Well, one thing's for sure," said Heath ominously. "Whoever killed Tracy knows about the connection between the knife and the mirrors. It's too much of a coincidence that Odolina and Tracy were killed by the same knife while in full view of the mirrors."

"M.J.," said Gil, "did you get anything else on this sinister character Odolina was captured by?"

Because the young Portuguese girl had impressed her energy on me, she had also shared a bit of her memories. "He wasn't Portuguese," I said. "I know he spoke the language, but I swear he was a Turk."

"Did you get a name?" Gil pressed.

I closed my eyes and concentrated. "Or . . . ruck," I said, trying to sound out the name I'd heard in the background on the ship when his men had addressed him. "But I think his first name was Bubba."

Gilley and the others laughed. "Did he shoot the jukebox?" kidded MacDonald.

I smiled. "I know, I know. But I swear that's what it sounded like when his men were addressing him by name."

"I'm on it," said Gil as he hurried off to try to dig up anything he could find on this pirate.

"What do we do until then?" asked Heath.

As if in answer, MacDonald's cell rang, and he looked at the display. "London calling," he muttered, before putting the phone to his ear and walking off to talk privately.

"Should we try to do some more ghost hunting?" Gopher suggested.

I shook my head and sighed. "I say we stay put for now, because I'm not up for any more ghostbusting tonight."

We sat in weary silence for a while, listening to the rain. At some point Gopher got up and went behind the bar to see if he could get the espresso machine to work, and just as our nostrils filled with the delicious scent of coffee, MacDonald came back looking as though he'd hit the jackpot.

Making a point of staring at me, he said, "You are not going to believe what I just found out."

"Do tell," I said, sitting up from my slouched position.

"That was Sophie's supervisor at Lloyd's. About two months ago Sophie reported to him that she had received a letter from Faline Schufthauser, the art thief. In the letter Faline said she wanted to strike a deal. Turns out she'd been working with a partner, a guy she was involved with who would arrange to fence the items they stole once the heat settled down.

"But Faline was becoming increasingly afraid of her boyfriend. I guess the guy had a real dark side. She wanted to meet Sophie and turn over some stolen artifacts in exchange for a good word with the authorities. A few items on the list that needed to be returned were a set of four mirrors, and a knife that once belonged to a member of the Ottoman Empire, which were stolen out of the private collection of a wealthy Turk!"

"Wow," I said with a grin. "I'm good!"

MacDonald laughed. "Yes," he agreed, "you really are. But, as I was saying, on the day Sophie and Faline were supposed to meet, Faline was murdered."

"Whoa," I said. Thinking about the freaky timing, I then asked, "If Faline was killed in Germany, what was Sophie doing here in San Francisco?"

MacDonald ran a hand through his hair. "That's what was so upsetting to her supervisor. He says that when he found out that Faline had been killed he took Sophie off the case, deciding it was too dangerous for her to continue with the investigation, and to pay the claim for the stolen property instead and let the authorities handle it. Sophie was understandably upset by the ordeal and asked for some time off to visit her sister in Sussex, which was where everyone thought she'd gone."

"But she continued to work the case and came here on the trail of the mirrors and the knife," I surmised. "I mean, it *can't* be a coincidence that she and the stolen artifacts were all in the same place at once." I was going to tell MacDonald that he needed to talk with Beckworth—and soon—when I heard a shout from across the lobby.

We all turned to see Gilley hurrying toward us. "Who's your daddy?" he called as he approached, a smile as big as Texas plastered onto his face and some paper in his hand.

"You found something?" I said, very surprised that he'd come up with anything in such a short period of time.

"Wikipedia," he said, taking a seat on a chair opposite me. "It never fails."

"So tell us what you've got!" I was anxious to put more of the puzzle together.

"Oruç Reis was an Ottoman pirate and lived from 1474 to 1518. He was better known as Baba Oruç, or Father Oruç, which is why M.J. thinks he's out of a country song."

I laughed and rolled my eyes.

"Still, that's a pretty amazing hit," offered Mac-Donald, who I swear was quickly becoming my biggest fan.

"Anyhoo," said Gil, "this Oruç character was a nasty beast of a man. He pretty much terrorized the coast of Portugal for his entire adult life, but there is one thing that I noted of particular interest here, and that is that Oruç had a taste for the occult."

"He did?" Heath asked.

"Yes," said Gilley, his eyes flashing with enthusiasm. "It seems that Oruç had spent time along the Barbary Coast and in the company of a particularly powerful witch. Baba became well practiced in dark magic, and it was said that he carried a special dagger to help him conjure up evil spirits to use in battle against his enemies. This dagger was also supposed to give him immortality, and it had a taste for virgins."

"So the dagger kept its side of the deal," I said. "The spirit of Oruç lives within the dagger."

MacDonald said, "And it did kill Odolina—I'm assuming she was a virgin?"

"I'm sure of it," I said, remembering the girl's terror about being ravaged by the Turk, and the fact that she was on her way to her betrothed. No way would a young girl of noble birth have been anything less than virginal in those days.

"Tracy clearly wasn't a virgin," Heath pointed out. "I wonder why she was killed with the knife."

"Yes, she was," said Gopher, and we all turned to him in surprise. He blushed and shrugged his shoulders. "That's why I moved on from hanging out with her. I could never get past third base."

I scowled hard at him. "You're disgusting," I said.

"I know, I know," he replied. "I'm a real shit. And I've turned over a new leaf since she died, I swear." We all looked at him skeptically. "Seriously!" he said, holding up his right palm. "I've sworn off women."

"Me too," said Gilley, bouncing his eyebrows.

I gave him a level look and got us back on track. "Gil, whatever happened to this Oruç character . . . I mean, he's obviously grounded and very attached to this dagger, so I'm assuming that despite his belief in its protection, he still died violently?"

Gilley's eyes lit up. "Oh, man!" he said. "I forgot to tell you the best part! In one hell of an ironic twist it turns out that our guy Baba was murdered in his sleep by one of his concubines. He was stabbed in the heart with his own dagger by a woman believed to have the ability to communicate with the spirits of the dead virgins murdered with the knife!"

"No freaking way!" I gasped.

"Way," he said. "Which is why Baba might have such a strong vendetta against the likes of you."

"So what about Sophie?" Heath asked. "What does she have to do with all of this?"

I turned to MacDonald. "I think we need to have a lengthy conversation with Mr. Beckworth."

"We do?"

"Yes," I insisted.

"Why?"

"Follow my logic here," I said, standing up to pace the floor again. "Sophie learns that Faline has been murdered and is formally taken off the case. But she doesn't want to give up; she's too close to catching up with the stolen artifacts. And say that she discovers that the mirrors and the knife have been fenced; someone with a lot of money has purchased them and taken them out of the country. She follows that trail and it leads her here, to this hotel where the mirrors are displayed in plain view. She also discovers that Beckworth—the owner of this establishment—has purchased them. She has the evidence and prepares to confront him. They meet in her room—which is why there was no sign of forced entry—and argue. He realizes she's got the goods on him and a struggle takes place. He strangles her, and ransacks her room trying to find the evidence she's got against him.

"He either locates the evidence or she's hidden it so well no one can find it, and then Beckworth realizes that Sophie's waking up. He panics and throws her over the balcony!"

There was silence around the seating area for several long seconds as everyone sorted through my theory. Finally Gilley played devil's advocate. "But how does an old guy with a cane heave a woman over a balcony railing like that? And why would he leave her room so ransacked? And for that matter, why leave the mirrors in plain sight until you came along and said something? Why wouldn't he have taken them down immediately?"

"And why would he mount them in the hotel at all?" added Gopher. "I mean, if they're really worth as much as you say they are, wouldn't he have hung them in areas less public? Anyone could grab one and run out the door with it. A busy place like this? They'd be gone in a flash."

I sat back down on the couch and frowned. "Fine," I said. "So my theory has a few holes. But we're not going to know for sure unless we talk with Beckworth."

"Do you have his number?" said MacDonald.

"No, but the assistant manager probably does," I said, pointing over my shoulder to the depressed guy at the front desk.

"Okay," said MacDonald. "Sit tight and I'll see what I can find out."

Chapter 13

Beckworth turned up about ten minutes later, and he and MacDonald moved off to talk privately in his office. The rest of us went to our rooms to watch television and hang out. None of us had yet decided what to do about the other ghosts on our list, but my thinking was that this bust was a bust.

I wanted nothing more to do with the hotel, the murders, or the ghosts. I really just wanted to go home. Gil and Heath knocked on my door, ready to discuss that very topic, and noticed my suitcase on the bed. "Packing?" said Heath.

"Yeah," I replied. "I'm antsy to get this job over with, and I want to be ready to leave the moment we wrap it up."

"Me too," said Gilley.

"Me three," said Heath with a sigh. "That last encounter with Oruç nearly did me in."

"Imagine it from my side," I said, then instantly regretted it, especially when I caught Heath wince. "Hey," I said, setting my packed suitcase on the floor. "I'm sorry. That was rude."

There was an uncomfortable silence until Gilley said, "At least you've got luggage to pack."

"Did you hear from the airline?" I asked, thinking it had been a while since Gilley had complained about his lost sweatshirt.

"Not since they told me it had been rerouted back to Boston," he moaned. "I'm waiting for them to call and let me know when it should arrive here."

Just then my room phone rang. I looked at Gilley with raised eyebrows. "Maybe that's them now."

"It's me," said MacDonald when I picked it up.

"Are you through with Beckworth?"

"Not quite," he said. "Can you come down here and talk with us for a little while?"

Heath and Gilley were both looking at me expectantly. "Sure," I said. "But I'm bringing the gang with me."

"That's fine," said MacDonald. "Bring them along. We're in Beckworth's office."

I hung up and told Gil and Heath that we were expected in Beckworth's office.

"What's *that* about?" said Gil.

"I don't have a clue," I admitted. "But MacDonald sounded serious, so I don't think we should keep him."

We took the stairs, crossed the mezzanine, and passed the front desk. The manager on duty wasn't at his usual post, which made me happy that I didn't have to explain our business to him as we entered the back hallway leading to Beckworth's office.

I gave a knock, heard a "Come in," and we went in.

Beckworth was sitting in his large wing chair looking stately but concerned, and MacDonald was on the sofa with his notebook open, talking on his cell phone. Beckworth nodded for us to be seated, and we sat down and waited to be addressed.

MacDonald clicked off a moment later and looked at Beckworth. "Your alibi checks out, sir. Thank you."

One of Beckworth's eyebrows lifted. "Of course it does, Detective. I told you I had nothing to do with the tragedies that have befallen my hotel guests of late."

MacDonald turned to us. "Mr. Beckworth has provided me with a confirmed alibi during the time of both Sophie's and Tracy's murders."

"Good to know," said Gilley, flashing Beckworth a smile as though he'd known it all along.

"Mr. Beckworth has also told me that he had absolutely no idea that the mirrors he bought at auction were so valuable." MacDonald lifted a paper receipt off the coffee table in front of him and handed it to me. "This is the bill of sale for the mirrors," he said.

I took the receipt and studied it. It appeared Beckworth had purchased all four mirrors for about ten thousand euros. I knew that if I was right and those frames were solid gold, their real value was about a hundred times that, if not more.

When I looked up at MacDonald again, he said, "Mr. Beckworth has also stated that he was never told that the mirrors might be haunted by a woman named Odolina, and that he never gave the order to have them dismantled and/or disposed of."

My jaw dropped. "But you told Anton earlier that you were going to get rid of them!"

Mr. Beckworth sighed as if he were very tired. "I have had no such discussion with anyone regarding those mirrors," he said. "Nor would I have ever suggested the idea of getting rid of four beautiful mirrors that I had paid almost fifteen thousand dollars for."

"Then why would Anton . . . ?" I stopped myself as a dead silence fell upon the room.

"M.J.?" Gil said. "Why would Anton what?"

I stood up and looked at MacDonald. "Ohmigod! It was him all along!" I exclaimed. "I can't believe I missed it! It was Anton, Detective! Of course it was him!" I then swiveled over to Heath and said, "And you even came up with the initial A when you were tuning in on Sophie's murder! It all makes sense!"

I looked back to MacDonald, who was staring at me as if I'd grown three heads. "I'm not following," he said.

"Anton comes from Europe! He even speaks with a French accent! He must have been Faline's partner! *That's* why Sophie was here in San Francisco! She wasn't following the mirrors; she was *following Anton*!"

As I looked around at all the wide eyes, I realized I was going to have to explain my theory a little more slowly. "There was no sign of forced entry into Sophie's room when she was murdered. As a manager, Anton had access to any room in the hotel. He could have easily entered her room when her back was turned. He was also on duty the night Heath and I were first attacked by that serpent *and* when Tracy was killed, and he would have had access to the security cameras! He could have corrupted the tapes before the police had a chance to review them! And I'll bet you that whole incident with him getting hit on the head and being taken to the hospital was his way of throwing suspicion off himself! I mean, how else could he explain his absence from the front desk for so long?

"If Anton set up the auction for the mirrors to be sold and taken out of Europe, he could easily have followed them here and waited for a time when he could steal them again. I'm sure he thought he was really lucky when he learned you all were looking for a new night manager!

"And when I talked to him yesterday about wanting to inspect the mirrors, he knew he had to fake going in to talk to Mr. Beckworth in order to get me to back off, and while we were out at dinner, he was the one who dismantled them and removed them from their mountings! The only one he didn't have easy access to was the one in the ladies' room because it'd been sealed and padlocked!"

MacDonald's face went ashen. "Oh, shit," he said quietly.

"What?" Heath said.

"The padlock," said MacDonald. "I forgot to re-lock the door!"

There was a collective gasp, and then everyone was in motion as we all scrambled out the door and ran back down the corridor and over to the ladies' room. MacDonald got there first, and he pushed the door open and flipped on the light. I knew what'd happened before I ever saw inside based solely on the look on his face.

"Damn it!" he yelled. "Son of a bitch! That *son of a bitch!*"

The mirror was gone. Behind us I heard Beckworth's cane tapping the marble floor. He didn't look happy.

MacDonald had his hands on the sides of his head. "I'm in so much shit!" he was mumbling. "The lieutenant is going to demote me down to traffic cop."

"Hold on, now; let's not panic yet," I said, feeling really bad about asking him to break the seal so that I could get inside to look at the mirror. "Maybe they're still on the property."

"What do you mean?" Beckworth demanded.

"Well," I said reasonably, "they're heavy, right? And they're big and bulky, right? It'd be pretty obvious if Anton were to just walk out the door with them. Maybe he's hidden them until it's safe to move all of them out."

"Where would they be?" asked Gil. "I mean, M.J., they could be anywhere, and this is a big hotel."

I looked at him with conviction and said, "I know exactly where they are, Gil."

"Where?"

"Room three-twenty-one."

"What?" MacDonald gasped. "Sophie's room?"

"Yes," I said, feeling I was on right on target. Turning to Heath I said, "Do you remember what Carol said to us when she wanted time to think?"

Heath cocked his head to the side. "That she wanted to be alone?"

"No," I said. "She said to you, 'keep the staff out of my room.' "

"Okay . . . ?"

"The staff! She meant Anton! He's probably been going in and out of there with the mirrors all day! And where else besides a crime scene would you be certain things weren't going to be disturbed?"

"That means he'd have to break the seal up there and remove the padlock," MacDonald told us.

"Come on," I said, already moving toward the Twilight Room to retrieve my tool belt. "I'm not going back up there unarmed."

"I've got a gun," said MacDonald.

I looked over my shoulder at him. "Which won't do us any good against a demon. Nope, Detective, for this we'll need grenades."

Ten minutes later we were riding the elevator, and gripped tightly in Heath's, Gilley's, and my hands were magnetic spikes. MacDonald was looking at us as if he was a little unsure about our weapons of choice, but Beckworth seemed to take it all in stride.

MacDonald asked him, "Can you believe all this?"

Beckworth replied calmly, "I come from England. You can't swing a dead cat without hitting a ghost there."

Gilley stifled a giggle, and I had a new appreciation for the billionaire. The bell at the top of the elevator dinged, and the doors opened slowly. The hallway was now well lit, and I spotted my cell phone at the end of the corridor. Everyone held back to see who would be the first brave soul through the doors, and I finally stepped out and held the spikes up defensively. "I think we're all right," I coaxed. "Come on out."

The boys all stepped out and waited as I trotted down the hall to retrieve my cell. The battery appeared to have died, but otherwise it looked okay. After going back to the group I walked next to Mac-Donald, Gilley was with Beckworth, and Heath brought up the rear.

He and I had already discussed keeping our sixth sense wide open, just in case. We got to room 321, and MacDonald inspected the seal on the door. "It's intact. My initials cover the seam." I squinted and saw that between the door and the seam on the piece of paper sealing the crime scene were the initials A.M.

MacDonald then moved his attention to the padlock. "The lock hasn't been tampered with either, and I'm the only one with the keys."

"Okay," I said. "Can you get us in there?"

"No," he said.

I looked at him in shock. "Why not? You got us into the restroom downstairs."

"Yes, and that was obviously a mistake." He gave me a pointed look that said it would be useless to argue. "There's no way I'm breaking a sealed crime scene again without a *much* better reason than a hunch."

"But—" I began to argue.

"No buts," MacDonald insisted. "I mean it, M.J.: You're not going to get me to break this seal, especially when it's clear to me that it hasn't been breached. The mirrors aren't in there. They're probably not even in this hotel. Anton or whoever could have taken them to the loading dock out back and driven off hours ago."

I opened my mouth to say something but decided against it. MacDonald had a solid point, and I figured I'd already landed him in enough trouble. "Okay," I said, giving in.

"This is most distressing," said Beckworth. "I'm off to call my insurance agency, but without at least one mirror here there's no way to prove their value.

Detective, I'm afraid I've little choice but to have a word with your lieutenant."

MacDonald blanched. "I understand, sir, but the mirrors in question were likely stolen property, which meant you were out the cash either way."

Beckworth scowled. It was obvious he didn't like being reminded of that, and he turned his frustration on us. "And I would appreciate it if the three of you packed your things and departed first thing in the morning. I will pay you for the time you've spent here so far—I'm assuming you were able to get rid of at least a few of the poltergeists haunting this hotel?"

"If you give us until the morning, sir," I said, "we'll clean out all the grounded spirits for you." Gilley gave me a look as if he didn't approve, but I figured it was the minimum we could do for things turning out so badly for the old man.

"I'm in," Heath whispered to me, and I nudged his shoulder and smiled.

"Very well," said Beckworth. "You'll have until eight a.m."

I glanced at my watch. It was currently eight p.m.—we had twelve hours.

"In the meantime, sir," MacDonald said before Beckworth could shuffle away, "would you mind giving me the address and contact information you have on this Anton character?"

"Of course," said Beckworth. "Come with me, Detective, and I'll have the assistant manager look that up for you."

As MacDonald and Beckworth left to go track down Anton, Gilley rounded on me. "Have you lost *all* your marbles?"

"It was the right thing to do, Gil."

Gilley crossed his arms and worked himself into a nice little huff. "The man gave us the perfect exit, M.J., and you practically beg him to hang out here in Hotel Hell for *another* night of fun and laughs while we run for our lives!"

I leveled a look at my partner—the drama queen. "Gil," I said, adding a rather exasperated sigh. "We can do this, and it doesn't mean putting ourselves at further risk. The only thing we'll have to remember is to stick together in groups, and at all times one of us should have our hands on the grenade caps. If anything even *remotely* demonish shows up, either Heath or Gopher or I will pull the plug and it's bombs away."

Gilley continued to glare at me. "You're up to something," he said to me.

I forced myself to laugh heartily, but the truth was that Gil was absolutely right. I *knew* the mirrors were still here, but I also felt just as strongly that if they weren't discovered soon, they'd disappear. I couldn't help but worry what would happen then.

I had little doubt they'd be destroyed and their frames melted down, and what would that mean for Odolina? She was so attached to the mirrors, wanting to get them to her beloved fiancé and all. I felt that she would suffer even more if the mirrors came to a bad end, and there would be little I could do for her once they disappeared.

Odolina had affected me more than I was willing to admit. It was just such a tragic thing that happened to her, and more than anything I wanted to stall for time and hope that we got lucky and, in ridding the hotel of its otherworldly residents, maybe, just maybe, we'd find the mirrors.

"Come on," I said, glancing at my watch and wanting to put an end to the argument. "We've got eleven hours and fifty minutes to cross as many of these guys over as we can."

Without another word I walked purposefully toward the elevators and smiled when I heard both Heath and Gil following close behind.

"You're sure this thing is going to prevent me from being possessed again?" asked Gopher as he stared rather doubtfully at the crystal I'd placed in his palm. We were standing in the lobby, putting on our gear, and Gilley had moved his monitor and much of the other equipment into that area, deciding that he wanted to be in full view of the manager on duty and the security cameras lest anything creepy be haunting the conference rooms.

"Close your eyes," I said to Gopher.

"Why?"

I sighed. "Because I asked you to. Come on, Gopher, play along for a minute, will ya?"

The producer closed his eyes, but the frown he'd been wearing for the past twenty minutes held firm. "Okay, they're closed," he said.

"Great, now tell me how you feel."

"Nauseous," he said. "I can't believe I'm agreeing to go on another one of these busts."

"You're the one who wanted to turn us into movie stars," I reminded him.

It was Gopher's turn to sigh. "We all know I don't make great decisions," he said.

I smiled. "Besides the nausea," I said, "tell me how the rest of you feels."

Gopher took a moment to answer, but eventually he said, "I don't know, kind of heavy. Like I'm weighed down."

My smile broadened and I plucked the crystal from his palm. Immediately Gopher said, "Whoa!"

"Lemme guess," I said. "You're feeling lighter?"

Gopher nodded. "That is freaky!"

I placed the crystal back in his hand and closed his fingers over it. "Now, keep that in your pocket at all times, okay? As long as you're carrying it your energy will be too dense for Oruç to enter you. He won't be able to take you over at all."

"Got it," he said, opening his eyes and tucking the sphalerite into his pocket. "But why aren't you guys going to be carrying some of it?"

"Because we'll need to keep our energies nice and light to communicate with the ghosties."

"Doesn't that mean that Baba can enter you, though?"

Heath and I shared a look. "It does," I said. "And that's why you've got to carry a few of these too." I handed Gopher three grenades. "Don't take the cap off until something scary happens," I warned. "Otherwise, you'll ruin our chances of crossing someone over."

"I'm supposed to carry these and film you two?"

"We'll all be carrying them, and we'll all be filming. Gilley brought along a set of cameras we use in our regular busts too. We'll give you full access to the film from those cameras to use in your show if you want."

"Okay," said Gopher, and I could tell he was trying to work up his nerve.

"What's the plan?" asked Heath when Gopher was armed and ready.

"We'll start in the old dining hall," I said, "and work our way up to the fifth floor. Then we'll give our friend Carol one more college try before we call it a night."

"Why did she have to be on the third floor?" moaned Gilley. "M.J., I vote for you to skip Carol."

"If we keep standing around arguing we'll have no choice but to skip her," I said impatiently, making a point of looking at my watch. Gilley rolled his eyes and went back to his monitors.

"I have good reception on all three electrostatic meters, and I've got clear pictures on cameras one and two," he told us, indicating on the bar the small digital recorders that Heath and I would carry.

I picked up the nearest one and handed it to Heath. "This switch converts the picture from normal view to night vision," I said, showing him the switch. "The rest of it is pretty straightforward."

"Too cool," he said, turning the camera over in his hand. "And I'm locked, loaded, and ready to go."

"Great," I said, stuffing several grenades, my electrostatic meter, and a bottle of water into it my tool belt. I then donned my headphones and microphone and said, "Let's roll."

I'd taken a few steps when I heard Gilley call my name. I turned and he said, "Please be careful?"

I gave him a winning smile and a thumbs-up and led the other two to the dining hall.

We entered the darkened room and flipped our

cameras to night vision. I took a moment to record
the massive room where the hotel held its wedding
receptions, and as I scanned the tables and chairs,
something appeared to flutter across my screen,
then faded by a table and chairs.

"Over there," said Heath, pointing in the exact
spot where I'd seen something.

"Yeah," I said. "I just caught an orb. Come on,
Heath, let's check it out."

We crossed the room to the far corner near the
stage, and immediately I felt the presence of a young
woman who was telling me she wanted to sing me
a song.

"Hi, there," I said happily. The woman's energy
didn't feel upset or troubled at all; in fact, she felt as
if she were a bundle of fun.

"I like her," said Heath. "She's a hugger."

I laughed. Sometimes in my line of work we come
across folks who just loved life on this plane so much
that they want to continue to engage in it. They resist crossing over because they were having so much
fun here. "It's the wedding receptions," I said. "She
loves the energy of them."

"I feel like she's a big romantic," Heath said, then
looked at the stage. "And a performer."

In my head I heard the name Molly, and from
somewhere toward the back of the stage we heard
what sounded like a woman singing.

"Whoa," whispered Gopher. "Do you guys hear
that?"

"Can I get a status?" said Gilley in my ear.
"Over."

"We've made contact, Gil," I said. "Heath and I
are getting ready to talk her into crossing."

"Now we know why people feel like they're being touched in here by unseen hands," said Heath, and in my viewfinder I watched the orb appear onstage and move from the center over to the left and down the steps to weave in and out of the tables.

"It's like she thinks she's in Vegas," I said with a laugh. "Man, I really like her."

"So let's get her where she belongs," Heath suggested, "to perform in front of an audience that can appreciate her."

"Cool," I agreed. "Do you want to take this one?"

"Can I?"

"By all means!" I backed up to give Heath some space and record him through the viewfinder.

It took Heath and me about a half hour to convince Molly to cross over. The lovely woman wasn't easily convinced that leaving a gig like this was in her best interest, but eventually, with Heath and me each taking turns, we were able to talk her into going by telling her a little white lie. We implied that we'd booked her a special show with a nice big audience. Of course, we'd had to pull some major strings to get her the exclusive gig, we'd said, but we'd heard how amazing she was onstage, and that she didn't have much time before the show was to start. We told her that the elevator was about to go up if she was willing to take the ride. "You can always come back if it doesn't work out," I said—which was a bit of a fib. Soon after that, Molly was on the joyride of her life, and Heath and I were slapping high fives with each other.

"Status, please?" said Gil as we were leaving the dining hall. "Over."

"We're on our way to the fifth floor," I said. "We'll be coming through your area in a few seconds."

We came out of the hallway and passed by the front desk. I was surprised to see Knollenberg seated there at this late hour. "Hello, sir," I said as he looked up at us.

"How is the ghostbusting coming along?"

"Two down, two to go," I said with a big smile, then noticed how worn-out and exhausted he looked. "What are you doing here so late?"

"I'm down a manager, so I'm helping by rotating in a shift," he said. "Your Detective MacDonald was unable to confirm the home address that Anton gave us—apparently it's an empty lot. And Anton's passport and visa are fakes."

"So he's our guy," I said, feeling it in my bones.

"It appears," Knollenberg said moodily. "I really should have done more of a background check on him. But I'd been so busy with the construction and hotel affairs and he came so highly recommended that I didn't vet him properly. Mr. Beckworth is quite displeased."

"Sorry," I said, then felt Heath nudge my elbow and make a point of lifting his watch up. "Okay, I'm coming," I said, then left Knollenberg with, "We'll be up on the fifth floor taking care of Gus."

"Do you need me to power down the lights in the hallway up there?" he asked.

"No," I said. "We're going to want to keep the lights on for now."

"Splendid," he said. "Good luck to you."

We didn't pause to speak to Gilley, but continued on our way to the elevators. We piled in, and Heath and I took point position at the front of the elevator with our hands on our grenades. The doors opened and I took a cautious step forward. Immediately I heard running footsteps down the hall and I froze.

"What is it?" Heath said behind me.

I held up a finger and said, "Shhh," while I listened intently. The footsteps had gone out of hearing range, so I motioned to the others to follow, but quietly.

We walked slowly down the corridor, Heath and I each holding tightly to a grenade while Gopher filmed over our shoulders. As we rounded the corner I gasped. I had seen a shadow, quick as a flash, dart through a doorway. Behind me I heard Gopher squeak in surprise.

"Did you see that?" he said in a hissy whisper.

"I did." I relaxed a bit now that I knew the source of the shadow. "That's Gus."

"Hopefully you can convince him to leave this time," said Heath. "He didn't want to listen to me."

As it turned out, Gus was one stubborn old coot. We worked on him for two solid hours before I came up with a rather ingenious idea. Sending Gopher down for a deck of cards, I told Heath out in the hallway that the best way to get Gus to cross over was by tricking him. "He needs to lose a bet," I said. "If we can beat him at a game of poker, then we can get him to cooperate!"

"What if he wins?" Heath argued.

I frowned. "You're right. I hadn't thought of that. I'll admit that my plan is slightly flawed."

"So what do we do?" he asked.

"We don't lose."

Heath smiled. "You're a blast to work with, you know?"

"I have my moments," I replied with a smirk.

When Gopher returned Heath and I made ourselves comfortable at the table in room 518 and made a *big* show of having a great time playing a game of poker. At first Gus was intent on peeking over our shoulders and offering us advice, but we staunchly ignored him, and every time we did, the one of us he was advising lost the hand. This frustrated our ghostie to no end, so when I offered to deal him in he took the bait easily and barely blanched when we told him that the bet was that the loser of the next hand had to do as the winner instructed, down to the letter. That left Heath and me with a little better than a thirty percent chance each that we'd be able to get Gus across.

Heath ended up winning the hand, and not even ten minutes later the score was three down, one to go.

"That was awesome!" said Gopher as he followed us down the hallway. I figured he was referring to the point during his filming when Gus lost his hand and the table had begun to rock back and forth without anyone touching it. Gus was a bit of a sore loser.

I glanced at my watch as we got to the elevator. "That leaves us with four hours to tackle Carol," I said, yawning.

Heath looked at me in surprise. "Is it four a.m. already?"

"It is."

"Okay," he said, as the doors to the elevator opened and we got in. "But I say we work on her for no more than an hour, then take a break. I could really use a cup of coffee."

Heath and I took up our point positions as the

doors to the third floor opened. "Keep your eyes and ears open, boys," I whispered as we stepped cautiously off the elevator.

We hovered next to the double doors for a few long seconds, listening intently for anything that might indicate we were in danger. When nothing happened, I waved everyone forward.

With great care we proceeded down the hallway. This was the floor where so much crazy stuff had gone down that it made me more than a little nervous. We rounded the corner and walked to room 321. Standing in front of the crime-scene tape, Heath and I pocketed our grenades and concentrated both of our sixth senses on calling out to Carol.

After a few minutes I said, "I've got her . . . and boy, is she pissy! Something's got her rattled—can you feel that?"

Heath didn't answer me, so I opened my eyes and glanced at him. He wore a deep frown, and my fingers immediately closed on my grenade, ready to pop the top if he so much as flinched. "Heath?" I said, keeping my tone even.

"Status, please?" Gilley said into my ear. "Over."

"Not now!" I snapped softly.

Gilley's voice lowered to a whisper. "M.J.," he said, "I've got electrostatic energy spiking all around you. Over."

"I'm aware," I whispered back, growing annoyed. "Now please shut up for a few, will you?"

"Okay, okay," he said, and finished with a tiny, "Over."

Heath turned toward me then and whispered, "Someone's in there."

My eyes widened.

"Who?" asked Gopher.

Heath shook his head and shrugged his shoulders. "Feels male."

I grabbed him by the shirtsleeve and pulled him away from the door as I ordered quietly, "Let's back out of here slowly. Keep your grenades close, guys."

We took one step, two steps, three steps back down the hallway when all of a sudden Carol Mustgrove came out of room 319 and practically jumped me.

"Holy crap!" I squealed as I felt the full weight of her energy cling to mine.

"What's going on?" said Heath as I struggled to push off the intense feelings of being tackled by her.

"It's Carol!" I whispered. "She's all over me!"

Heath stepped in front of me and put the grenade up close to my head. He eased the cap open just a fraction and Carol let go, but I could still feel her spitting and reeling and fighting to get to me.

I placed a hand on Heath's grenade, pushing the cap back down over the opening. "Thanks," I said, "but I think she's trying to tell me something." With my heart hammering hard in my chest I said, "I'm going to give her exactly ten seconds—if anything weird happens, pull that cap back off, okay?"

Heath nodded, and I closed my eyes. *Carol?* I asked her in my mind. *What's the matter?*

I saw it! I saw it all! she said. *He came in with that awful dagger! The poor man didn't have a chance!*

I opened my eyes, and both Heath and Gopher were staring at me intently. I felt Carol tug me *really* hard toward the door of room 319, and I wavered between getting the freak out of there or trusting my instinct to investigate.

"M.J.?" I heard Gilley whisper. "Electrostatic is spiking off the charts! I want you guys to get the hell out of there! Over."

Heath asked, "What are we doing here, M.J.?"

I pressed my lips together, trying to find a few extra ounces of courage. "I need to go in there," I said, pointing to room 319. "And I'd appreciate it if you two had my back."

Heath's eyes widened, and Gopher gasped. Meanwhile Gilley hissed in our ears, "Heath! Don't let her do it! Drag her out of that hallway if you have to! I insist that you guys get out of there, *now*! Over."

I reached up and clicked off the volume on my headpiece. "Are you coming?" I asked, reaching for the door.

Heath gulped but said, "I've got your back."

I used my master key card to swipe the lock. The small light on the handle turned from red to green, and, taking a deep, slow breath, I pushed the door open.

Chapter 14

The room was dark, and a mixture of aromas lifted to my nostrils. There was the smell of antiseptic from the bathroom, a mustier scent from the carpet locked in an airless room, and something else that was foul and metallic. Through the viewfinder I surveyed the room. It was larger than mine on the fourth floor had been, with two double beds and a small kitchenette to the far right. A seating area was set up near the window, and a chest of drawers and bureau lined the remaining wall.

Without switching on the lights I stepped inside, feeling Heath's body heat close to my back. "Okay, Carol," I said very softly. "Show me why we needed to come in here."

Behind us in the hallway I could hear Gopher talking rapidly to Gilley. "I don't know what's going on, man!" he was saying. "They've gone into room three-nineteen, and no one's telling me what's happening." There was a short pause before Gopher said in a squeak, "How am I supposed to do that? It's not like I can pick them up and carry them down the hall!"

"Shut the door, please," I murmured to Heath, and a moment later I heard a satisfactory click behind me. "Come on, Carol," I sang sweetly, pulling out my video camera and holding it out in front of me so that I could see the details of the room in the night vision. The bed, side table, curtains, etc., all looked normal.

"Is she talking to you?"

"No," I said, frustrated and ready to leave. "Carol," I called more firmly. "If you don't show us what's so important in here, then we're going to leave."

I'd barely stopped speaking when Heath and I heard a set of knocks from the corner of the room by the bureau.

"Over there," whispered Heath, pointing to where the knocks had come from.

My legs were trembling with nerves, and I hoped that I had the strength to walk the few steps over there, but after taking another deep breath I managed to put one foot in front of the other. Still looking through the viewfinder, I swept the bureau for a clue. Nothing at all struck me as odd or out of the ordinary.

"Okay," I announced. "We're leaving." I was about to turn when three *very* loud knocks sounded on the wall right next to the bureau, and I noticed for the first time that there was a narrow door there. "Wonder where that leads?" I asked, but almost as soon as I'd gotten those words out both Heath and I said together, "To room three-twenty-one!"

"Holy shit!" Heath exclaimed. "That's how the mirrors were moved into there!"

Without thinking I hurried over to the door and

tested the handle. It wasn't locked. "It's open," I whispered.

"M.J.," Heath cautioned, "don't go in—" But it was too late; the moment I'd turned the handle the door released and something heavy pushed it ajar.

I jumped back, and I heard Heath pop the top of the grenade, and the slide of the magnetic spike as it came out of the lead tube.

Instinctively I pointed the camera and the night-vision viewfinder at the door. There was a thump and I moved the lens down. On the floor, half in the door, half out, was the body of a man.

I screamed, and Heath flipped on the lights. Outside the door Gopher was pounding. "M.J.! Heath! Open the door!"

"Jesus!" Heath gasped as we leaped away from the body and yanked open the door.

Gopher stood in front of us, his eyes wide in surprise. "What's happening? Gilley says he saw a body on the monitor from one of your cameras!"

"*Run!*" I yelled, brushing past him without explanation. The three of us took off down the hall as fast as our legs would carry us.

We bypassed the elevators and headed straight for the stairs, our footfalls sounding a bit like machine gun fire. Almost out of breath, we burst through to the ground floor and found Gilley nearly out of his mind with worry. "What the freak happened to you guys?" he screeched. "Jesus Christ, M.J.! What . . . *Who* was that falling out of the door up there?"

I grabbed Gilley by the hand and pulled him and the others back into the stairwell. I was out of breath from the shock and the run, and was about to speak when the door was yanked open and Knollenberg stared at us with surprise. "What's going on?" he demanded.

"Nothing!" I said, forcing a smile to my lips. "We just had a bit of a scare with Gus on the fifth floor, that's all. Man, that is one irritated poltergeist, and he's got some serious tricks up his sleeve. If I were you, I wouldn't let any of your future guests check into room five-eighteen. Anyway, we're going to call it a day for now, Mr. Knollenberg. So sorry if we disturbed you."

He looked at us oddly for a long moment, but finally closed the door and left us alone.

Three faces stared at me as if I'd gone completely insane.

"Have you gone *completely* insane?" said Gilley. (See? I told you they were looking at me that way.)

"Shhhhh!" I said to him, then motioned up the stairs. "Follow me."

"I'm not going back up there," Gopher insisted.

"Just one flight up," I assured him. "I want to be out of earshot."

We got to the stairwell of the second floor and I explained quietly, "That body belonged to Anton."

"*No way!*" Gil and Gopher gasped together.

"Way," I insisted. "I caught a good look at his face when Heath turned on the light."

"But if he's dead, then who killed everyone else?"

"Knollenberg," I said.

"*What?*" they all asked.

"No way!" said Heath.

But I was convinced; everything seemed to point to him, so I told them my theory. "I think that Anton and Knollenberg might have been in on it together, but when things started getting sticky, Knollenberg needed someone to take the fall, and that guy was Anton."

"I don't know," said Gopher. "I mean, Knollenberg doesn't seem the type."

"Think about it, guys," I pressed, knowing I'd need a little more to win them all over. "Knollenberg was the one who hired Anton, and when Anton looks suspicious he claims that he didn't vet him properly—I mean, who doesn't do a thorough background check on a foreigner looking for employment these days? Wouldn't you think Knollenberg would have actually checked with the establishments Anton claimed he worked in and all of his personal references, with the reputation of the hotel at stake?"

"She's got a point there," Gilley agreed.

"And," I continued, feeling more confident, "we know that whoever murdered Sophie, Tracy, and Anton needed to have full access to the hotel and likely had intimate knowledge of any out-of-the-way areas where he could come and go without really being noticed. *Plus*," I said, the adrenaline still coursing through my veins, "who else knew about that door that connected rooms three-nineteen and three-twenty-one? Only a staffer would know that!"

"So you think that Anton brought Knollenberg in on the deal and that the general manager killed him?" Heath asked.

"Yes," I said. "Yes, I do."

"Jesus," whispered Gilley, looking over his shoulder. "If you're right, then we're really in trouble."

"Why's that?"

"Knollenberg is the only one here with us tonight. He said to me a few hours ago that he'd sent the other assistant manager and the security guard home to avoid the extra overtime."

"We need to call MacDonald," I said.

"Yes!" said Gilley. "Get him to bring the cavalry down!"

I pulled out my cell and dialed quickly. MacDonald answered on the fourth ring. "This had better be good!" he barked.

I spoke quickly and quietly as I told him that we thought we had discovered Anton's body up on the third floor.

"You are shitting me!" he yelled so loudly I had to pull the phone away from my ear.

"I'm actually not," I said, more calmly than I felt.

"Christ!" he said. "Are you sure he's dead?"

I paused before answering. "I'm pretty sure," I said. "I mean, it was dark and all, but I really believe he's been murdered."

MacDonald was silent for a few beats. "Here's the problem, M.J.," he said soberly. "I've been taken off the case."

"*What?*" I said loudly. "For God's sake, why?"

"Beckworth talked to my lieutenant," he explained. "The thing with the unsealing of the crime scene and the missing mirror didn't go over well. Hell, I'm lucky I didn't get suspended."

"So who's been assigned to the case?"

"An idiot," MacDonald said. "No joke, the detective they've assigned to take over has only been in our department for three weeks."

"So now what?" Again MacDonald was silent for

so long I actually thought I'd lost him. "Hello?" I called into the silence.

"I'm still here," he said, and added a sigh. "Okay, so here's what I think we should do: I'm going to put my ass on the line and come down there and check this out for you. If Anton really is dead, then we'll call nine-one-one and get some uniforms on the scene. I know a couple of guys on duty tonight who could keep my involvement a secret and make sure the case isn't bungled by some new kid on the block. You guys meet me out back by the loading dock, but don't let Knollenberg know I'm on the premises, *capisce*?"

"Got it," I said. "Let us handle Knollenberg; you just get down here as fast as you can."

I filled the guys in on what MacDonald had said, but they didn't look too thrilled about his idea not to bring in the troops right away.

"Gil," I ordered, "you and Gopher go down to the lobby and stall for time."

"Huh?" he said, his eyes big and buggy.

"Make a show of putting away the equipment— make it take a while, to give us time for MacDonald to arrive."

Gilley's frown deepened. "Even if I dragged it out, that would still only take me fifteen or twenty minutes—tops."

"We could go over the film," offered Gopher. "You and I could review the footage we've taken and start editing something together."

"Genius!" I said to him. "Yes, you and Gilley do that while Heath and I get MacDonald inside." I pulled out my maps of the hotel from my jacket pocket and sorted through them quickly. "Here," I announced, pointing to the loading dock. "Heath, we can have MacDonald come in through the dock in the back of the building and get him up to the third floor using this back stairway. Knollenberg will never know he's here until it's too late for him to run."

"What if Knollenberg leaves the front desk?" Gilley asked nervously.

"Follow him," I ordered. "But don't get caught. If we're lucky and he leaves the front desk, he may lead you right to the mirrors."

"Or he may kill us, like he did Anton and the others," grumbled Gil.

"Right," I said. "So again, try *not* to get caught, okay?"

Gilley gulped, but Gopher clapped him on the back and said, "It might not be so bad, buddy. He'll probably wait for everyone to go to bed before he makes his escape."

"Yeah, why would he still be hanging around if he was the one who killed everyone?" Heath asked.

"Because I believe that at least one of the mirrors is still here," I reasoned. "And with the four of us roaming the hotel, there's no way he'd want to risk getting caught with it. Trust me: He'll wait for us to check out before he bolts."

We left Gilley and Gopher to go back to the lobby, and I instructed him to make sure he mentioned to Knollenberg that Heath and I had turned in for the night, but that he and Gopher were going to go over some film for about an hour before retiring. That way Knollenberg wouldn't think we were up to anything . . . at least, that was what I *hoped* would happen.

Meanwhile, Heath and I used the map of the main floor to make our way over to the loading dock and avoid being seen by Knollenberg. I had my headset back on, and Gilley was going to warn me if the general manager moved away from the front desk.

Heath and I used our key card to open the back door to the loading dock and waited until a black sedan came to a stop right in front of us. I felt my shoulders relax, and I said to Gil, "MacDonald's here. Just keep your eye on Knollenberg, okay?"

"Copy that. Over," said Gil.

MacDonald got out of his car and hurried up the stairs to us. He was unshaven, rumpled, his eyes were bloodshot, and he had a serious case of bed-head going on.

"Morning!" Heath and I said to him, both of us trying to sound bright and sunny.

"So where is he?" MacDonald barked, his mood as rough as his looks.

"This way," I answered, and Heath led the way for us to the back stairwell and up to the third floor. As Heath pushed through the third-floor door, he and I didn't worry about taking up our point positions— Knollenberg likely had the dagger on him as well, and Gilley hadn't said that Knollenberg was on the move, so we felt relatively safe.

"Down here," I said, taking over the lead, but about five yards from our goal MacDonald pulled up short.

"Tell me you haven't broken that seal," he demanded.

Heath and I both turned and looked at him in surprise. "We haven't," said Heath, and when Mac-Donald still looked skeptical he added, "Detective, we promise. But there is something in the room next door that you have to see."

MacDonald continued to stand frustratingly still in the middle of the hallway, his hands on his hips and a scowl on his face.

"Please?" I said. "I swear, Ayden, this is really important!"

MacDonald let out a loud sigh when I heard Gilley say in my ear, "M.J.! Knollenberg is on the move! Over."

I put my hand up to my earpiece and commanded, "Follow him!"

Gilley squeaked in fear, but said, "Okay. Over."

I turned back to Heath and MacDonald. "You've got to trust us and move to the room right *now*!"

Heath hurried along ahead to room 319 and used his key card on the lock. He held the door open as I trekked through, avoiding the door on the other side of the room and the body still lying there.

"He's heading toward the back," whispered Gilley in my ear. "Over."

"Okay, if he sees you, then you and Gopher split up and run for it."

"Gopher isn't with me!" Gilley whined.

"I'm still in the lobby," came Gopher's voice.

MacDonald appeared at that moment in the doorway, and his eyes immediately widened in alarm.

"Why didn't you go with Gilley?!" I demanded of Gopher, as a tickle of fear shot up my spine.

"Because we thought one of us should stay here in case the other one lost Knollenberg and he came back this way," Gopher explained.

"What the *hell* is going on here?!" shouted MacDonald, and I winced.

"Heath," I said, "shut the door!"

MacDonald raced over to Anton and placed two fingers on his throat, but it was quite obvious the guy was dead. His shirt was drenched in blood, and there was a large open wound in the center of his chest. "Gilley," I asked into the microphone, "what's your twenty?"

"I'm in a back hallway," whispered Gilley, and there was real fear in his voice. "And I've lost Knollenberg! Over!"

"What do you mean, you've *lost* him?" I said, noticing that Heath had moved over to the detective's side and was trying to explain everything to him.

"I mean," said Gilley, breathing hard, "I saw him round a corner, but I didn't see where he went after that. There are a bunch of doors off this corridor, M.J., and I think he went through one of them!"

Just then, from my tool belt I heard a blip and a buzz. Heath heard it too, and his eyes shot up and locked with mine. I pulled out my electrostatic meter and gazed at it—the energy reading was intensifying.

"Hey, guys," I heard Gopher say in my ear, and his voice sounded alarmed. "I'm looking at footage from the first day of shooting *Haunted Possessions*, and you're not going to believe this!"

"Not now, Gopher!" I snapped.

"M.J.!" Gopher insisted. "Just listen! It wasn't Knollenberg! It was that other guy!"

I was about to ask Gopher what the hell he was talking about, but suddenly there was a loud hiss directly in my ear, and the headset shorted out. "Yeow!" I said, knocking the gear off and onto the ground.

"M.J.," said Heath cautiously.

I rubbed my ear and looked at him. "Yeah?"

Heath held up his meter. The gauge was in the red zone. "Son of a bitch!" I swore, and glanced at the door to the room.

"We gotta get outta here!" Heath warned, but even as he said it I could feel the air cool by at least forty degrees, and goose bumps formed on my arms as the hair rose on the back of my neck.

I moved over to the door and listened. I couldn't be sure, but I thought I heard heavy footsteps out in the hallway. I cut the lights and whispered, "Heath! Turn off the meter!" while I flipped off mine.

I then moved to the back of the room, and my eyes locked with MacDonald's. "Get over here!" I whispered as loudly as I dared, while waving him over frantically.

Heath jumped up to join me, but MacDonald stayed rooted right next to Anton. I couldn't understand why and was about to go over and grab him to pull him out of sight of the door when there was a click and the door began to open.

I held my breath and felt Heath stiffen beside me. I reached down for my grenades, but then I remembered that I'd given them to Gilley in case he needed to chase after Knollenberg. I hadn't wanted him to be caught unarmed.

From the corner of the room there was something like a snarl or a growl, I'm still not sure which, but when my eyes darted in that direction I saw MacDonald get up, his gaze trained on me. His mouth opened and words came out, but they weren't anything I could recognize.

I realized with horror that Oruç had returned, and he'd taken a new prisoner. Before I had a chance to do anything, Heath was in motion; he flew across the room and hit the intruder coming in the door with the full weight of his body.

In the darkened room, chaos ensued. Heath and the intruder fought and tumbled around while I stood frozen for a few heartbeats before my wits came back and I made to help Heath. My way was blocked, however, by MacDonald, who reached out and grabbed me around the throat. I tried my karate-chop move, but MacDonald was far too strong. His elbows bent but his grip on my neck held firm.

I kicked and struggled, real panic now settling into me as I realized how much stronger MacDonald was than Heath had been when he'd attacked me. I pushed and slapped at him, and we banged into the rear of the room, where the little kitchenette was. My fingers flailed along the countertop, looking for any kind of a weapon.

My hand grabbed the coffeemaker, and I hit MacDonald on the forehead with it. It didn't even faze him. Instead, he lifted me off the ground and squeezed tighter. I was losing consciousness and knew that at any moment there would be a point of no return. I clawed at the counter, trying to find anything that would help me. My hand hit a dial on the microwave and it came on, illuminating Mac-Donald's twisted face in an awfully sinister way. But then in an instant that scary face was gone completely, and he immediately let go of me.

I fell to the floor, gasping for breath.

"What the hell?!" he said, then squatted down and said, "Jesus! What was I doing to you?"

But I couldn't answer him. I was still simply trying to breathe. Behind MacDonald there was more crashing, and I realized Heath was in big trouble. Using much of my remaining strength I jerked MacDonald's shoulder and pushed him toward Heath and the intruder. MacDonald jumped to his feet and tackled our suspect.

A moment later the lights were turned on, and Gopher and Gilley stood in the doorway, panting and flushed. "We came up here as fast as we could!" Gopher said. "I saw that guy on the dailies from the earlier shoot and realized he *had* to be the guy we were after."

My eyes moved over to where Heath and MacDonald were holding the other assistant manager who'd been so grumpy. Next to him was Oruç's dagger. "Gil . . ." I said, my voice hoarse. "Gimme a grenade!"

Gil handed me the one clutched in his hand, and I struggled with the top. Behind me the microwave dinged, and I knew that if I didn't get the lid off now I was also out of time. With trembling fingers I tore off the top and tipped out the spike, tossing it over toward the dagger. It landed right next to it, and I collapsed on the ground.

The cavalry arrived about five minutes later. MacDonald called in any and every available backup unit, and the hotel was soon overrun with cops and CSIs. I was checked out by EMS techs, who asked if I wanted to go to the hospital (I declined); then I was approached by a heavyset man in a trench coat, who asked if I'd like to make a statement and have Detective MacDonald arrested.

I blinked at him while holding an ice pack up to my throat. "Why would I do that?" I asked.

"Along with returning to work a case he had been removed from, my detective has admitted to using unwarranted force against you, ma'am," he said.

"Who are you again?" I was pretty sure the guy had introduced himself, but my brain was still a little foggy.

"Lieutenant Crenshaw," he said. "MacDonald's boss."

I looked at Gil, sitting beside me and holding my hand, his face both guilty and concerned. "Well, Lieutenant," I said, "I don't quite remember it like that. I mean, to begin with, I was the one who asked MacDonald to come down to the hotel. When he initially refused, because doing so would be going against a direct order, I tricked him."

Crenshaw's eyebrows lifted skeptically. "Tricked him?"

I nodded vigorously. "Yes, sir. I told him that the producer of the television show was working on some background shots for the production, and we just needed to get a nice shot of the detective in front of the Duke. When MacDonald arrived I tricked him again into coming inside and heading up to the third floor, telling him that, because of the rain, we had moved the shoot up there."

Crenshaw frowned. "I see. And what about those bruises on your neck?" he asked, pointing at them.

"Well, you see, sir, when all hell broke loose up there, it was pretty confusing, and there were four of us in a small room with the lights off. I'm pretty sure I got injured by your suspect and certainly not by Detective MacDonald. So of course I won't be pressing charges, and you may take that as my statement."

Crenshaw's face—which comprised a bulldog's jowls and a Doberman's intense stare—was unreadable for several long seconds. Finally, however, he shrugged and waved at MacDonald, who was standing by a group of uniforms, looking for all the world like a rejected puppy. "MacDonald!" Crenshaw barked. "You're in the clear here, and I want you back on this case. I'm putting you in charge, so don't screw it up again." Then he announced, "I'm going back to bed."

MacDonald jumped, staring first at his lieutenant, then at me. I gave him a big, fat smile to reassure him we were still friends, and he seemed to relax. "Yes, sir," he said. "On it, sir!"

The rest of the morning was spent watching the techs and police come and go and getting pieces of the puzzle from MacDonald, who filled us in when no one was looking. It turned out that the assistant manager, whose alias had been Joe Fresco, had been hired just one month prior to Anton, and it was Joe who had vouched for Anton to Knollenberg. Knollenberg had only called the most recent employer on Anton's résumé, a hotel in Berlin, which checked out, and Joe was able to convince his GM that Anton would be a perfect fit for the Duke.

Joe and Anton had indeed been longtime partners, their career in crime dating back a decade, when they teamed up to work as valets at a popular hotel in Paris and fleeced the hotel guests of any loose change and valuables they kept in their cars. The pair eventually worked their way up and became part of the hotel management. They had a long history of working for short stints at several of

Europe's finest hotels, where they established a pattern of stealing from the hotel guests and blaming it on housekeeping.

It was while he was working in one of these hotels that Anton had met Faline, and those two moved on to bigger and better heists, but Anton and Joe continued to keep in touch. When Anton found that his girlfriend was ready to turn him in, he'd called on his old friend Joe to help him secure an alibi for her murder and dispose of the stolen mirrors.

It was Sophie who'd done most of this detective work on Joe and Anton's background, and she'd meticulously documented all of this on the flash drive stolen from her room and found in Joe's hotel locker.

During her investigation, Sophie had discovered that Joe and Anton had come up with the plan to spray-paint the mirror frames with an antique gold enamel to disguise their value; then the pair set up an estate sale and sent an invitation to Mr. Beckworth, who was known to attend such functions. The mirrors were attractively priced, and Beckworth took the bait, purchasing the mirrors for a fraction of their real value and unwittingly assisting Joe and Anton by getting the mirrors safely through customs and out of Europe. Joe had then followed Beckworth and the mirrors to the Duke and was able to land himself a job almost immediately. Two months later, Anton joined him and the pair kept a close eye on the merchandise until the international heat died down.

When Anton learned that Lloyd's was going to settle the insurance claim by the wealthy Turk whose collection they had stolen from, the pair figured the mirrors were safe to remove from the hotel, and had even made local arrangements to melt down the gold. But Sophie showed up just as they were about to follow through with their plans, and she nearly ruined everything. When she was taken care of, the pair then had to wait for an opportunity to remove the mirrors and get out of town fast, but our group kept making it difficult for them.

Still, through persistence they had actually been able to take down the mirrors one by one and hide them in the perfect spot, room 321—a place where no one was allowed to enter, and where Anton and Joe felt the priceless bounty would be safe until the smoke cleared.

However, Oruç's dagger and its influence over Anton kept botching things and making it difficult for him to make a clean getaway. It seems its dark influence had exerted quite a bit of control over Anton, who'd grown very unpredictable with it in his possession. He'd murdered Faline with it when he discovered she'd been in contact with Sophie, and it'd been Joe who'd managed to get the knife back by paying off one of the German police clerks. Anton had then smuggled the knife into the U.S., and he and Joe had argued about getting rid of it—that was the fight Steven and I heard out in our hallway the night we arrived.

Anton truly believed the dagger had special powers, however, and to prove to him that it was nothing more than an old relic, Joe had sneaked it onto the table during our television shoot when no one was looking. The dailies that Gopher had reviewed while Gilley was following Knollenberg (who'd actually gone to the kitchen to make himself a sandwich) had captured Anton and Joe coming in to watch the shoot, then a blurry few seconds of Joe near our table removing the dagger from his blazer.

To this day we're not sure which one of them killed Tracy. We suspect that one of the pair had been in the ladies' room scoping out the miror when Tracy walked in and recognized either Joe or Anton as having been on the set. Either way, we're pretty convinced it was just a case of wrong place, wrong time for the poor girl.

If it was Anton who was turning darker by the minute because he'd been so attached to the evil of that awful dagger, then he got what he deserved. Joe killed him either because he was sick of the liability that Anton was constantly creating, or because he got greedy. He never did confess.

In the end MacDonald was able to get him for the stolen mirrors, which had his fingerprints all over them, and for Sophie's murder. The flash drive taken from her room and his lone thumbprint found on her suitcase placed him there at the time of her murder. And because MacDonald had other evidence to rely upon to convict Joe and send him to jail for a very long time, he actually took a huge risk when he passed me something wrapped in newspaper shortly after his lieutenant left. When I peeked under the flaps of newsprint I was shocked to discover the dagger and the magnetic spike from the grenade.

"I can't let it near the techs," MacDonald explained. "I taped that spike to it, but there's no way that thing should be making its rounds at the crime lab, or anyplace else where innocent people might gather."

I was stunned. Not only could MacDonald lose his job for this, he could very well be brought up on criminal charges for obstruction. I closed the newspaper over the dagger and said, "Thanks, Ayden. I'll make sure this thing never sees the light of day again."

"I'd appreciate it," he said. "And can I ask you something?"

"Sure," I said, leaning back in the chair I was sitting on, weary down to my bones.

"How did you get me to come back?"

"You mean how did I get Oruç to let you go?" I said, knowing that MacDonald was talking about the point when he was strangling me. "I turned on the microwave," I said.

MacDonald blinked a few times, clearly not understanding. "Huh?" he said.

"Microwaves have two really powerful magnets," I said. "When you turn the oven on, you activate the magnets. Anything sensitive to a magnetic field within ten to fifteen feet of the microwave would be affected when it's turned on."

"Ahhh," said MacDonald. "Well, thank God for that, huh?"

"You ain't kidding," I said with a smile.

"Again, M.J.," he said soberly, "I'm really, really sorry."

I laid my hand on his. "It wasn't you," I reassured him. "So there's no need to apologize."

At that moment Heath came over and sat down next to me. "I was just upstairs," he said, a small smile forming on his lips.

"Oh, yeah?" I said.

"On the third floor."

"How come?" I asked.

"Carol. She actually came down here and tapped me on the shoulder. When I followed her upstairs, she said she's had enough of all this racket and wanted to know how she could cross over so that she could get a little peace and quiet."

I laughed heartily for the first time in days. "That's a new one!" I said. "So she's gone?"

"She is."

"Sweet," I said, then turned to MacDonald. "Have the mirrors been taken away?"

"They're in the evidence van outside," he said.

"Can I have ten minutes with them?"

"You thinking about Odolina?"

"I am," I said, then turned to Heath. "You up for one final bust?"

"Bring it on," he said, and we followed after Ayden outside.

Three weeks later our checks arrived: one for twenty thousand from Mr. Beckworth and one for five thousand from Gopher. I convinced Gilley to let me give most of it to Steven, who promptly tore up my personal check to him. "I don't need this money," he insisted. "You do."

My heart went all mushy as I stared across my desk at him. "You know . . ." I said, finding it hard to form the words.

"Yes," he said gravely, "you love me. You can't live without me. Life would not be worth living without me. You say it too much, and I'm tired of hearing it."

I laughed. For the record, none of those words

had ever crossed my lips, and I suddenly wondered what I'd been waiting for. I got up from my desk and came around to sit on his lap. Crossing my arms behind his neck and looking into his eyes, I whispered, "Steven . . ."

"Yes?"

I opened my mouth, ready to really pour my heart out, when the door to my office banged open and Gilley burst inside.

"Ohmigod you are *not* going to believe it!" he squealed, before noticing our rather intimate position. "Jeez, you guys, get a room."

I cleared my throat and got up from Steven's lap. "Do you ever think to knock?" I knew full well that Gilley never thought about something like that . . . ever.

"Whatever," he said dismissively, then got to his point. "I *just* got off the phone with Gopher," he said. "And you are *not* going to believe what he had to say!"

I sat back in my chair and sighed. Anytime Gilley began with a line like that, it was never good for me. I waved my fingers at him. "Spill it."

"Gopher's shown the footage of our busts from the hotel, and I guess the bigwigs at Bravo are *so* impressed that they want to give you and Heath *your very own show*!"

Gilley was hopping up and down with excitement, and my jaw fell open. Before I had a chance to even react our phone rang. "That's Heath!" Gilley said, punching the speaker button. "Hello?" he said, while I blinked hard and tried to take in the dizzying pace of these unfolding events.

"Gil?"

"Hi, Heath!" Gilley sang. "I'm here with M.J. and Steven."

"Did you hear the news?"

"I did!" said Gilley with enthusiasm. "Just got off the phone with Gopher. Are you in?"

"For that kind of money? Hell, yeah!"

"What kind of money?" I asked.

"Ten thousand dollars per episode!" Gilley yelled.

In the corner Doc squawked. "Cuckoo for Cocoa Puffs!"

"Whoa!" I said, and held up my hand, wanting everyone in the room to slow the hell down. "Gilley," I said sternly, "as usual, this is the first I'm hearing of this. Why haven't you told me about this before?"

"M.J.," Gil said patiently as he took a seat next to Steven, "I'm in charge of business development, and this whole thing fell under that category until we got the green light. And now that we have it, I can inform the talent!"

I nodded and pursed my lips. "I'm assuming I'm the talent?"

Gilley flashed me a big, toothy grin. "You are, indeedy!"

"So what's this show about? Is it a camera crew following us on ghost hunts?"

There was a palpable silence that followed, and I was immediately concerned.

"Sort of," Gil finally said, and his voice got that squeaky quality that told me there was much more to this, and that I wasn't going to like it at all.

I looked at the phone, hoping for a straight answer. "Heath? Want to fill me in?"

"The show is called *Ghoul Getters*," he said. "As I understand it, the production crew is researching reports of particularly nasty poltergeist activity where they think something much stronger and more dangerous than your average ghost haunting is taking place. You and I will visit these locations and do our thing."

My eyes flashed over to the safe in the corner of my office, the interior of which was packed with magnets and one cigar box, which held a certain dagger and a portal to the lower realms. I didn't immediately respond, so Gilley chimed in with, "Think of it, M.J.! If you do just twelve episodes, your condo could be *paid off*!"

"I won't do it if M.J.'s not on board," Heath said through the speaker, and I realized that I held not only my own financial future in my decision but his as well.

My eyes roved to Steven.

"I would rather you didn't," he said softly, "but only because I worry about you and don't want anything bad to happen. But I must admit that having Heath on your back makes me feel better about this offer."

I smiled as the picture of Heath on my back formed in my mind. I closed my eyes and thought for long seconds, weighing the pros and cons. Finally I said, "Okay."

Gilley squealed loud enough for Doc to flutter nervously about his cage. "Really?" My partner giggled. "You'll really do it?"

"On a trial basis," I cautioned, and leaned in to look directly at Gilley so that he couldn't misunderstand. "The *moment* this gets too dangerous or I feel our safety is being compromised for ratings, we're done. I want an open-ended contract, Gil, with that as part of the escape clause, or no deal."

Gilley didn't look happy, but he nodded. "Got it," he said.

"And I want fifteen thousand per episode," I said, feeling rather ballsy.

Both Gilley's and Steven's eyebrows rose. "Really?" Gil said.

"Really. They'll probably give us twelve-five—but if we don't ask for more money, then we look weak."

"Got it. Anything else?"

"Heath and I approve all locations beforehand. No dumping us in the middle of nowhere without any knowledge of what we're up against—especially if the activity we're fighting is that combative."

"Done," said Gil. "Anything else?"

I smiled and sat back in my chair. "I'm good. Heath? Anything on your end that you want?"

"I think you've covered it," he said.

"Great. Gil, go make your call."

We hung up with Heath, and Gilley rushed out of the room to telephone Gopher. When all was quiet again I got up, rounded the desk, locked the door, and took my place back on Steven's lap. "Now," I said softly, stroking his hair. "Where were we?"

Read on for a sneak peek at
Victoria Laurie's next Ghost Hunter Mystery,

GHOULS GONE WILD

Coming soon from Obsidian.

I'm not really put off by the skeptics out there—people who believe that, for someone like me to call herself a psychic medium, I must be a fraud. They see me sitting across from a client, struggling to come up with the name of a deceased loved one or a relevant, specific detail related to that loved one, and it's easy to believe I'm making the whole thing up.

But they don't know what I know. They don't feel what I feel. They don't hear what I hear or see what I see. And they never will. Well, at least until *they* cross over, of course.

One of the best readings I have ever done was for a woman who had just lost her father—and by "just," I mean earlier that very morning. When she came to me, desperate to know that her dad was okay, I took pity on her and fit her into my schedule right away. When I sat down, her father came through immediately, and all he kept saying was, "Holy cow! This stuff is real!"

Turns out that for seventy years he'd been the biggest, loudest atheist you'd ever want to meet and

was convinced that people like me were charlatans.
So imagine how surprised he was when he died and
discovered a whole new world—*literally*.

And really, because of that experience, I no longer
worry about the snarky little side comments I get
from folks who think what I do is a big charade. They
just don't get it, and maybe they're not supposed to
until they too drift off into that great night.

But none of that is going to slow me down or even
give me pause. There's *way* too much work to do for
me to linger on what other people think.

I've got my regular work as a medium—connect-
ing the living with their deceased loved ones—and
my other job as a ghostbuster for a brand-new cable
TV show.

It seems that there's a growing fascination among
television audiences to understand things that go
bump in the night. And, truthfully, our world is
chock-full of those poor souls who haven't made it
across yet. I'm talking about grounded spirits, better known to most as ghosts. There are millions and
millions of them out there, wandering aimlessly
about, and some places are more heavily populated
than others.

Take Europe, for example. You can't walk a mile
anywhere on that continent without bumping into
a ghosty or two—they're *everywhere*. Which is why
our production company wanted my two partners
and me to trek some three thousand miles across the
pond to do a little ghostbusting for must-see TV.

Gilley and Heath—said partners—were really
geeked about the idea. But I wasn't so keen, mostly
because of who I'd be leaving behind.

My sweetheart, Steven, would have to stay in

Boston and work, plus my beloved bird, Doc, would have to be looked after by a trusted friend. Doc and I have been together for more than twenty years, and in all that time we've never spent longer than a week apart. The show's filming schedule had us out of town for the next six to eight weeks. Which is what had me so glum about the prospect of leaving. And it must have been obvious, because as I sat in my office waiting for a client, Gilley came bounding in, took one look at me, and said, "Don't pout, M.J. You'll develop frown lines."

I sighed and said, "Way to cheer me up, Gil."

"Are you still moping about the trip?" he asked.

"Doc's going to think I've abandoned him," I said moodily.

Hearing his name, my bird gave a loud wolf whistle from his play stand in the corner and said, "Nice bum! Where you from?"

"He'll be fine," Gilley insisted. "Plus, look what came from FedEx!" I noticed then that Gil was holding a CD in his hand.

"What's that?" I asked.

"Location footage," Gil said. "Remember when you insisted on approving each location before we committed?"

"Yes, and I thought I already approved all of them," I said, distinctly remembering the three hours Gil, Heath, and I had spent viewing each location that'd been chosen by the production company to film episodes of *Ghoul Getters*.

Gilley nodded enthusiastically as he came around my desk, propped open my laptop, and slid in the CD. "Gopher called me yesterday," he explained, referring to our producer/director. "He found a new spot that he thinks we should film at first. He said the location team that scouted it is still freaked out about what they saw, and he says we can't pass it up. It's the scariest place on earth!"

"Great sales pitch," I grumbled, still pouting about having to leave home for so long.

Gilley ignored me and hit Play. My computer screen filled with the image of a drizzly gray landscape. Old-looking brick buildings lined a narrow cobbled street as rain dripped off thatched roofs and collected in puddles.

Someone off camera began speaking in a lovely Scottish brogue. "Before us is the infamous Blair Street, the most haunted lane in all of Europe and maybe even the world. And below our feet are the world-renowned caverns where countless thousands lost their lives to the Black Death, starvation, fire, and murder. Pain lines this street and seeps up from deep underground. Here, the earth is so thick with it that nary a beast will tread these cobbled stones. No bird, stray cat, or dog will venture here. Only humans are fool enough to walk these cobbled stones."

I wanted to roll my eyes at the theatrics, but before I even had a chance, a man appeared on screen holding a cute, cuddly black puppy that was shivering in the rain. The man, dressed in a long black raincoat with a black bowler, wore something of a wicked grin that I immediately didn't like. "What's he doing?" I whispered as the guy came forward and held up the puppy to the camera so that we could get a better view of the adorable face.

"Aw, it's a pug," Gil said. "M.J., you love pugs!"

Gil was right. I did love puggies, but something

told me that this guy was up to something, so I didn't reply with more than a nod. And sure enough, in the next instant the man set the little pup down on the ground, securing a leash to his collar before he announced, "I've selected this adorable puppy from the local shelter to demonstrate what happens when any animal finds itself on Blair Street."

And with that the man turned and began to trot on the cobbled stones, leading the puppy behind him. At first the pug was all too willing to follow, but then, about ten yards into their walk, the puppy stopped abruptly and tried to sit down. The man looked behind him, smiled, then stared into the camera. "They all attempt to resist in exactly the same spot every time," he said.

I hoped it would end there, but it didn't. The man pulled cruelly on the leash, dragging the puppy along as it began to squirm in earnest, and the far-ther the man tugged it down the street, the more ter-rified the puppy became. Its eyes bulged wide and it began to bite at the leash and growl and whimper and snarl. Five more feet had it resembling some sort of rabid animal—it was so terrified that it was nearly unrecognizable as the same dog who'd been held up to the camera only moments before.

"That son of a bitch!" I roared as I stared in hor-ror at the computer screen. I could feel my hands curl into fists, and I wanted nothing more than to reach into that image and punch the guy in the nose. But he managed to anger me even further when he picked up the wriggling, squirming, snarling puppy and held it suspended for a moment while the cam-era moved in for a close-up.

Gilley and I sat there in stunned silence; I couldn't

believe the cameraman was cooperating with this clear-cut case of animal cruelty! A moment later the man began to walk slowly back toward the camera, and the second he got to within about five feet of the cameraman, the puppy suddenly calmed down and settled for just dangling in the mans hands, shivering pitifully from nose to tail.

I closed the computer screen and rounded on my partner. "Get Gopher on the phone," I roared. *"Now!"*

Gilley was already dialing, and after three rings we were rewarded with Gopher's enthusiastic, "Hi, Gilley! Did you get the CD?"

"What the *hell* was that?" I yelled, not even bothering to announce that I was in the room with Gilley.

There was a pause, then, "Hi, M.J."

"Don't you 'hi' me, Gopher! How could you let them do that to an innocent puppy?"

"It wasn't my idea," he began, but I wasn't interested in his excuses.

"Of all the stunts you've pulled, Gopher, this has to be the lowest, most underhanded, most ridiculous . . ." My voice trailed off and I got up from my desk to pace the room. "You're lucky I don't quit over this. Do you hear me?"

For a long moment Gopher said nothing, which was probably wise, and I knew that he was likely waiting for me to calm down long enough to hear him out. Finally Gilley said, "You didn't have to use the dog to get us to agree to the location shoot, Gopher."

We heard Gopher sigh; then he said, "You're right. But I swear to you, it wasn't our idea. I sent Kim and John over there to do some more scouting because I wasn't really excited about our first pick. They found a few spots that were just okay, but when they got to Edinburgh, Scotland, they called to tell me they'd hit the jackpot.

"I guess the guy you saw on the footage is some local who does these ghost tours, and he picks up a new dog or cat every week from the pound to demonstrate what happens when you try and walk an animal down Blair Street. From there he took John and Kim down into the tunnels and caverns right below the street, and the footage gets even freakier. Did you guys happen to see that footage?"

"No," I snapped, still angry about the pug. "And I'm not planning on watching it, Gopher. That was just sick. Do you hear me? *Sick!*"

There was another long pause, and another sigh from Gopher before he said, "Okay. I understand, M.J. We'll stick to the original plan and fly you guys into Yorkshire."

That got my attention. "No," I said firmly. "Now that I know what's happening there, we're absolutely doing Edinburgh first."

"We are?" said Gil and Gopher together.

I nodded. "Definitely."

"Fantastic!" said Gopher, and he began to say something else but I cut him off.

"We'll go to Edinburgh on one condition," I said. "And that is that you call ahead to find out where that puppy is and if he's okay."

"Er . . ." said Gopher.

"Further, that you let that tour guide know that I want a meeting with him specifically."

"Ummm," said Gopher. "M.J.?"

"What?" I snapped, reading his tone.

"Are you sure that's a good idea?"

"Positive," I said. "Get me that meeting, Gopher."

"Okay," he agreed. "I'll do that, but watch the rest of the footage, okay? There was some really amazing and creepy stuff happening belowground that I know Kim and John are still really freaked-out about. It'll help prepare you for the shoot."

"When was the footage taken?" I asked, still worried over the trauma the puppy had experienced.

"This past weekend," said Gopher.

I didn't reply, and Gilley took the lead. "Sure thing, Gopher. See you tomorrow at the airport."

After Gilley had hung up I hit the Eject button on my computer and handed him the CD. "Burn this," I ordered.

"To another CD?" he asked.

I smiled. Only to a computer geek would the words "burn this," not include the thought of fire. "No, honey," I said. "Destroy it. Make it into barbecued brisket or chop up it into a million pieces. I never want to see it again."

"But Gopher said to watch the footage," Gil whined, refusing to take the CD from me.

I scowled at him and walked around to my shredding machine, where I fed it into the grinder. It made the most satisfying noise as it was gobbled up. "I guess we'll have to go in blind."

Gilley looked at me skeptically. "I never like it when you say that."

I smiled. "Come on, honey. Let's go pack."

Also Available From
Victoria Laurie

Demons Are a Ghoul's Best Friend
A Ghost Hunter Mystery

Northelm Boarding School on Lake Placid has
the worst bully of all—a demon by the name of
Hatchet Jack. M.J. Holliday, along with her
partners Gilley and the handsome Dr. Steven
Sable, are ready to send him back to the portal
from whence he came. The school's summer
construction, an uncooperative dean, and the
very tempting Dr. Delicious are all trying to
distract M.J. from her ghost hunting. But with a
demonic disturbance as great as Hatchet Jack,
she must focus and show no mercy to send him
to detention for an eternity—in hell.

**Available wherever books are sold or
at penguin.com**

FROM

VICTORIA LAURIE

The Psychic Eye Mysteries

Abby Cooper is a psychic intuitive.
And trying to help the police solve
crimes seems like a good enough
idea—but it could land her in
more trouble than even she
could see coming.

AVAILABLE IN THE SERIES

Available wherever books are sold or at
penguin.com